MW00386933

# THE CLEANSING

## WAYNE C STEWART

The Cleansing
The Zeb Dalton Military | Political Thrillers Volume 2

Copyright © 2017 Wayne C Stewart

This is a work of fiction. Any names, characters, businesses or places, events or incidents, are used fictitiously. Though some of the named characters may be real persons, their portrayal and inclinations are merely a product of the author's imagination and serve only to tell a fictitious storyline.

All rights reserved. No part of this book may be reproduced or transmitted in any form or by any means, electronic or mechanical, including photocopying, recording or by any information storage and retrieval system, without written permission from the author.

waynecstewart.com

https://www.facebook.com/authorwaynecstewart

*To the poor in spirit, regardless of station*

# ONE

*Sharp tropical grasses parted, creating an eyes-on-target view from only seventy-five yards out. Brushing blades aside, the lone figure set himself for devastation, and in his mind, greatness.*

**He was a believer.** At this point in his worldview trajectory, it would be anyone's best guess as to when he'd stepped across the line from compassion into murder. To him, the distinction blurred so much as to not exist. Life was precious, this was true. But it was also true that to save life one must extinguish it from time to time. Not in a protective sense. More like weeding, on the larger scale of humanity. These maxims, deeply embedded, had ushered the young man to this moment. And he was committed now to giving his last full measure in execution of such self-evident truths. Nothing he observed from behind these dunes persuaded him otherwise.

Fifty-three men and women gathered on this northern Caribbean atoll, busying themselves with the luxuries of their station. Food and drink flowed freely, as did their momentarily fluid commitments previously spoken to those not present. Vows? Shed as easily as the minimal items of clothing they bore with them on these slim, snow white beaches. They were celebrating yet another banner season of using others' money to make money themselves. For a storied London investment firm like Langston & Wyche, nothing out of the ordinary. They'd been wildly profitable every year since the reign of Charles I. But while the occasion might be rather regular, the location was not. At eighty-three nautical miles northeast of the Belizean coastline, this coral-ringed patch of earth poked above the waterline for only three weeks annually in late autumn. And though everything here had to be shipped in, none of it looked particularly portable or cheap.

The young man glanced back to where blue-green waves lapped against the shoreline. So beautiful. A perfect contrast for such depravity. Completely unaware of their place, their crimes. That these people blithely consumed the world's most gracious provisions with no sense — not even a base consideration — of the suffering of so many others, galled him. Yet it remained more than that in his heart. More than simple, anger-fueled justice. The next few moments would bring a balance to the system. A small adjustment, yes, but a beginning. Like the precarious nature of this small island ecosystem, the same care need be applied to the human condition. For too long the invasive beliefs and acts of those with power and means had held their brothers and sisters in check. No more. New beginnings were indeed possible. All that was required was death.

Moving from beach to the center of the gathering took less than thirty seconds and, as planned, the sight of an uninvited guest among the revelers had been met more with curiosity than fear. Though a few armed security men approached, it was far too late. Slipping the vials from pants and vest, the would-be revolutionary broke their seals, dropping the now unleashed contents to the ground. He smiled, hands high in mock surrender; another diversion.

Among the festive throng, initial cries of painful disbelief became quickly subsumed in a cacophony of bodily failings. Though too massive and grotesque to be processed in realtime, the experience was the same for each victim. A small prick. Nothing more at first. But what normally required the swatting away of a tiny, winged perpetrator and rubbing the lightly swollen bite space transformed instead to an immediate seizing of the central nervous system. Rigid, unresponsive. Men and women fell where they stood, convulsing, until overtaken by an eerie biological calm, leaving only their eyes to assess what had happened and what was to come next. Mercifully, or maybe justly, they would not wait long. Large, cyst-like expansions of their abdomens burst, spewing bile and flesh outward, staining every square inch of the weekend paradise and bleeding them out in the process.

On his side as well, and with legs and arms splayed aimlessly, the young man's smile remained. Bereft of the body's sensory feedback loop, his only window to the world — just as the others — was the power of sight. Head lolled to the side. Gross motor control absent. Yet his eyes still blinked, refocusing in the confusion and haze of what he had done. While accessing no further than twenty or so feet ahead, including the sideways range of his peripheral vision, he surveyed the carnage; his mission successful. An assumed rightness glowed within, warmly coloring his fading consciousness. Then it was his turn. He didn't feel his midsection explode. And, in the absence of pain, the smile endured — even as all faded to darkness.

# TWO

*The Majority Leader brought the Senate gavel down on hardened mahogany. For the first time in history the tone signaled that most ominous of political proceedings: the removal of a sitting American President under Articles of Impeachment.*

**The instrument itself** supplied an irony of major proportions. Oddly hourglass-shaped and with no handle, its sculpted ivory stood as replacement for the traditional piece broken in a 1954 late night session by then-Senator, Richard Millhouse Nixon. Though that defamed President avoided officially answering charges from America's populist representatives, something about him shattering this icon of the upper house's practices seemed fitting—if not prophetic. And while voluntary resignation stopped formal removal in Nixon's case, this current president would not travel the lighter path to ignominy.

He held no intentions of resigning. None at all. The House drew up the articles, passing them to the Senate for trial. The vote wasn't even close. True, a handful of Senators remained faithful to the doomed executive, but for who knows why. Only two years ago this man had chosen to sacrifice unknown but presumably significant portions of America's soil and people in a maelstrom of light and heat. The

Chinese occupation of the greater Seattle area pushed him down this decision matrix. In his estimation, all-out nuclear war remained the only apparent solution to growing aggressions from the East. Having weighed the options, he'd fated America to rise again from ashes, even if tainted for the foreseeable future with post-apocalyptic residues. So, there the man stood, an accounting before the full Senate, and as convinced of his choices as ever.

The gavel hit home again. From C-Span's long camera shot it appeared he winced slightly. Government broadcast production value wasn't the equal of major network or cable efforts. Still, there was something basic, fundamentally appealing in a moment like this. No show. Just the Founders' system doing its job.

The pronouncement was stunning in its simplicity, considering all it achieved in a few short sentences. American presidents endure long months on the campaign trail. Hundreds of millions of dollars spent to get them into office, to nudge the people enough to vote them in on normally slim majorities. Unarmed takeover and transition remains the grace and beauty of the process. And once sworn into office, the position holds enormous responsibility and power, not just for the fifty states and her citizens, but also to a world where its only remaining superpower still does much of the heavy-lifting. That these things could be stripped from the holder of this high office in such a manner was unexpectedly jarring.

While none tuned in expected anything different, their leader's remonstration before the eyes of the nation cut deeper than anticipated. He had done the unthinkable. Now, the unthinkable had completed its orbit. Justice? Likely. But the sting and shock would linger for some time in the American psyche.

*Karen Spurrier* **watched** from the Vice President's Office, in the West Wing of the White House.

Her office.

Having served under the now-removed president for the last six months, she knew the tempest coming. The previous VP resigned over a year and a half ago. While such an interim unsettled, it did not signal a constitutional crisis. Assuming the worst and then wagering that association with the defrocked chief executive would do his ascendancy no favors, the man *a breath away* made a supreme show of his "principled" resignation. Most people perceived it as a play toward a later run. Most also agreed at a visceral level with the disassociation.

Spurrier—actually *Eisenhower-Spurrier*—responded differently. When offered the post, the strong presumption of impeachment and censure hovered on the near horizon. This fifty-eight-year-old niece of President Dwight D. "Ike" Eisenhower understood: she would be forever linked to this man's misdeeds; a scar not assuaged easily, if ever, from her decades of tireless public servanthood. Four years would come and go with little to show for them, other than the fact she was not him. Still, love of country and the reality that someone had to do the job, summoned her forward.

*The first female president.*

She so wished this moment to be under more stable circumstances. A genuine appeal to the electorate on her own merits and initiatives. Maybe even a matchup of two female candidates from the major parties. That would assure a contest of ideas, a truly historic event where the winner could proceed with confidence on their platform. No, these were not the circumstances under which she would assume the role. Then again, maybe true leadership would now arrive as the balm and strength the nation needed so desperately.

The expected knock on the door. Her chief of staff entered.

"Madam Vice President."

Rising from her desk, she straightened her jacket and skirt. Told she would look more formidable in a pantsuit early in her political career, the former National Security Advisor rebuffed the advice. Power clothing or great legs had been the choice. She scoffed, deciding she could carry both and still thought they looked pretty decent. Her husband concurred.

"The Chief Justice of the United States Supreme Court."

While the room itself wasn't imposing, the declaration signaled a most important occasion. The chief justice approached, a well-hidden smile arching at the very corners of his mouth. The moment required gravity—especially so this time around. Still, he knew the woman placing her hand forward to take the oath, seeing her as an especially good fit for the post and the need.

"Vice-President Spurrier. Please place your left hand on the Bible and raise your right hand, repeating after me."

She heard herself say them. Still, the words hung somewhere in the distance, muted in the surreal, existential nature of the moment.

*I do solemnly swear.*

*That I will faithfully execute the Office.*

*Of President of the United States.*

*And will, to the best of my ability.*

*Preserve, protect, and defend.*

*The Constitution of the United States.*

*So help me, God.*


**The White House photographer's** flash brought her back to the present.

"Congratulations, Madam President."

The Chief Justice's extended hand met a firm return shake from the new leader of the free world. A few more words and the entourage left, leaving only Spurrier and her administrative and policy team behind.

"Madam President, this way please."

Her chief of staff led her to the Executive Wing, through crowded hallways filled with onlookers, eager for a story to pass to their grandchildren. A mere two minutes later the thick, reinforced doorway opened. Holding her breath, she stepped over the threshold and into the world's most famous office space. Spurrier stopped mid-room to take it all in. Three, large south-facing windows; perhaps the most iconic elements of the room besides its functionally oval shape. The fireplace at the north end. Four doors, leading to either administrative support, private study, or the long portico walkway — featured in so many famed presidential photographs — terminating at the Rose Garden.

"The speech draft is on the desk, Ma'am."

"Thank you, Richard."

Spurrier walked over, brushing her left hand on the front edge of the desktop. Images of the seat's prior occupants ran through her mind like a slide show carousel. Kennedy's children playing beneath the desk and his national address during the Cuban Missile Crisis. Nixon speaking to the Apollo 11 crew live during their moonwalk, and then his somber resignation. Ronald Reagan's reassuring smile and unbound optimism as well as comforting presence in reaction to the Challenger disaster. Bush 43, confirming our worst fears in the wake of 911 and charging the nation to act. Life. Mortality. Mortalness. The surface of the desk was smooth, level. Its inhabitants found the work to be done behind it neither predictable nor manageable. Yet a guarded optimism hung from every contour, each bend in the room. Like it's shape — an unbroken ellipse — a hope of enduring nature lived here comfortably. Certainly not due to her residents. Many had been fine leaders and human beings. A few bore the deeper flaws often revealed by history alone. But they had all come and gone in their own time. Their moment. The Office of the Presidency persevered, never borne by an outright despot or dictator, in all these American seasons of life. That was something to be proud of, even in this darker moment of the country's body politic. And it weighed on her now as equal summons and caution.

"We are scheduled to go live in half an hour, Madam President."

Spurrier walked around and took her seat. Picking up the speech draft, her eyes took in the first two paragraphs and then she paused, resonating internally with the words and ideas she would soon place before the country.

"Fine. Let's do our best to make this a transformational moment. The world and our nation wait to see what measure of friend or foe they still have in this office. They expect little. We'll give them much more than that."

"Ma'am," was all the senior aid need say, knowing full well the person he had served under, these many years.

# THREE

*Small clusters of students watched their new leader speaking. She talked of healing, purpose, and a future. They'd heard it all before.*

**They gathered at sleek couches** in the Soderblom Center Commons, wary but oddly hopeful. While not of their specific ideological stripe, Spurrier had crushed the ultimate in glass ceilings. Surely that amounted to something deserving of at least a minimal political and social leash.

They were bright, thoughtful, and very passionate. This was, after all, Cal Berkeley. While much of the country misidentified this fine research institution with the flower power happenings of the 60s, the campus remained one of the most difficult in the nation to gain acceptance to, proving even more strenuous once inside the doors. They landed here as the promise of their generation. Many would go on to head up new fields of discovery, entire sectors of emerging economies. Some in the broader culture discounted them as beholden to privilege—the participation trophy and friendship tournament rounds kids. Yet, these young men and women had somehow gained a sharpened awareness of the human condition, especially its injustices and failings, that smoldered within. Maybe in time they would become as jaded as their forebears, insulated by their own circumstances and affluence. Maybe not. Could be they knew too much to simply be quiet. And this specific cohort kept asking the most significant question: *why*. How was it the world they had been born into could manifest such suffering? What kinds of thinking allowed this to go on, millennia after millennia? It spoke well that they took as seriously the just-absorbed World Religions talk as their seemingly endless rounds of statistics and engineering coursework.

**The older man, viewing the same speech from a few feet back,** was not one of them. Though sitting through the identical class over the last hour, *Zeb Dalton* played the role of onlooker. Not officially enrolled, he was taking advantage of the ongoing education options Berkeley provided its local residents. While auditing added no credits to his collegiate total, he didn't really need them. With an undergraduate degree in Computer Sciences from the University of Washington and a Master's in Digital Sciences Theory from CalTech, Dalton had invested more than enough time in the classroom. While the early 2000s were all study and research, and then applying his particular knowledge and skill sets in America's armed forces, this round of reading and thinking was more personal, born of crisis, and as vague a journey as imaginable.

Zeb reached down, unconsciously brushing the right front pocket of his jeans. Still there. It always was. The small, toy-sized wood carving of a Northwest Native American totem pole reminded him of what he was doing here and brought back flashes of memory from the closest he had come to death in his 35 years on the planet. Recalling the long weeks of recovery in the ICU of Seattle's Swedish Hospital, it also reinforced the promise made to himself in the aftermath: to ask questions, to explore areas left behind years, if not decades ago.

Carrying the fate of millions while seated at a small, outdated computer console in a remote military installation, he had been confronted with the question of whether he had the right—no, the moral station—to push the proverbial "button." When honest, he thought it likely he would have followed through. That is, if not for the incursion of another computer operator on the other side of the world, unknowingly posing the one odd question calling his bluff.

*Do you fear God?*

Dalton didn't hold a well-reasoned response. His *yes* was purely visceral, but at that moment true, even if in a limited state. The affirmative response served as his first step, though only that. And as he typed the simple word into the flow of code before him the other side—just as eager to fly their warheads over crowded American cities—backed off. Of course, the former Army Lieutenant only came to know this later, as his typing in the old bunker was met immediately with gunshots, pain, and darkness. Physical rehab crawled, taking most of the prior twenty-four or so months. His very average 5'10" frame granted him no spectacular advantages in the repair his body needed. An age-appropriate weight and muscle mass only sloughed off in the waiting, leaving him more sickly than thriving.

But every time he looked over from his hospital bed, and then therapy unit couch, to the small trinket on his side table, he remembered the vow, however nascent. He would investigate what stood atop *his* totem pole, metaphorically speaking. If he were not fully in charge, more than enough challengers desired the post. Growing up under the watchful eye of a Baptist pastor, he understood the game. But a whole new perspective dawned now in these vaunted halls of academia, a very different conversation than his previous studies allowed.

**"Hey, *grandpa*, what do you think?"**

Dalton looked up and laughed. He would have had to sire offspring at the age of ten to have grandchildren by now. Still, his relationship with the young man asking the question was warm enough to sustain the beating.

"About what, exactly?"

"You know, Spurrier."

"Well," Zeb poked. "What's trending on Buzzfeed and HuffPo? Isn't that where you kids get all your news?"

"Yeah, true," the student shot back. "But I had to. Already checked and dismissed the fake news I found on your favorite flag-waving blogs."

Dalton liked this kid.

At twenty-two, Joey Schumer was bound for one of the nation's finest law schools in another year or so and likely to actually do something that mattered with his *Juris Doctor.* Having sat in enough breakout conversations with the young man, Zeb assumed he would find his way through the maze of big firm money and appointments and move onto something more substantial, both for himself and his community. He talked briefly of interest in an organization, *La Guardian,* that seemed to be doing good work in Latin America.

"Hey, you hungry *Gramps?*"

Dalton had to admit to the ill effects of only a single cup of coffee in his system as the noon hour approached.

"Yeah, sure. What you got in mind?"

"Blondie's?"

"The pizza place? I hear it's good."

"Oh, man. How long you been here, old man? No Blondie's yet? We gotta make that right."

The deal was struck and they exited the Soderblom, en route to what Dalton assumed would be the best slice of pie he had ever experienced. Semi-awkward silence painted their first few minutes of travel across the southern edges of campus. Stepping past the corner of the MLK Student Union, Joey got it started again.

"It's all about authority, right?"

"Huh?"

"The lecture. Geez, you old guys struggle keeping up, don't you?"

"Oh, yeah," Zeb engaged again, recalling some of the last hour's conversation. "I guess so. I mean, sure, you have to start somewhere. And to know that where you've started is reliable."

It sounded so esoteric coming from his own mouth. Far too loose for his normal lines of thinking. This kind of processing came slower for Dalton than numbers, scenarios, and probabilities. Much slower, in fact. Peering inside Zeb's head while he was assessing factual data and scenarios would be shocking, incomprehensible for most people—even someone as bright as Joey. Dalton's analytical prowess was his gift, crunching data in ways quite profound, sometimes mysterious. Amounting to a large 3d field in his mind's eye, he had no problems processing simultaneous, multiple-threaded streams. It was the reason he ended up in the military in the first place. Well, maybe not the sole reason, but certainly the thing the Army wanted. Far surpassing the power of the most advanced field computers, Zeb's brain gave them immediate, on the ground abilities, setting them above every enemy combatant in the world.

Numbers, options, probabilities? No problem.

Truths? That played a bit further out than his depth.

Another hundred feet down Telegraph Ave the duo walked through the older wooden doorway and took a seat at the counter, ordering up a couple of lunch specials. In just seconds the aroma hit their noses, stomachs growling in unison. They dug in.

"Clearly, it all comes down to authority. The problem is, does humanity possess the capacity to enact a good order? And under what set of rules? That's still out for verdict, historically-speaking," Joey opined.

Zeb nodded. It made so much sense when spoken from this young man's pizza-filled mouth. Somehow it rattled around in his own heart and head like an ever-spinning top.

*It's true. Everybody wants to believe we can make this thing work,* Dalton thought to himself. *But at some point, you start to wonder if we're just burning up time, with no real progress to show for it.*

Dalton looked up and laughed quietly.

"What's so funny?" Joey said.

"The sign," Zeb pointed. "Maybe not a bad idea after all."

The younger man's eyes went to Zeb's reference, above them on the wall.

*Blondie's Pizza: Make Pizza Not War.*

Dalton appreciated the sentiment, Yet, he understood the aphorism as probably a bit too naive. He had seen virtuous people do everything they could to stave off the advances of those hell bent on dominion and destruction. Fallujah, Tikrit, even his home town of Seattle. Every battlefield reminded him that, in fact, there were bad people in this world. Ignoring that truth did nothing to stop the slaughter of innocents and the revolving door of tyrants, both local and international.

Zeb took another bite of the thin crust pie, processing as much of the heady conversation as he could while enjoying the cheese and sauce the place was famous for. Washing it down with a swig of Diet Coke, his phone rang, bringing him back out of the ramblings in his head. Though not recognizing the number, he answered anyways. What came next surprised, to say the least.

"Lieutenant *Dalton? Zebulon Dalton?*"

A series of clicks and tones indicated the establishment of a digitally secure line. Zeb knew enough to step away from the counter for this one. He nodded to Joey while keeping his ear to the phone and backing around behind the kitchen access and by the restrooms.

"Yes... speaking."

"Please hold for the President of the United States of America."

# FOUR

*President Spurrier held the mute button down with her right forefinger and leaned out over the massive desk. Her look questioned one more time whether this was a good idea.*

**Mike Stevens knew exactly** what she was getting at.

"Ma'am," he reassured. "He is indeed the man you want to be talking to first on this. I know, he's been through a lot. We all have. But this bird was made to fly. He might just need to experience the world outside the cage again."

The president enjoyed Stevens' homespun metaphors. Most of the time. Right now, she stared down an unfolding crisis not twenty-four hours into her term and needed certainty the right people were added to the team. Her first move had been to call Mike — General — Stevens.

One of the first to go public with the former executive's actions, Stevens' fate became discharge from field duty, sent to languish in the netherworlds of the Pentagon's lower levels. Highly decorated and roundly respected, Stevens watched over the indignities of forced removal of his men and women from the Seattle area, with Chinese soldiers moving in as the protectors of their new province: *Penghu*. Stevens reset some 30,000 warriors on the other side of the mountains and then provided the training and mission support necessary for a small team to head back over the Cascade Range, into the enemy's lair. Against all hope he did his job and led his people well, refusing to imagine that his home would forever now be occupied, foreign soil. And in the process, he'd come to appreciate and respect an odd, retired lieutenant who believed he had a chance at returning a sense of normalcy to their world. Still, there lingered a more intimate loss in this whole, crazy scenario: he and the now-removed president were longtime personal friends. Calling out his Commander in Chief was not an easy decision, one that would remain an open wound for some time. The president responded understandably but uncharacteristically in sidelining Stevens from the very things at which he excelled. In the end, testifying against his friend was the right thing to do. Whatever else could be said about Mike Stevens, when he owned a sense of moral clarity he would act, no matter the consequences.

**The line was clean,** an abrupt pause of silence signaling to go ahead with the conversation. Spurrier lifted her finger from the mute button.

"Mr. Dalton, this is *president*... "

She paused, as this was the first time making her title known, and the weight fell on her suddenly. A measured, confident breath and then she continued. "This is President Spurrier. I realize this may seem out of context but I appreciate you taking the call."

"Absolutely, madam president. Talking with the leader of the free world while tossing back some pizza is a bit different than I imagined how this day would unfold, but I am glad to."

"Yes, Blondie's is one of my favorites, as well... whenever I am in the area."

Zeb's head snapped around. He swept the street side windows and the crowded room in a mere second. Dalton tensed, knowing he was being watched.

"Okay," he turned back to the phone. "I'm listening."

"Mr. Dalton. You and I have never met. But I do know your story. General Stevens here insisted you be my first call. As he is one of the few people I trust at this early stage in my tenure, I am inclined to give his recommendation some weight."

"Understood, madam president."

"Very well then. I have something I'd appreciate your assessment on. Are you getting the video feed now?"

Dalton pulled the phone from the side of his head and glanced at the screen.

"Yes, it's coming through."

*What the...*

"The split image you are viewing is from two separate incidents, one offshore the nation of Belize and the other a resort on the Baltic in Montenegro. The timestamps will give you more clarity but the best timing we have is that Belize is three to four days ago."

She stopped the narration in a way that told Zeb something important was coming next.

"Montenegro is live. Realtime."

**Though the dual sets of images** came across small on his phone, the scenes bespoke something unmistakably tragic. Body parts lay in piles, a gory mass of flesh where the torsos of each should have been. It was like someone had taken a smudge tool to the pictures from their upper chest areas down but stopped upon reaching the arms and legs. Faces frozen in shock and pain. Whatever happened, happened fast. Violently so.

She couldn't see it from the Oval Office but Zeb's face held a far-off look. His mind went into overdrive, summoning server farms' worth of stored data on the effects of various kinds of biological and weapons agents. Nothing matched. At least not closely enough to give him a sense of certainty as to what they were witnessing.

"Ma'am. On first appraisal," Dalton felt bile elevating as he forced himself to scrutinize the horrific display. "I don't see any entrance or exit wounds. Spent ordinance would tear them apart more uniformly, albeit chaotically. A straight up bio weapon would be more of an internal collapse, so the… pardon the phrase... exploded areas of their midsections would still be intact. Honestly, I just don't have an initial categorization for this kind of destructive pattern. Whatever it is, it did the job with unusual speed and violence."

Zeb stared at the horrors again, quieted by the scene and its implications.

"Thank you for your analysis, Mr. Dalton. Now, let's get you on a plane to Montenegro."

"Whoa, hold it," Dalton shot back. "I mean, respectfully, ma'am. I retired from active duty a long time ago."   .

"And yet you stepped back into the fray a mere twenty-four months back, when your country needed you, didn't you Mr. Dalton?"

"Sure... but…" Zeb knew he was splitting hairs at this point. "That was different."

"Mr. Dalton. Clearly, this situation has not landed on American soil... yet. But we are in a unique position, a gatekeeper if you will when it comes to this kind of thing. We have no idea what level of threat we are looking at here, not even whether this is something natural or of human invention. And if it is man-directed, what is the intent and scope of the person or persons behind it? Terror? Major geopolitical players? Could be random occurrence of a viral strain not yet encountered. Maybe just an odd flash in the pan of humanity's strife, though the means of death are so closely parallel from the two that makes for a very rare possibility. Might be over in a day or two. Might be the beginnings of something on the order of a new plague. Given what you see in front of you, do we want to take any chances?"

Dalton couldn't erase the images. Embedded now, both visually and emotionally.

Spurrier let the words sink in, counting on what she had heard of Dalton's moral compass as indication he would serve again.

"Give us a week, *Zeb*," she tried with a more direct touch. "Get on the ground. Get as much data as you can and we'll know what to do next. Neither Belize nor Montenegro has hit the mainstream news yet but that won't last long. Families and coworkers are going to require answers. It will only spread from there."

The new leader paused, realizing this might be the first time she would need to weigh complete openness in respect of the dead against the ability to contain fear in the general populace. She'd received the favored cover stories already. Amazingly, there were people whose specialty was just this sort of thing—creating a probable cause or narrative surviving scrutiny. They'd forwarded their recommendations to her in the last hour. Belize would become a tragic accident at sea. Montenegro? A food-borne illness, unique but contained.

"We can stay ahead of the curve but we can't wait around," she finished. Time to close the deal. "Lieutenant, can I... can *we*, count on you?"

Zeb looked down at the screen one more time. The images were like nothing he had ever seen and he had seen much failing of the human body and its attendant miseries.

A slight groan on Dalton's end. It was the signal Spurrier was looking for.

"Very good, Mr. Dalton."

"Aghhh, okay," Zeb replied, pressing a palm to his right temple. "But I'm gonna need some support on this before I agree to anything."

Spurrier waved Stevens forward. He stepped over to the desk, within vocal range of the speaker phone.

"Alright, LT," the major general asked. "What do you need?"

Zeb smiled at the sound of his voice.

"Not so much what, general. More the question of *whom*. And you and I both know the answer to that could be a challenge."

# FIVE

*Her right eye focused, unwavering, through the Leupold Mk 4 LR/T M3 3.5-10-40mm variable power scope mounted on her older M24 rifle. She preferred a more traditional approach to her work: the same duties engaged in for the better part of humanity's story. Stalk. Assess. Act.*

**But her goal was not that of the hunter.** Unless, of course, claiming a trophy led to the release of someone held against their will. No, *Jessica Sanchez,* highly skilled and recently retired asset with a decade-plus of valor and service in the US Army, watched for very different reasons.

The woman's small but serious frame tensed and relaxed at the same time. She let the scene unfolding through the reticle produce just enough anger for her to focus but not so much as to cloud her judgment. In this case, that would prove no challenge at all. The sad grouping of ten boys had none more senior than eight years old, some as young as three or four. The small clearing, only thirty yards from her position, hosted an unseen yet unbelievable setting. The "government man" still tried to negotiate. The three men with semi-autos held a different idea of what was to happen here and made this known with the end of a hot barrel. Bullets flew skyward. There remained no question in their minds: this transaction was complete.

The boss man in the jeep at the edge of the clearing needn't say a word. A blank look from behind aviators signaled his approval, as well.

Sanchez moved stealthily, approaching the armed guards, quite unseen. The deep, heavy foliage allowed her to get right up and behind two of them while a slight pause lingered in the air from the discharge of their weapons. The moment of peace would not last long. A balled right fist attacked the lower kidney area on one of the men. Hard, knuckled bone structure met soft tissue. Pain resonated throughout his nervous system, sending him immediately to the ground, knees buckling. Man number two turned but far too slow as her left hand swept in an arc both graceful and punishing. The sound, again — resolute concussion of cartilage against flesh. Soon, he was in the dirt with his partner, not only writhing in pain but gasping for breath. Dispatching the third guard required a formal use of Sanchez' weapon. She would not take this action prematurely but he loitered far enough from the cluster; too much distance to cover if she were to use a non-lethal move in subduing him. After pulling the trigger, she turned back to the two men at her feet and sent them to dreamland, denting the backs of their heads with the butt of her rifle.

Boss man sized up the scenario and fled, as assumed.

Cowardice. Plain and simple. Most people exercising this kind of power came from the same bag of miscreants. A quite dependable factor in her line of work.

All told: less than thirty seconds at the office.

Sanchez looked down. Government man wet himself, curled up in a ball. So much for the windfall he assumed for this day. More likely, he would occupy a small, barred room for quite some time, instead.

A wash of air blew past her dark, long hair. The ex-fil had arrived, her part of the mission now over. Waving upward to the pilot of the large, army-issued helo, she glanced back one more time at the young boys. A single smile confirmed today's efforts would not be in vain. One boy seemed to be taking stock of her presence and acts, as if setting himself to repay for others at some future moment what had been done for him. She smiled back. A beautiful and heartening smile.

And just like that, she was gone.

**Ten hours later Sanchez sat alone at a patio table,** awaiting contact. The sun set behind the low-built structure as she poked away at local fare and a cheap beer, almost as if she were on vacation. A group of four made their way past her table, brushing close, between her and the other few customers. In quick succession, the expected envelope slid under her plate, but also—quite surprisingly—a phone appeared, landing softly in her lap. She called for the check. Leaving both the cafe and its quiet end of day scene behind she lifted the phone casually to her ear, receiving the same series of clicks and beeps Dalton had earlier.

The rundown from President Spurrier took about the same amount of explanation but far less convincing. Sanchez held for Dalton to come on the line, processing the political realities unfolding while she had been incognito, half a world away.

Seriously? First female president? *Represent, ladies.*

Sanchez knew Spurrier by mere reputation. What she had gained through the ex-military grapevine made her think this to be much more than a token appointment. Smart. Tough. Witty. Neither blindly ideological nor spineless. Principled but playing the long game at the same time. Now that she thought about it, why hadn't this woman run on her own before this whole mess came down? Probably timing, like most things in life, she thought.

"*Wellllll, Sanchez...*"

The snark was clear, even from this distance.

"Why does it not surprise me at all that you're off doing God knows what, somewhere it took the finest intelligence assets the United States could muster to slide a phone call into your busy schedule."

"Dalton," Sanchez returned. "Charming, as always."

They both smiled lightly.

"Well, wherever you are," Zeb added, more judiciously. "It's good to hear your voice again."

Jessica knew he meant it, even though the last time they'd seen one another had been beyond awkward.

She was the one sitting with him for the long days it took the rescue team to show up, watching the man almost bleed out on the dusty floor of the old comm bunker in Washington State as Chinese troops hovered nearby. Then, she served as frequent visitor and sometimes demanding coach as Dalton took his first, long steps into recovery. In the process, she had come to appreciate his mind, his history, and a profound sense of loyalty that pervaded all he put his hand to.

It's not uncommon for people sharing tragedy and life or death circumstances to connect on a deeper level than mere friendship. So, it seemed quite natural to say *yes* to an evening of dinner and drinks. Looking back on it now, it was no wonder the night ended early and abruptly. No measure of common struggle or extended empathy could overcome the hot mess Dalton had going on in his head and heart. They both tried to be polite but it became painfully obvious — and embarrassing for Zeb — to accept the fact that though his body was getting better all the time, his soul still boiled in a fury of loss, alienation, and anger. He didn't have the words to get it out, so it sat there underneath the surface, clearly poisoning any chance at engaging on deeper levels. Not even half way through their entrees they exchanged a sad but knowing look and simultaneously got up from the table. That beautiful June evening on the Seattle waterfront was the last time they'd spoken.

"Thanks, Zeb" she replied. "Great to hear you too. Where you at these days, Berkeley? I caught rumors you'd gone south."

"Yeah, the Bay Area's not so bad. I mean, a little rough being a 'Hawks fan here but the Niners suck so I'm pretty happy with that."

Sarcasm. Fences. Same thing.

"So, I hate to interrupt the old gang get-together," General Stevens jumped in. "But, we've got something we need to address. Ms.

Sanchez, Dalton here is our op lead and he insists on having you along. The physical evidence at Belize has been lost to the seasonal tides, so all you'll have is the video we got from in-country intel. Their overflight was more timely than first imagined. We got lucky on that one. Montenegro is fresh, so to speak, but we need you on the ground as soon as possible. Sanchez, hoof it to the airport and grab a ride on TransAfrica Air. It's a company-owned outfit." He paused for recognition.

"Yep. Got it."

"Montenegrin authorities are keeping the place sealed up for the time being and the both of you are now food safety agents, on loan to our allies. Welcome to the USDA. You should be in place by later evening, local time tomorrow. This is an eval and analysis op. Dalton, you'll be getting reams of data on your overflight to put in that crazy head of yours. I trust you'll enjoy that."

"Sure," Zeb offered. "Just so I can take in a few bad, late run movies as well."

President Spurrier appeared ready to jump in, chastising Zeb for his lack of seriousness. Stevens motioned with his hand gently, asking for understanding and receiving a stay of the lecture. He wanted to keep Dalton on task. He also wanted to keep the new president reasonably removed from issuing specific orders on this thing. Though the head of the American military, and this could be formally construed as an official op, it was better at this point she maintain some political deniability. A good deal of flexibility in the actual work needing to be done wouldn't hurt, either. Belize was leaking now and families were being informed of the tragic "sinking" of their loved one's vessel. Soon, the same calls would go out in Montenegro, only with a different cover story.

"Very well. Dalton. Sanchez," Stevens said. "You'll both be receiving secured texts and email traffic over the next twelve hours. Reestablish contact when you are eyes-on and have something to report."

With that, the line went cold.

# SIX

*Following an uneventful Atlantic crossing at 30,000 feet the team set up shop in a side office of the Uprava Policije, the Montenegrin National Police. Their conferenced video signal dangled somewhere above the atmosphere before making its way back down to an untraceable location, known only as The Vault.*

**"Mort, what have you got for us?"**

The request came from Dalton, leaning in close over the desktop call unit.

"Labs so far are real basic, Zeb. Tissue and blood samples. Nothing all that helpful yet. Starting to investigate the possibility of a biologically-based neurotoxin, still un-named. Likely something in the category of a snake venom. No markers yet to confirm this as our cause of death, but we gotta start somewhere."

"Hold it, Mort. This thing is far more trouble than a cobra bite causes. I mean, the most... "

"Oh," the tech stepped in, "you would be so lucky as to nab a cobra on this one. First off, not even close. The most common snakes don't even crack the top ten in toxicity. Wayyyy more to worry about than that. Southeast Asia and Australia remain the scariest places to encounter a nasty, angry serpent."

Though the newest add to their crew, *Petty Officer Third Class Craig Mortensen* had earned his stripes as a skilled, senior member of the Pentagon's deep-tech service, performing invaluable assessment work in the Chinese code debacle a few years back. The man's station was officially non-existent—buried under both physical layers of the famous five-sided building as well as a mountain of bureaucratic misdirection—but vital in America's ability to combat cyber incursions. *The Vault* did work few knew about. And even among those privileged few this most recent attachment to Zeb and Sanchez would be a masked affair. Spurrier needed intel, their best assets deployed and returning fruitful data and analysis. What she did not need was a bloated process, placing her efforts into lower gears unnecessarily. Mortensen was the best. He was also a bit scattered at times.

"Take, for instance," he continued, "the little understood Belcher's Sea Snake, erroneously popularized as the most venomous snake for years. This one will really do some damage. But the tests misled because nobody thought to distinguish between modes of transmission. Like a subcutaneous and intramuscular venoming would be the same thing. Ha! What were they thinking?"

"Mort?" Sanchez tried to break the flow, without success.

"Anyways, the one you never, ever, *ever* want to come face to face with is the Inland Taipan from Down Under. A shy species and therefore unlikely to garner much human contact. Still, trust me, I've seen the postmortem images," he shuddered. "Not pretty."

Silence.

A strange counterpart to Mort's breathless recitation of his research.

Another pause.

"Hey, guys. *Guys?*"

"Okay," Dalton asked. "We finished with the Wikipedia review?"

"Almost… " came the dejected reply.

The away team couldn't see Mort's puppy dog face from all the way across the ocean, but it was a good one.

"Look, Mort," Dalton reassured. "We're kinda under pressure to find some answers quickly. If we can't at least narrow down the type of bio-threat we're looking at, we might as well make blind guesses and call it good. I doubt that will be helpful to anyone."

Dalton caught the chagrin of Sanchez, just as he finished the mini-lecture.

"What?" Zeb asked.

"Like you didn't enjoy that little spin around the block of useless facts? C'mon, Dalton. I could see your brain doing its thing while Mort geeked out on the other end of the call. You two are brothers from different mothers. And here I am watching DweebFest 2015 while dead bodies pile up in an emerging pattern, thousands of miles removed from each other."

This time Dalton took the hit and flushed slightly. Throwing up his hands — guilty as charged — he returned to the call station.

"Thanks, Sanchez. You always were my favorite."

"No problem, Mort. Now, please continue."

"Well, the first event is a bit more settled and you guys are on the ground there, so I made some contacts in Belize, checking into possibilities nearby. Diplomatic sources led to some locals, which led to some other locals who gave us a trail to head down for more info. Gotta say, though: even from first steps, it leads to a place much weirder than just snakes."

"Yeah? How weird are we talking here?"

"You might want to sit down."

**Five minutes later,** their collective silence matched the topic's strangeness and the place it had traveled. Dalton literally scratched his head, easing back into the government issue desk chair and considering whether to give any credence to the tall tale just relayed to him. Zeb's hand moved to his chin, rubbing stubble that had gathered from the harried schedule of the last twenty-four hours. It was in moments like this that Dalton's eyes — a curious, warm amber tone — seemed to resonate with analytical activity. He shot them over toward Sanchez in a quizzical expression, probing her level of interest in following up on such lunacy.

She was actually thinking it over.

"Mort," Zeb said. "I want to hear it again. What you're saying is that some Ancient Mayan King is behind this?"

"Are you kidding me?" Mort shot back. "Is that all you got out of the last few minutes?"

"Okay, no. There's much more to the story but essentially what you're hinting at, right? Ancient rival nations go to war and the winner brings back the loser king's *actual legs* to keep them from rising in vengeance. That's a powerful image. I will grant you that. But, that somehow this act of ill-fated diplomacy triggers a curse and their unlikely and widespread demise some hundreds of years later is the result? And that our situation is connected to all this?"

"I didn't say it was logical, Zeb. Just telling you what I heard. Folks in Belize have kept this tale alive for a long time. Like most myths, there's a certain substance to it, even if the story only gives some form of mystical outlines to a part of their past. Think of it like a way to fill in a canvas, where only the barest of sketches hints at the finished portrait."

"I don't know, Mort."

"Wait a second, Zeb. I agree in part," Sanchez said. "The surrounding narrative is out there. *Way* out there. But what about the glyphs? The murals?"

Zeb looked back down at the images Mort had sent while reporting what he'd discovered.

*Severed legs and a mystical revenge. Really old stones with pictures resembling our victims' bodies in both Belize and Montenegro. How in the world do I get myself into these kinds of things?*

Dalton shook his head incredulously. That nudged the former signal corpsman's thinking into gear. At the very least, the story needed to be eliminated from contention, whatever the real-life parts of it turned out to be. Multiple tours in Afghanistan and Iraq – not to mention the whole Chinese takeover craziness in Seattle – taught him he had not seen it all. Probability of any real connections? Extremely low. As in, possibly not worth calculating in the first place. Still, they might as well debunk it and move on.

"Alright. I am no expert at decoding ancient artwork but I agree, the pictures sure resemble what we've viewed so far from our two current events."

Zeb nodded toward Sanchez, looking for her take.

"Yep. Super weird. We have to at least follow up," she assented.

"Who was your contact, Mort?"

"Interestingly, the locals all directed me back to an American husband-wife research team. They've been the primary archaeological presence at *Caracol* – the major Belizean Maya ruin – since the mid-eighties. People say they're your best bet for any potential ties to what's known about the place. They're not on the dig site again for another month but you can reach them at their teaching posts at the University of South Florida."

Zeb glanced at the screen of his phone once more.

Primitive figurines, yet clearly human. Extremities rigid and playing at odd, unnatural angles. Distended bellies. Many of them opened violently but not as if cut into from the outside. That approach would only signal a normative, if maybe even ceremonial violence. The ancient artist-historians in this case had depicted something far more unsettling. Indeed, these mortal wounds portrayed an inward-out bodily catastrophe.

Dalton stood and walked away from the table. Turning back, he confirmed what they all suspected.

"Alright then, looks like we need to make a little side trip to the Sunshine State on our way back to DC. Sanchez, I hope you packed some sunscreen. For me, not you."

# SEVEN

*Another set of eyes scoured a separate, private video feed from Montenegro. This time, instead of standing aghast at the death toll and carnage, the man behind the eyes was pleased. Very pleased.*

**He scrubbed the transport controls back to the beginning again,** once more for timing. The fast-motion of the event made it seem almost comical. That is, if it weren't for the human lives snuffed out in the process. No bother for the viewer. The man noted timestamps on this pass.

*14:16.*

The grand ballroom, extending outward to a terraced area overlooking the Baltic Sea. Three-hundred-some guests. Afternoon cocktails, yet a richly appointed, nearly formal dress code. A lone figure enters the frame from lower left, clambering over a large hedgerow.

*14:17.*

Security approaches, weapons drawn. Intruder drops something to the ground. A tiny burst of gas, appearing more like a small vaporous cloud on the Romanesque tile work. One by one the guests freeze, an odd rigidity displayed before falling where they stood, drinks and caviar in hand.

*14:32.*

Hundreds of bodies, strewn at odd angles with telltale distended and ruptured midsections.

**Satisfied, the man closed the laptop lid**, placing both hands at rest on his black onyx desk.

A knock at the door.

"Yes."

"Sir, are you ready?" the voice probed without entering.

"In a moment."

The man stood from behind the desk and walked toward the door, pausing for just a second before opening it. To the right of the handle he glanced up, to one of the many artifacts lining glass-encased shelves in the room.

A miniature replica of what appeared to be the Easter Island Heads. A smallish stone with hieroglyphics gracing its ragged face.

The man stared.

And then knelt.

Rising a moment later, he grasped the chrome handle and exited the office.

**The small auditorium hosted stadium seating** and a front stage area serving as one gigantic screen—a seamless concave surface. The crowd awaited in an air of anticipation, one of those strange but tangible social interactions registering somewhere between the highly emotional and vaguely spiritual. The MC wrapped up, having done his job to raise the excitement level just below fever pitch. Now, his role was to hand off without losing any momentum.

"So, there's no reason to make you wait any longer. Here he is. I'd give you an introduction but that would be pointless. Our TED Talk conversationalist for today: tech entrepreneur and global social change advocate... "

He waited a beat.

"*Matthew Donneleigh!*"

Bodies shot from seats like rockets off launch pads. Enthusiasm was not the right word. Not quite the chaotic emotion of the Beatles nor any other demigods of the entertainment world. More like hope. Maybe too much like that. Maybe too much for any man to carry for his fellow humans.

It took a full minute and a half of gesturing to get the crowd back into their theater-style seating, though once the applause and shouting ended there remained enough unspent energy in the room to inflame it anew at a poignant turn of phrase or lofty ideal.

"Please, please," the forty-five-year-old pleaded, torso bent in a sort-of Asian bow, hands clasped. "I am humbled and appreciative. You have no idea how much that means to me. Thank, you."

"Matthew, I'll have your babies!"

All present laughed. Donneleigh seemed to blush. It only helped his cause.

"Ah, yes. Well, thank you... I think."

Disarming as always. He had them right where he wanted them.

"Okay. What do you say we start that over."

Another chuckle, this time more reserved. Though sporting a basic tech CEO wardrobe, his words couldn't be received with any more seriousness than the crowded room already granted him. Their countenances spoke resoundingly: this was the most important thing these men and women might do with their time and energies. More revival than rally, his statements shaped their reality, providing them something greater than a job. More than a vocation, even. Something on the order of a mission.

"First off, thanks so much to the TEDS folks for letting us host this talk here, at Quantech Headquarters. I really, really wanted to do this topic and our current innovation schedule made it a bit of a challenge to get out to anywhere else. And honestly, I think this conversation needs to happen now. There is an urgency in our world. One we can't put off for production schedules and quarterly reports any longer."

Looks of affirmation. The faithful nodded with a seriousness and commitment, an almost apostolic authority conferred upon the man. With every new sentence their fervor mounted, white hot in moral zealotry and readiness for action. This was so much more than a technology update. Everyone knew that. And no one should be surprised. It was the logical outcome of a world enamored with innovation and newly-inspired to the boundless reach of their collective efforts. The internal reasoning followed a fairly straight track: if people envisioned such wonders as these, surely the human condition was on the rise, an undaunted ascent toward a world where tolerance, creativity, and fulfillment reigned for every inhabitant of this blue-green globe. For goodness sake, the ability to converse directly with someone hundreds — or, if need be thousands — of miles distant was a given and increasingly a universal reality, regardless of location, nation, or economic challenges. Seventy years ago these advances would have graced the pages of science fiction. A few hundred years back and you may have been burnt at the stake for claiming a power of long-distance communication. Prior generations engaged their world as if filled with mysteries, unsolvables. Their forebears considered themselves minor actors in a great divine storyline. Sometimes the immortals were benevolent. More often they played at a distance, unpredictable, fickle. But now, having unlocked the great unknowns of matter, bending it to their desires and needs, this new greatest generation saw nothing but glory ahead; a humanly perfected dawning on the horizon. It could be. It must be. If only they all banded together and left older thinking behind. And men like Donneleigh, though half a generation their senior, pointed the way. They would follow him anywhere. At any cost.

**Exactly twenty-eight minutes later** Donneleigh exited, stage-left. He would not return for an encore. Probably be too much for them to take in, anyways. His words had moved them to the exact planned pitch. In fact, so heightened was the emotional temperature in the room that in the aftermath nearly a third of the attendees felt compelled to engage in some form of amorous activity. Many went home to unsuspecting and surprised spouses. Some opted for the closest open cubicle or a backseat in Quantech's parking complex. Such was the effect of one Matthew Donneleigh.

The return trip to the man's office took only a few minutes. He walked quietly, flanked by two security guards, through mostly emptied spaces. The route: planned and cleared. Standard operating procedure for someone of Donneleigh's rank. His office door closed and the two men took up station, watching the corridor with blank, steeled expressions. Once inside, the tech guru came around, behind his desk again. With the laptop lid opened, he clicked a small icon in the quick-start bar. A rectangular subnet window appeared, flashing red, then orange, and finally green. A simple cue. The most secure digital communication net in the world readied. His line-command-style sentence was straightforward, at least to those on the other end.

*Caracol 3: proceed.*

Donneleigh shut down the subnet, erasing all traces of the command. Easing back from the desk, he swiveled in his chair. The view out back his office was of a specially curated garden, viewable only by himself from this space. The fifty-foot glass ceiling space boasted a beautiful and rare exposition of some of the world's most unusual floral bounty. The colors were untainted but begged disbelief, as if they must have been manipulated, engineered. The hues radiated with life, almost pulsating in their vibrancy. A coexistence of unbelievable aliveness.

*Almost Eden*, he thought.

*But not quite yet.*

# EIGHT

*Zeb caught a sideways glance at Sanchez. With eyes closed, her head rested against the airplane window's oval portal. Static electricity set strands of her hair slightly above the others, almost levitating. She seemed so peaceful.*

**Dalton had tried for some shuteye as well,** but the pace of their op and the things he was learning kept his mind in high gear. The upside of a brain like his was obvious. The downside? An extremely hard beast to shut down, once fully engaged. Proving a futile exercise since departing the Montenegrin airport, he leaned back in his seat and let it go.

The mental rush came hard and fast. Data streams breached like storm surges on a New Orleans waterfront precinct, pulsing in and out with abandon. A flow of information so heavy that any sense of discernible patterning vanished, at least momentarily. Soon, clusters of statistics and variables began to form, allowing a more precise reckoning. Of particular attention were the toxicity numbers and effects Mort researched and passed to them. They didn't add up at all. No, more than that: they didn't seem to fit. While accounting for the paralysis each victim experienced, the whole stomach thing stood as a mystery. Zeb looked again, deeper.  Natural poisons. Virulent strains. Infections. Nothing causing this level of neurological distress carried an accompanying gastric event.

*Almost seems like whatever got in and did all the damage also wanted to exit almost as fast. But that makes no sense at all, Dalton. Toxins don't think and act, they merely spread and affect, ferried along by the body's own natural pathways to tissue and bone. And why? Why would they want to leave?*

Dead end, for now.

Zeb sighed and focused up the aisle of the big commercial jet. Nearly everyone else was asleep, just like Sanchez.

*Lucky stiffs.*

Donning earmuff-sized noise canceling headphones, Dalton reached forward to the chair-back screen and perused the entertainment options. The *Bourne Legacy* seemed a good match, approximating his mood and the amount of flight time remaining. A reticent fan of the genre, Zeb noted that danger and adventure in real life seldom came across the same as in books and movies. He found it more difficult to suspend reality, since he had lived so much of it. And his experiences were often distressing, gritty, and confusing. No easy answers. Almost always undesirable choices. Still, the exotic locales and beautiful people on the screen helped him set aside what he knew to be true. Like a roller coaster, he decided to just strap himself in and enjoy the ride, visions of distorted dead bodies removed for now from his consciousness.

**"Mr. Foreman, has the jury reached a verdict?"**

The ominous memory returned, amplified and distorted in the restlessness of the last thirty-six hours and a wash of overactive brain chemicals. The judge's face in the dream, disproportionate to his body, loomed menacingly. His words from the bench echoed and sharpened, assaulting the teen's ears. Dalton heard his mother's cries but for some reason couldn't turn his head to see her face. Heartbreaking. Her sobs remained muffled and he sensed she lay doubled over in her seat. Zeb tried to rise from where he was, to go to her. His torso would not agree. The young man's heart reached out to her but his body refused to move. He struggled against unseen bonds, knowing he should be at her side in this moment. One last, monumental effort to escape the weight capturing him. No. Nothing. She sobbed even more and it broke the teenager into pieces, equally from shame at his father's sins and his mother's pain.

"Your honor, we have reached a verdict," came the expected yet unwelcome response from the jury box.

Dalton stared over to the defendant's table. His father stood, orange-clad in jail garb. The older man's face remained blurred as well.

"We find the defendant, James Murifield Dalton... "

*No. No!*

"No!!!" Zeb screamed, this time for real, awakened from sleep. Odd, startled looks from the five rows closest to him.

"Dalton? Hey, Zeb."

Sanchez' tone carried concern and for a second Dalton felt cared for. That feeling came and went quickly, as all seconds do.

"You okay, Zeb? Must've been out good. Eyes all crossed and mouth open. I waited for the drool but you held it together. At least, until you started the *screaming like a frightened schoolgirl* bit."

"Aghh. Thanks, Sanchez," Zeb shuffled some in his seat, trying his best to reclaim awareness and maybe a bit of honor. "Can always count on you. Reassuring to know there are some constants in this world."

"Exactly what I'm here for, buddy. Um, I mean team leader."

Zeb rubbed his eyes and face, flushing the skin with blood flow.

"Oh. *That's* what's bugging you? You've been pissy this whole trip. Well," he considered, "When you think about it, I guess that is something. The newly elected president needs help. First call? Well, we know how that went down."

"Shut up. You're an idiot."

Sanchez had a way of ending a conversation that meant "we're done, no really"; not to be debated or challenged. Zeb hated to admit it but if he plowed ahead, things were about to deteriorate rapidly. She was a formidable verbal sparring partner; one of the reasons he so enjoyed her company. There was also her loyalty. Unheard of, really. And then, there was always the fact she might literally stretch across the armrest, incapacitating him before he could even reach the call button above his head.

She gave him the look.

*Back off now and we'll all be better for it.*

Dalton was especially good at probabilities. In no arrangement of the data in his head did he see a win coming from pursuing this interaction.

*Awkward Sanchez because of a crappy date. Angry Sanchez from being undervalued.*

*Yeah, I'm screwed.*

**The remainder of the flight was uneventful,** if a little edgy between them. Approach and landing: completely routine. The rush and flow of passengers at Tampa International appeared about normal for a weekday afternoon. With deplaning, airport transit, and an Uber ride behind them, the duo now stood in a parking lot astride the Social Science Building on the campus of The University of South Florida. The beige and red structure left something to be desired, aesthetically speaking. Some collegiate settings boast grand, historic architecture or innovative design and interaction spaces. USF's blandly named housing for all things soft science was not one of those places. The dual-tone, nondescript multi-level structure sported twin paved paths, leading to parallel, uninspiring entrances. Balanced, yes, but not very inviting. Neither Zeb nor Sanchez were art snobs, so it looked like a normal college building to them. Through the doorway they were met with another academic mainstay, the black punch board with white attachable lettering, hosting the name and location of the faculty's offices across both floors.

*Drs. Martin and Constance Hendricks: SS234 and 236*

The wide stairway took them up and just outside the stippled glass doors of their interviewees. To the left and right of the doorways: posters and postings of the Mayan ruins at Caracol. Good. Exactly what they came for. Time to run this story down a bit more.

Dalton knocked, leaning through the half-opened doorway.

A small woman with wiry white hair and startlingly bright eyes looked up.

"Oh, hello. You must be the couple from DC."

"Yes," Sanchez started, "But we're not a ..." and then wished she'd kept that one in.

"Hello," Zeb extended his hand in greeting, covering the awkwardness. "We are indeed your appointment from DC. I trust you have been briefed on the sensitive nature of our visit?"

"Why certainly," floated a voice from the adjacent room. This one came with an older man, sporting a medium build but obviously someone still active in his later years. "Here's your tea, my dear," he turned to the woman, handing over a small cup and saucer.

"You're so sweet, Mart."

"I hope your flight was good," the older man offered to the duo. "Coming back that direction is always the hardest. Hopefully you can get some rest and back to your normal schedule soon."

Dalton had been around a veritable sea of PhD's in his almost four decades of life. None had been remotely as winsome as this gentleman. If their relationship were to be any extension of this first sixty seconds, he knew he'd like this guy a lot. Zeb caught Sanchez with a shrug of his shoulders. The conversation had started off a bit differently than anticipated but pleasant, nonetheless.

The smallish woman took a sip of the hot liquid, proclaiming it perfect by her satisfied air, and then moved her glasses down her nose. She glanced from Jessica to Zeb and back to Jessica again.

"I don't know, sweetie. There's something about this one," tilting her head toward Dalton. "You could do worse."

*Oh, lady,* Sanchez turned, rolling her eyes this time. *There's something about this one. Just nobody's figured it out yet.*

# NINE

*Sanchez felt like she was interrupting a lot.*

**"Okay, so the ruins at Caracol** — you found *what* story, again?"

Constance was a patient woman; a fine academic and even finer person.

"Sure, Ms. Sanchez. Ongoing warfare between Caracol and their next largest rival Tikal continued for centuries. Many of these battles were of a limited nature, minor incursions to remind the other they still existed. Preemptive in an ancient sort of way, maybe with the consideration that a smaller fight every now and then would keep things in balance. Then, about 600AD a major engagement between the groups ensued, much larger than usual and with an unheard-of scale of loss in life and treasure. Caracol won. To make their point beyond the battlefield they severed the legs of the Tikal enemy king and brought them back to their people, intending for them to always be on display as a sign they had and would conquer again, whenever necessary."

"Got it. The same story passed to our contacts stateside from locals in Belize. But you relate it as if it were history, not myth. How exactly do you know the dates and the details?"

"The ruins, dear. Mayan history is all carved into stone. Stelae —
large rocks throughout the city — serve as an ongoing, visual history
lesson. We've been quite busy on that front. Unearthed about 100 tons
worth over the last thirty years."

"Okay, so the legs. Intended to be a lasting image?
Mummification?"

Martin jumped in. "Essentially, yes. But different than more
familiar Egyptian rites and methods. The prevailing theory is they
used a unique chemical bond, based on Yucca from the deeper
Amazon basin. It does the job quite well."

A brief pause lay between them all in the small office space
overflowing with maps and books until Martin spoke again. "So,
that's what you came here for? All the way from the Baltic? The legs
story?"

"No," Zeb replied. "We came here because of this."

Dalton placed his phone down on the desk so the professors could
eye the video streams, side by side, in simultaneously gruesome
fashion. Constance blanched and put her hand to her mouth, more
out of the horror of what had happened to actual people than the
vileness of the scene. After the initial shock wore off, the long-married
couple gave one another a knowing expression. An understanding
born of decades of toil and study.

"You don't think?" Constance murmured.

"Sure looks the same to me, dear."

Martin took two steps toward a filing cabinet and removed a legal
sized, perfect bound journal. He opened it for all to survey.

Aging photos, hand sketches from the field. Yellowing pages with
long past dates and scribblings. Still, the match was unmistakable.
The couple's visual discoveries from underground vaults were a
valuable, if inexact pairing.

Another half-hour of pleasant and informative conversation ended
with Zeb and Sanchez heading back to the airport for their connecting
flight to the Capitol.

---

Washington, D.C.

**The private office served as more of a side room,** a quiet, set aside place in contrast to the heavily trafficked Oval Office. Used at times in suspect activity by former executives, today it was simply a better space to get things done.

The four of them had been going over the intel from the trip for almost an hour now. The president, Stevens, Zeb, and Sanchez searched for connections, commonalities. Dalton, as usual, sped out ahead of everyone else, narrowing the immense field of data into a few concurrent streams of reasoning and possibilities. And yet he waited. This was something he was learning lately, but well. Though his abilities got him places faster than most others, he had started to value contributions and angles brought by a more collective process. Sure, at times, especially in combat, his advantage needed to be leaned into significantly and immediately. But he was beginning to accept that the backgrounds and experiences of co-laborers could be useful as well. The simple fact that they were *not him*, did not have his mind, was a component part of good strategy. Though still difficult to slow down enough to gain from it, Dalton willed himself to try.

"Okay," Stevens queried. "Blood work inconclusive?"

"Correct," Zeb said. "The paralysis leads us one direction but the distended, destroyed bowel makes no sense."

"But the rapid seizing," Spurrier jumped in. "I mean, do we know of anything that acts so quickly and uniformly?"

"No, ma'am. Not according to the findings from Mort. Some rough parallels, but again the equation doesn't add up. We are still waiting for a fuller analysis. Last we talked, he thought we should get it anytime now."

A small green light flashed on the bottom of the wall-hung LCD screen. Sanchez caught it first.

"Well, there you go," she said as a picture in picture emerged, taking up roughly a third of the space. Mort's still-young looking face appeared. He seemed breathless and held a few loose papers.

"Hey, soldier," Dalton probed. "You okay? They got you doing real sprints along with the coding kind?"

Mort would have laughed but currently was fending off the effects of having been more desk jockey than active warrior for the better part of the last decade.

"The... " he swallowed hard. "Aghh." after another big breath, holding the papers out front of his heaving chest. "Crap. Stupid printer is broken. Had to... run up and down a hundred steps."

The four of them, having enough collective government experience to know the fate of the world could hang on something as banal as a busted printer cartridge, accepted it, waiting for him to calm down.

"Final report, madam president," Mort eventually got out.

The screen filled with another set of images. None of the four were trained in the medical arts, so it didn't immediately occur to them the significance of what they were seeing.

"Mort, this looks like radiologic imaging. But what part of the body are we looking at here?"

"Let me rotate and pull out a bit," Mort said.

Though their collective "aha" stayed unspoken, he knew they were tracking so he zoomed back in again.

Dalton looked over to Spurrier.

"Ma'am. You're seeing this?"

"Yes, Mr. Dalton. I am."

They looked at one another this time, literally speechless. The realization sunk in. It all started to make perfect if incomplete sense.

"So, Mort, correct me if I'm wrong," Zeb continued. "But those look like a grouping of incredibly small bite marks on the basal ganglia of Victim Doe."

"Yep. You got it, LT. And not just small. Microscopic. Which means... "

Sanchez completed the thought, "... which means two things. The paralysis is not coming from a toxic infusion. These people had the core of their nervous systems severed. The cut is thorough but ragged. Which also indicates... "

This time the general theorized. "... must have been hundreds, if not thousands, of biological entities at work here."

"For sure," Mort confirmed. "The docs are telling me they don't have a classification for this but the evidence suggests a parasitic infestation; one that has a two-fold trajectory. Once in the body, crazy, but these little buggers, whatever they are, go for the top of the spinal cord first and then make their way down through the venous system to the larger organs in the lower trunk. Once there, they agitate the stomach lining in an explosive fashion. Hence, the burst effect."

Dalton put the streams of intel together. He had that look.

The others saw it, wanting him to voice it for everyone.

"New host."

He paused before continuing, considering the gravity of the situation.

"Exit wound. They're done with the body and are looking for a new one."

"Yeah, and one more thing," Mort said. "We have a party-crasher on this one."

"Go on," the president prodded.

"Couldn't see it from the original footage, bad angle. But, in going over the guest list, an unidentified body lay among the attendees with a small, spent aero-cannister within reach. The residue of some form of gelatinous substance indicates this is likely the carrier for the bio entities. Completely clean now. Problem is, we can't ID him."

"What do you mean, Mort?" Zeb tried.

"Dental implants. Fingerprints scrubbed. DNA analysis also coming up zero. No records whatsoever this person, who wasn't supposed to be here, actually exists."

"Well," Sanchez finished. "Anyone thinking this is still possibly a random act of nature?"

No one spoke.

"Didn't think so."

"Okay," Spurrier processed out loud. "We have a probable means of death and certainty that someone, somewhere is behind this. It was an attack. Scope? Too early to tell. The two events, though disconnected geographically, have some traces of similarities. And then there's your strange tales from Caracol, Dalton. Seems more like a loosely hovering aspect of this whole thing. Could be a wild goose chase."

"Yes, ma'am," Zeb returned. "But then again, the pictures are uncannily alike. Now, whether the story has any operational bearing in our case, who knows but I'd like to follow up on the researcher's leads. The Caracol story intimates a connection to a deeper Amazon basin setting. There's always been a component that somehow the Tikal King's revenge emanated from within the recesses of the river's ecosystem. From what we know of the biological basis of many plants and animals from there, it seems we might gain some insight by checking it out. We are discovering all kinds of healing properties from the Amazonian context. Seems there could be some equally nasty stuff lurking, as well. We know this micro-parasite likes to eat through the human basal ganglia. Could our mystery in the jungle be the same thing? No idea, but I'd be remiss if we didn't run this one down to a dead end. There is even a particular, very remote setting that present-day storytellers claim as the genesis of the 'curse.' Seems a good place to start."

Stevens stepped back from the small grouping, gathered in front of the screen. He arched his back and stretched, almost as if clearing his mind in the process of adjusting his body.

"Madam president. I concur. Our footing now is the assumption of imminent grave harm. Not much to go on, but a whole lot to be concerned about. Let's get Zeb and Sanchez down there and see what we can uncover. In the meantime, we need to do some more work on threat analysis from the Vault."

"Very well then," Spurrier ordered. "Until our next steps are a bit clearer, this is still need to know, and only for this cohort, until otherwise stated. Preliminary assumptions of possible tactical response and range of options should begin, simultaneous with further investigation of the causes and agency of the individuals behind these two attacks and the bio-parasite angle as well."

She paused, once more measuring the team.

"Are we clear on our jobs for the next number of hours?"

A *yes, madam president* resounded, even through the video call screen.

# TEN

*She was a believer, too.*

**Listless.** Barely conscious with a heart rate well under normal. The attractive, intelligent young woman spent her last few breaths somewhere nearer brain dead than self-aware. A sleek silver cannister lay at her feet. She had fallen back into a semi-upright position after losing all control of her torso. A short side table caught her drop to the floor and it was here she viewed the first moments of her life's last efforts, her final contributions to the world her parents had ushered her into, some twenty-eight years ago.

Born into an upper middle-class family in the very middle-America city of Omaha, she was loved and cherished. The fifth and only successful effort of this couple to bear children, she stepped into an especially thank-filled environ; one promising every advantage to be placed upon her cherubic face and the curls she wore until her first haircut, age seven. A comfortable home. The best in private school education. Vacations. A top-tier college and studies abroad. One would imagine this young one to continue the ways in which she had been reared. Good job. A good family. But it wasn't enough. Somewhere along the way she discovered an emptiness that nothing in her well-manicured life could fill.

Though fading quickly now, what remained of her eyesight focused downward, fixed lazily at her waist. Numbed by the gross failures of her nervous system, her rapidly growing belly seemed an odd sight but nothing in her body's hard-wired warnings screamed *trouble*. So, quite abruptly, layers of flesh forced their way open. She bled out and her heart ceased its steady life-rhythm.

**The chaos was greater this time.** Some five thousand Haitians sprawled in a grotesque portrait of the coldness of death. The force of bodies, all surging toward the exits of the stadium, caused a bulge at the gates. No one ran free. The locks had been set three minutes before the event. Upon realizing they were trapped, nearly a hundred souls clamored up and over the wire fencing. None of the would-be escapees made it out that way either. Performing what looked to be some strange, drug-induced dance, their arms and legs flew to the sides and back onto the unsuspecting, next in line.

In a last, futile attempt to escape their unknown and unseen killer, hundreds headed for the middle of the soccer pitch. Aimlessly, they threw themselves forward, even as their eyes widened at the fate of their neighbors and fellow countrymen. They'd come for a special playoff match of their local team versus a semi-pro club from Port Au Prince. It was to be the classic David vs Goliath scenario. Instead, a well-fought contest heading into extra time became a nightmare of unimagined proportions and the tragically violent ending to mostly harsh lives. This game, and the free admission offered, provided a small blessing in an otherwise bleak existence. Little did they know the afternoon's respite would be their final release from earthly toil as well.

That's the way Donneleigh saw it, too.

**"Visual confirmation in ten seconds, sir."** The flight tech's voice came through loud and clear, though originating over a thousand miles away.

The AirStrato Pioneer approached the open-air structure with stadium seating for 5400 at its top speed of 106 mph. A half mile to target, the Romanian-produced UAV began descending to the planned surveillance pattern of wide arcs over the field. Slowing to under 85 and dropping to 200 feet, her twelve-meter wingspan floated gracefully over the macabre happenings below, all the while sending back a wide-angle view of a crowded ballpark gone silent.

"Initiating heat signatures and motion detection analysis."

The same voice, again.

"Commence zoom and hold for east end of target zone."

This time the tech had to lean over, away from his station. as his stomach responded to the utter horrors on the comm screen. Men. Women. Children. Then he reminded himself of the pay grade bump from regular air force to some unknown employer. His services were valuable in the new world of unmanned flight and intelligence acquisition. He was only responding to how things were changing for the better, at least for his bank account.

"Ah, we are confirmed," he finally got out. "All targets dispatched."

"Good. Complete the run and transmit secured analysis within the hour," came another voice, to this point silent on the line.

The last image lingered and *Dr. Anthony Bartollo* stepped back from the lab station screen, a bit shaky.

"Doctor?"

Bartollo caught his balance on the edge of the table and gingerly made his way back in front of the giant touch screen computer's camera.

"Doctor, you don't look well to me. Or is it the lighting there?"

"No, I am," the scientist attempted a recovery. "I am fine, sir."

Donneleigh knew when to push and when to soften. He opted for the latter in this circumspect moment.

"My dear doctor, I am repulsed by what we witnessed as well but we have what we need now. At least on first appraisal, the ratios are workable, are they not?"

"Yes," another pause for a minor clearing of the doctor's throat. "A thousand to one works, as in our projections. With the environment reasonably secured we should achieve similar results, and with minimal overkill."

The eminent biologist allowed the numbers to placate his conscience. It was only partially working.

"Well, then," Donneleigh replied via video link. "It seems we are green light to produce and set our efforts in motion."

"Very good, sir."

The last response left something to be desired. Donneleigh was not convinced his key science adviser held no lingering reservations about their work.

"Dr. Bartollo. *Anthony...* "

"I know, sir. Forgive me. I know what we are doing here is right. It's just that these people are not the problem. They caused no harm to our world. If anything, they should be the ones given a new chance at simply living."

"You are right, Anthony. Their lives were noble, as is their sacrifice for the untold others like them taking new places of meaning and order in a remade world. A better world. The world that should have been from the beginning. Caracol 1 and 2 were small learnings but righteous action. British financiers and some of Eastern Europe's faux royalty had it coming. Caracol 3? Necessary to confuse the pattern to anyone who might notice. Surely no one will. At least, not with any kind of clarity as to what is really happening until we have fulfilled our mission. No, my friend. We will prevail. And these fine, shining examples of humanity will have played a most critical, though unnoticed role. After all, we need not sacrifice in this manner again, correct? How long now to get things in place?"

The scientist felt no better. Still, there was a commitment to their actions that went deep, far too deeply for a slight twinge of misplaced morality to unseat.

"Three weeks, sir. Twenty-one days from now."

"Perfect, Anthony. You may rest assured; our testing phases are complete. Every act from this point forward is in execution of our plans."

"Yes, sir. I understand."

"Good, now onto our organizational phases. I have word from our third partner that the communication elements are ready. Tomorrow will be a very new day, Anthony. A corrected course for all we hold dear. That is all for now, my friend."

Matthew ended the transmission and breathed deeply, satisfyingly.

"Let it be so," Donneleigh intoned.

*Yes, let it be so.*

# ELEVEN

*The email icon wouldn't stay in the trash.*

**The young royal called for his servant.** "Get in here!" was the formal understanding of the Arabic. The contextualized meaning came across somewhat saltier.

*Prince Aman* was not a patient man. Then again, nothing of his circumstance required nor shaped such a disposition. Fourth in line of the world's few remaining royal families and their billions, the nineteen-year-old had no time for things that didn't work. Immediate gratification was simply the rhythm of his days. The word *no* or *stop* rarely filled his ears, and then only from a more senior member of his family. Work was an afterthought. Education a formality, with little to no justification for the things he absorbed, and that only when he felt like it. In all honesty, he was a bit bored with it all. But, then again, he knew — at least on a very factual level — that the rest of the world did not live in this manner. So, while he was not a thankful man, nor was he compassionate toward those whose lives were framed in struggle, neither did he wish to trade places with anyone, anywhere.

So, the minor irritation on the screen was not just that. It was an affront. Like a bad magic trick, the single message in his inbox performed a maddening re-appearance act, while hiding every other message he had received over the last few days. He had had enough of the joke.

"Pharook!"

His voice boomed and his personal assistant entered.

"Hmm," the tall, older man leaned over, trying the identical commands as his charge. A few more clicks. Nothing. Shut down the email client. Re-open. Syncing new messages.

There it was again, all by itself.

"My lord, do you recognize the sender? Have you opened anything from them before?"

"No. Never. Make it go away."

"Yes, my lord. Have you clicked on anything in the body of the email yet? There is a lone link here."

"Don't you think I see the same thing?!!... "

The young royal ended the phrase with another colorful term, this one as unflattering as the first. Though thoroughly modernized in every other way, the heir still preferred thousand-years-old insults, the generational vocabulary of the Bedouins before him. This time Pharook stepped back, just slightly. He knew his place but also understood he was the only immediate help in this situation. The servant waited, calmly. Prince Aman gestured for him to proceed. Having made his point without breaching protocol, Pharook continued.

"Maybe you should take some time for yourself, my prince. A soak perhaps? I will keep working on this."

"Yes, maybe you have a point, my good man."

Thirty minutes later the young one returned from the baths, calmed and oiled.

"Well, Pharook. Tell me you've made some progress."

"Sir, unfortunately, no. At every turn, the system locks up, except for the live link. I restart and return here. I force the boot back to a former, healthy recall. It brings me back again."

"So, we need a new computer."

"I wish this were so easy, my lord. I called in our lead IT engineer as well. He logged on to your accounts from remote access points with the same results."

"What is he recommending, then?"

"Believe it or not, sir, he says to go ahead and activate the link. He has no means of entering otherwise. In his thinking, if clicking destroys everything, it is no different than never gaining access again. Logically, it appears someone is trying to gain your attention, not destroy your files. With this level of coding, they could achieve that end without ever alerting you in the first place."

"He says to click the link?"

"Yes, my lord. He says to click the link."

**The monitor switched to a basic black background.** Soon, darkness was replaced in a flurry of images and numbers, supported by a voice over and carrying the world's ills to the screen in front of the prince and his attendant. But, while the news was grim, the conclusion was strangely hope-filled.

*This is our moment, our hour to adjust the human trajectory, to replace tragedy and suffering with simple lives of honor and love. It can be done. Banded together, we hold the resources and knowledge to make things new again.*

*It doesn't have to be this way. A better path can be forged.*

The visionary language ended with a call to action, a voice behind a faceless avatar.

"You don't know me, but we are quite alike. We are the key to the changes this world needs. We've been given much. Now, much is required. So, please accept my invitation to a truly global event—*World One*—three weeks from now. People like us, coming together in a vital effort to make this planet a true, flourishing home for all humankind. Once gathered, we'll contribute our collective resources and talents toward a better future for everyone. Let's call it a tithe, shall we? An investment of a tenth of the world's greater resources. I am certain many of you will want to give more once you hear the plans, but we'll start there."

A Rorschach-looking mess of a QR Code came on screen, breaking and adding to the confusion of the message.

"This is your invitation. It is also your bond of trust. The choice is yours: attend *World One* and contribute toward a better future... or we take the other 90% of your wealth, leaving you with the tenth. Impossible? No, I think we both know this is entirely possible. You have not even been able to break the loop of this simple email. Be assured, our hold over your accounts and investments is much stronger and more immediate than this simple display."

A pause.

"Oh, and one last item. As the world becomes aware of this event, you will speak of it only in positive tones with no mention of the 90/10 scenario. Let's be careful with our words, shall we? All you have to lose is, well, almost everything. But think of it this way: what we can be gained is almost unimaginable. Your QR Code invite will arrive in your inbox momentarily. Once accepted, this message will forever be gone, untraceable by even the most advanced forensic efforts. Details regarding time, location, and preparation for *World One* will be forthcoming."

Pharook stood, mouth opened. Prince Aman was boiling.

"That is all for now. The date is set. Show up and join together for good, to ennoble the existence of untold hundreds of millions... or begin living a very different life, as well. The choice, of course, is yours."

---

New York, NY

**Benjamin Jacobs** leaned into the floor to ceiling window panes of his office at 1211 Avenue of the Americas in the heart of Manhattan's financial district. His shoulder and the side of his face warmed against the tempered glass as his gaze lingered out over the bustle of the workday below. Leaves were transitioning, colors showing their obedience to the rhythms of nature. The man wondered if this were a moment of change for him as well, the odd video message and invite he'd just watched still roiling in his head and heart. It was unsettling. But not completely off-putting.

"Mr. Jacobs?" The familiar voice of his executive secretary drew him back toward the present moment.

"Turner. Yes, what do you need?"

The young man was still shy of a year in this position and didn't want to screw things up. He loved the job, and knew there were ways to approach his boss and ways not to. And he was getting better all the time at discerning the difference.

"Uh. That quick summary of editorials. You asked me to pull the abstracts. Here they are."

"Oh yeah, that. Right," Jacobs breathed in and stretched himself taller, as if the small act might clear his mind and shed unspoken concerns from his frame. "Great. Thanks. You can just leave them."

"Sure thing, Mr. Jacobs. Door open, or closed?"

"Closed. And please hold any calls."

"Yes, sir."

A soft whoosh meant the large door had settled into its jam. The ensuing silence was pronounced, bordering on cavernous. It was also exactly what the man needed. Sitting down, Jacobs opened a new Word doc and began writing. What started flowing were sentiments and honesty, of a depth never imagined by himself or others who knew him well. It all took shape as if written by another, for him. All he was required to do was swipe his fingers across worn plastic keys and place black figures on a white background. He'd labor over a title later. For now, the familiar byline would get things started.

*Benjamin Jacobs, Editorial Staff — The Wall Street Journal*

# TWELVE

*The following morning, Matthew Donneleigh was one of the first to absorb Jacobs' words. What he saw pleased him, convinced even more that he tred the right track, was doing the right thing.*

**The tech executive couldn't help the smile** growing with every paragraph read. The piece was more than he could have asked for. It was especially powerful at the third paragraph in:

*... the Journal has long stood against tyranny in all its forms. Political, military, economic. There is no difference. "Free Markets and Free People": our mantra. I still believe it. But there comes a time when the measure of an ideal is its actual expression in the real world, the lives of people across the globe. Yesterday's anonymous transmission to some thirteen million of the globe's wealthy – now understood as having targeted those categorized as High Net Worth (HNW) Individuals (investable assets of a million or more dollars) – gives me pause.*

*Yes, I personally received the notice as well, the invitation to World One. While I first reacted as being held over a fire to give yet again to people who didn't earn my money, something in me stepped back for a moment. I realized it didn't matter. Go or not, whoever is running this thing grips me, excuse the crassness, by the balls. In that freedom of mindset, I began to wonder.*

*Maybe this is what's required. Let's be honest, everything else just maintains the status quo and our world thrives none the better with each generation of the same. Maybe I needed a kick in the groin. Maybe we all need a kick in the groin. Who knows. We have no idea the actual plans to be presented. Still, whoever it is demands our attention. At this point, I am going. Willingly. Maybe even hopefully.*

*Benjamin Jacobs, Editorial Staff — The Wall Street Journal*

**Donneleigh leaned back.** A flush of emotion overtook the normally staid man. He actually began crying. Two-plus decades of frustration unloaded in his office. Though the world viewed him as one of its most innovative and successful people, there was another chapter to Donneleigh that read a significantly less victorious one for those who followed his life, as well. It began with a simple question: what does one do after achieving many lifetimes worth of wealth and success by age thirty-five? In this case, you turn your attention to the world.

Matthew found it a simple thing to begin a philanthropic enterprise. He certainly had enough money. And he had hired all the right people. As a team, they targeted the most strategic of campaigns. Broadly spread across health care, nutrition, education, and micro business development, the foundation was up and running within twelve months.

Such hopes, early on. Each step built on another, momentum all heading in the right direction. But then timelines closed, and gains — though measurable and meaningful — landed nowhere near expectations. The humanitarian enterprise proved to be yet another example of the proverbial number of steps backward and forward, with not enough traction gained to solve the problems they were targeting. Looking at it from a distance, one might think the weight of humanity leaned heavily against itself, unwilling to be cured of its own ills. Plans and resources were not the issue. Implementation at the local level, constantly warring against corruption and political instability. These seemingly unmovable factors reared their ugly heads, time and again. The first time Donneleigh learned of warehouses full of vaccines held back for the highest bidder, he was undone. The he found out how many of these warehouses existed; the sad norm instead of anomaly. A pattern emerged. Some man — mostly men, but every now and then a woman — decided the hardships of their fellow countrymen signaled opportunity for them to prosper.

What to do in places where the law was fluid and those in authority often colluded, or outright led, these efforts at control by scarcity? Security services hired by Donneleigh suggested a more direct tack. The philanthropist in him blanched at the thought of using force to remove these human cysts from their communities. But there would be no more progress while these despots ruled. Increasingly, he made his peace with realities on the ground. *Better for one man to die.* His first time paying for a hit was met with vomit upon hearing of its success. Yet his stomach and mind responded ever more forcefully as each new boss assumed his place, usually within days. Soon enough, and after it seemed he employed a full-time force of small-time assassins, the realization settled in: this was not working. It was confusing. Everything else in his life had landed him on medal stand after medal stand. This remained an unsolvable problem. And so, not quite knowing what else to do, he left the work in good hands and returned to his first work — technology — ever uneasy about his foray into worldwide humanitarian efforts and wondering when, or if, he might happen upon the answer, the solution currently escaping him.

**Matthew wiped his tears** and sighed. A contented settling when a plan of action not only proves successful but carries with it an air of moral or religious fervor. Thinking back over those painful twenty years he realized again that everything that matters in life comes with its particular timing. He hadn't been on the wrong track, at least not as fully as imagined at the time. The strategy, the means of getting to a long-term solution, escaped him. That was then. Now, all was working.

Donneleigh brought up a subnet on his desktop and waited.

*Initiating...*

Dr. Bartollo's lab coat-clad image appeared.

"Doctor. Good morning. Have you any news for me? Anything I should be aware of?"

"Sir, we are on schedule for mass production. Two weeks is a tight window but we are on target," the scientist paused before continuing. "And, might I say, the communication end of things is progressing as well."

"I could not be happier, Anthony," he beamed. "Jacobs' piece is the fountainhead. Many will follow and the weight of opinion will shift in our favor. There is enough mystery surrounding *World One* to keep it in the media cycle, right up to the moment it begins. And enough of a call to empathy that many will respond positively."

"Certainly, sir. But do you think most will be as thoughtful as Jacobs?"

Donneleigh smirked.

"Oh, heavens no, my dear doctor. They'll come because I am forcing them to come. A tenth of their wealth is significant, no question. The misers so love their money. They'll consider it a small price to pay and move on with their lives. True, a few will show they possess a beating heart inside their chests, like Jacobs. But most? No. They will lay their tribute down reluctantly while presenting an air of concern for the plight of their brothers and sisters. And that's the issue, Anthony — the sickness I couldn't cure before."

"Yes, sir."

"And it's the reason we are doing this, my friend."

Matthew signed off and made his way across the office, stopping just short of the doorway. There he stood, silent, reverent before the statuette on the shelf. The face and eyes stared back, almost knowingly; the deep features more sad than stoic. Donneleigh felt it. Not joyous. Not celebratory. Just resolved. After a few minutes, his heart rate slowed and the familiar sensations appeared. Peaceful.

Calmed. And the next half-hour brought more of the same, only further embedding the rightness of his cause.

# THIRTEEN

*Sanchez held the red bandana in place, covering her mouth while making her way through the chaotic mass of bodies, unmoved since their untimely demise. Catching word of the Haiti event only five hours after it occurred, Zeb and Jessica's investigation in the jungle would have to wait until they'd made a thorough sweep here first.*

**She was familiar with death.** Army snipers either learn to separate themselves from the outcome of their efforts or wash out. She wasn't cold-hearted. When she pulled the trigger, it represented an act of defense, a means of stepping in on behalf of the powerless where other efforts failed. The thirty-four-year-old understood the gravity of her work and remembered every single time she dispatched an enemy. She was quite skilled at her job. In fact, had graduated out of field assignments, called in to prep the next generation of sharpshooters when that whole craziness in Seattle took place. Her recent employment had been contract work, serving those with resources enough to pay for her specialized expertise. The duties remained the same: protect, use force if necessary. Her accomplishments were a point of pride, even granted the end result of many of her missions. But this? This made her feel powerless.

Someone somewhere was ordering the gruesome deaths of innocents on a scale that her best stealth and a single bullet could not deter.

The stench of decay loitered on a level she had not yet experienced, noonday heat only accelerating the biological journey back to dust. The official story came just as quickly as Zeb's and her departure to the island tragedy: the world was learning of an Ebola-like outbreak, serious but contained by the natural confines of the stadium and a full five miles to the nearest village. Such was the effect from a distance. Closer to home the horrors only increased their painful reach. No loved ones could claim their family's dead, and so the mourning process stayed on hold. When fathers and daughters failed to return from the game and news spread about what happened, people put the facts in order, gauging this as another of life's many cruelties. Yet, it only pressed deeper and sharper for the surviving families to lay in some middle ground, at arms' length from making their grief real and calling their clans to mark time and legacy with a funeral.

Jessica surveyed the carnage. The bodies bore the same telltale signs as the other two events in Belize and Montenegro. She needed a break from the beating sun and rounded the corner of the field, walking toward the on-site op center, a single-wide pre-fab whose AC unit spun in overdrive, seeming as if it would lift the office from its cinder block foundation and fly away.

She closed the door behind and removed the bandana.

Where previously she and Dalton had been the sole occupants, there was an added presence in their midst.

"Who's the new guy?"

Dalton's head remained fully engaged in data collection, so he barely heard her.

"Oh. Yeah, Sanchez meet Mr. *Smith*."

"Seriously," she snarked. "When is the Agency gonna get a little more creative with you guys' names? And it gets confusing. You know, he's Mr. Smith. Oh, and he's also Mr. Smith. Geez, for all the tax revenue we throw at your bosses, we should demand more for our money."

Smith didn't move, not a word from the nondescript, probably thirty-ish male with no identifying characteristics — and presumably blank personality to match. Made to order from the SpooksRus catalog and the only model available, at least in the male version. No upgrades. No embellishments. All CIA, all the time.

Sanchez wasn't done yet.

"So, did your supervisors let you in on what happened the last time we had a little team of three going?

Zeb looked up at this one, clearly curious as to where this line of questioning might go.

"Hmm. True," he responded, nodding toward Smith. "Odd man out. Ended up dead. Three is a crowd, they say."

Smith appeared a bit thrown off because he was.

"Okay, *Smith*," Sanchez lectured. "Last time crap hit the fan hard, Dalton and I carried another partner. Short, stocky guy that could easily lift this entire trailer with one stubby little hand of his. Zeb's training buddy and by all accounts a fine soldier. Interesting accent and a snappy conversationalist. He turned bad. I had to shoot him. Dead."

The agent was no newbie but her straightforward account of killing a former member of their team sunk in.

"But," she finished. "I am sure you're one of the good guys, right?"

He finally spoke. "Look. We all understand how this works. This is an incident of international significance and with national security implications because we don't know what the hell is going on yet. I am here to make sure you loose cannons keep from misfiring. Both at the enemy and, also, yes, friendlies."

This didn't seem right.

"Does Spurrier know you've been assigned to us?" Dalton asked. "I mean, this whole sequence has been a no-tell affair to this point. Can't scare folks about something when we don't even have a handle on what it means. Bunch of theories with innumerable loose ends. Why now? We not doing a good enough job at saving the world this week?"

"I am not at liberty to divulge those in the loop. Let's say the president understands the precarious nature of her new administration and has been advised that a happening of this magnitude requires seasoned professionalism on the ground."

Both Dalton and Sanchez blew air through their lips at that one. Give him twenty more years in the field, maybe. But seasoned? Professional?

"Okay, Smitty," Jessica summed up. "You got a chance to walk the dead yet?"

His reaction told her no.

"Then be my guest," she gestured toward the door. "Take some more pictures. That's what they train you for at Langley, right?"

**Texting was not Dalton's thing.** Finishing what was supposed to be a quick summary to Stevens, he realized it would have been much faster to call him. Nope. Not allowed. Engagement rules. Mort had set up an ultra-secure line of communication. Problem was, it required a fingers-on-tiny-keys kind of approach. Zeb had retyped his message four times already. Good thing Mort hadn't programmed it for auto-correct: who knows what kinds of gibberish may have been transmitted.

Finally ready, Dalton hit *send.*

*Same physical indicators, merely larger numbers than previous events.*

*Five cannisters found on site near unidentifiable victims. Same story: teeth, prints, DNA matches. Nothing.*

*Not much more to do here.*

Dalton waited at the small table in the trailer, a worn Formica surface having seen better days decades ago, for the reply.

*Received.*

*Scope of threat at issue still unknown. Next steps?*

This time Zeb got it mostly right, the first time.

*Investigate origins. Follow through on Caracol leads. Won't achieve clarity until we locate and eliminate source.*

*Going after the "what" may lead us to the "who."*

**Back in D.C.,** Spurrier loomed over Steven's shoulder, the general actively communicating with the team this time. "Is he saying what I think he's saying, general?"

"Yes, madam president, he is."

"But you don't actually buy that whole story, do you, Mike?"

"Ma'am. I am inclined to let him follow where this takes him. I stopped questioning his instincts a long time ago. Sure, things get messy when Dalton starts heading off in god-knows-what directions but his track record is pretty solid. Real solid, as a matter of fact."

"Very well then, general. Tell him to proceed."

**Dalton stood.** Placing his phone on the table, he turned to Sanchez.

"Time to pack your bags, Sarge."

"Okay, back to plan A? As in *Amazon?*"

"Ughh, puns do not befit you, Sanchez. But, yes, the Amazon it is. Haven't you always wanted to spend some quality time in the Central American Jungle?"

"Come to think of it... no."

"See, now that's where you're wrong, Sanchez. There's always something new to experience in this world. I have one last check-in with our Haitian partners here. Shouldn't take long. Meet at the runway in ninety."

"You bet," Smith interjected, walking back inside and catching the last part of the conversation.

The duo's heads shot back at the new man, signaling a *no way, buddy.*

"What?" he questioned. "After all, it's a company plane, right? Well, meet your pilot."

# FOURTEEN

*Upon landing, the dirt strip welcomed the small plane and her passengers with ease. The burdensome heat and humidity extend no such hospitality, greeting the trio upon exiting the airframe in a much less accommodating fashion.*

**Smith had done a decent enough job** on the first leg of the trip. The last skip required a bona fide bush pilot, so he had been forced to take a small, rickety jump seat in the cargo end of things. Third man out, he looked like he had just spent the last three hours crammed in a space not large enough for someone half his size. He wasn't a large man. The narrowing end of the plane was hard, constricting, and with sharp metal edges to most every surface he bumped along the way.

Sanchez smirked at his stooped, lumpy, disoriented presence. But then her humor turned to concern he would quickly become a drag on their efforts in a very hostile environment. Not to mention they weren't even sure what they were looking for — besides a parasitic monster, so small they'd never see it coming.

It all tended toward the ridiculous when fully considered.

Here to run down a myth, in the chance some small piece of truth clung to the ancient stories. Something to help them unravel the mystery of Belize, Montenegro, and now tragically, Haiti. Dalton, on the one hand, was as considerable a skeptic as you might draw up on paper. Still, he had been around enough odd circumstances to see the value of keeping your nose to the path, even if it seemed to lead to fantasyland at first. Sanchez, conversely, remained open to the proposition of purpose in all things. Where Zeb surmised randomness, she saw strings attached at some unseen end. It lay there: cohesion. You just had to probe a bit deeper if you weren't seeing the connections quite yet. Dalton held out the possibility that seemingly disconnected data may end up as something helpful. More times than not pushing through the variants in his mind arrived at a reasoned next step. He merely denied any order behind it. While Dalton's experience of having the lives of millions resting at his command led him to the primary supposition he could not make that call himself, he was equally as wary of anyone who might claim that right for themselves. And so, he remained extremely leery of stories, especially old ones.

"Gear up. We've got supplies for the first ten miles in. Should hit a small outpost village there, restock, and meet our help at that time. Questions?"

The orders came from Jessica. Sanchez ran a tight ship, as always. Dalton was no slouch when it came to field experience either, but in this case—more survival and search than outright operational footing—she represented their best asset. While she could knock an orange off a goalpost from over a mile away, her value in this instance was the second set of skills all snipers hone to a razor's edge. Stealth, patience, creativity. These are the tools that earn you the shot in the first place. And the ones that carry you back home again after pulling the trigger.

"All good," Dalton replied, tugging downward on his flexpack straps. The lightweight carriage a great match for the terrain.

"Check," Smith added.

Their first steps, from reasonably level ground at the airstrip and into the jungle, were like walking into a wall. A clingy, wet wall, guarding the southernmost edge of the *Reserva de Biosfera Maya* and Guatemalan sovereign soil.

Officially designated in the early 90s, the reserve provided a vibrant home for an immense number of species, both animal and flora. With nearly 22,000 square kilometers of everything from wetlands to lower mountain ranges, the biosfera kept intact the largest area of remaining tropical forest in all of Central America. And while a growing ecotourism presence was welcomed, at least on the books, quiet incursions from foreign state agents were not.

"Whoa," Dalton whispered, looking wondrously at their surroundings.

"What's the matter, you grew up in the woods, didn't you, LT?" Sanchez prodded.

"Yeah, kind of. But the trees didn't reach down to swallow you whole back in the Northwest."

"You two are pathetic," Smith moved past the conversation, pushing his way through the heavy green until establishing the lead.

"Hey, buddy," Sanchez chided the newcomer. "Didn't your mom teach you any manners? Oh, I get it. You're the guy who doesn't even suck his butt in on the way down the movie theater aisle, right?"

Dalton laughed outright.

Smith held no expression on his face, whatsoever.

Wordlessly, he reached into his right front pocket, retrieving a small tube looking every bit like a flashlight. He pointed it forward and pressed the lone button on its slim exterior. The angry branches and ferns parted, opening a clearing the next thirty or so feet ahead.

"Uh, okay," Zeb stared. "Maybe we'll keep you for a while yet."

The team moved forward into unbelievably heavy overgrowth, a gentle wave of green opening as they advanced, and closing again as they passed by.

"What the crap is that?" Sanchez blurted.

Smith felt quite vindicated, enough to share some secrets.

"High-energy sound waves. Well, actually high-energy, low-frequency sound waves. They're the big bullies of the tone spectrum.

But, as you note, they don't break, just bend. Problem is, like all prototypes, it's flawed."

"What, we grow a third ear or something like that?"

"No. Completely harmless to us. Not sure about all the animals there are in this place, though. And the power source runs dry pretty quick."

"How long?" Dalton did the math in his head for their journey to come.

"Lab trials lasted 3-5 hours, but in a seriously controlled environment."

"Well," Sanchez finished. "Let's get going, then. We need to make our meet by dark anyways."

**All three were soaked in sweat.** Their ease of passage had ended about two hours prior when Smith's wonder-light ran out of juice. Now, they fought a battle of constant effort, arms endlessly slashing about with machetes and torsos supporting each footfall. The track had also turned less than level as of late. Foliage all around. Vines grabbing at their ankles. Every now and again, an unseen drop a few feet into a swampy creek bed. So, it was in this semi-exhausted state that the faint smell of a small fire of smoldering, wet, old growth branches took them by surprise.

Sanchez hit the deck, down to one knee and a closed fist in the air. The others followed suit, quieting their breaths as much as possible.

Making a contact this deep into the wilderness? Always a dicey situation. People generally live away from other people for two reasons. Either they were cut off from the rest of the world by their history and culture or they're here because the long arms of law and civilization had a rougher time wrapping around them in the woods. You never knew which situation you'd encounter. Could be an innocent indigenous villager. Or not. One man, poking at the lazy fire with a long branch, stirring some reticent coals. Dark hair, slightly matted. Simple clothing, worn.

Another thirty seconds. Sanchez was always patient. She'd seen too many friends step into trouble prematurely. A sustained breath and she began moving forward, toward the campsite. Dalton had experienced it before. Still, each time he marveled anew at her grace. Not a single sound. The flow of body and motion: astounding. He thought for a moment she would have been a singularly beautiful dancer, had she chosen a very different kind of art for her life's work.

A mere three feet back, about to emerge, and another hand went up.

"You are late," said the man by the fire, without turning.

She froze.

Never before had she been caught off guard this way.

"Come."

Her surprise was tempered by the softness of his voice and lack of physical aggression. Dalton squared up the scenario as safe, too, and moved out of the heavier flora, into the small clearing at the edge of the brackish river. Walking by Sanchez, he gave her a look.

*Well, that was interesting, wasn't it?*

The return glare was classic Sanchez. Shrugging her shoulders in acknowledgment there was a first time for everything, she proceeded forward as well. Smith emerged last and they took off their packs, taking a seat on the mossy forest floor.

"Don't get too comfortable," the stranger cautioned. "Expedite your timetable."

Though none of the team let it out, each groaned inwardly, hoping instead for a few hours rest before moving on. It had been a strenuous first day and they longed for a break.

"Sorry," the man answered their unspoken questions. "Drug runners, poachers, revolutionaries. Seems we have a jungle trifecta. We'll need to move quickly to stay clear of the unusual amount of activity in this sector of the biosfera."

The three stood, exhausted but knowing how this worked. There were rhythms to this kind of thing. The man motioned toward the riverbank. Dalton and the others surveyed the dugout canoe awaiting. Each of them thought the same thing: *somebody's gonna need to row that thing.*

Like a mind-reader, or maybe just someone with excellent people reading skills, the man answered the question preemptively.

"Yes, we'll all work the oars. Good thing we only require two at a time. A couple of you can rest and then we'll shift. We've got six hours in the boat, so let's move it."

"Okay," Zeb offered. "Sanchez and Smith, you take first rest."

Jessica knew Dalton would never treat her as a weaker partner because, in fact, she was not. Instead, she took it as a gentlemanly gesture. He did surprise, every now and then.

Smith looked relieved.

"Hey, what are we supposed to call you?" he asked, stepping into the dugout.

The man turned from his place in the bow.

"People call me *Padre.*"

# FIFTEEN

*Donneleigh's countenance gave away nothing.*

**"Seriously, though,"** the morning show host rejoined. "A pretty short list of people in the world could pull something like this off. And everyone respects your history of philanthropic work around the world. Still, you say you know nothing about this mysterious invitation received by so many, this *World One* gathering?"

If anyone was counting — maybe her agent for contractual leverage purposes — this was somewhere near her three-thousandth television interview. A career spanning ten years of regular, daily broadcast had gained her a wealth of experience and an especially sensitive BS meter. She could smell it from a mile away, even the subtler varieties of untruth peddled by those most skilled in its arts. Outright lies held no chance of even exiting someone's mouth before she pounced, tearing at the edges of a story until all came apart like cheap fabric.

So, given her gift, she had to admit it: she believed him. As did the other millions of viewers chewing on Poptarts and tossing back home-brewed coffee in preparation for seeking another day's dollar.

Such was Donneleigh's hold on those who breathed his air.

He'd figured it out as a teenager.

The pretty girl with straight A's should have won but her final speech was more pedantic than inspiring. Young Matthew stumbled into the discovery, ditching his prepared notes for something more off the cuff. There was no reason to abandon what he had down on paper. It was good. It was orderly. But it was very average. More recitation than anything else. So, while pausing to look out over the crowded auditorium of Panther Lake Middle School, he took a chance. Biting his lower lip, he spoke from the heart. It worked. The emotional temperature in the room changed dramatically. A focus emerged, nothing short of miraculous for those in the heady throes of pubescence. Even the two guys in the back row stopped throwing hard candies at the cheerleaders down front. Apparently, greater concerns than merely lunchroom policies and game night activities hovered over even those not yet able to drive. He had caught them off guard. Then he had them.

Donneleigh learned something crucial that fateful September morning: everyone cares. But you can't just leave them there. You need to tap into what they care about and then call them to action with urgency and passion. In a young world where hanging your heart out on your sleeve was completely taboo, he had some innate sensibility about how to do this effectively. Leadership. Charisma. No, more than that. A simple authenticity, focused toward real problems and promising concrete solutions. In the end that got him 85% of the vote for class president. He would no longer imagine his peers as an unconscious horde. That day he discovered a maxim: everyone knows how screwed up the world is. Even young men and women normally beholden to just keeping their faces from breaking out before Friday. So began the path of righteous causes for the newly elected leader of P.S. 36, Butte, Montana.

**"Samantha..."** he paused, perfectly. "I can assure you I have no idea who is behind this. But, I can say the prospect sounds pretty good to me. I am all for the collaborative efforts of people who can make things happen, especially on behalf of those less fortunate among us. Like you said, my record speaks volumes here."

"What about the stories of not so subtle extortion? We've all heard them. People's fortunes are at stake, whether they go or not? Isn't this more economic tyranny than invitation? Coercive tactics can't be a good way to go about something like this. Wouldn't you agree, Mr. Donneleigh?"

"Well," he countered. "No real confirmation of these claims has surfaced, Samantha. Many fine journalists, present company included, are finding a bit of a challenge in settling that, correct?"

"Sure, but there's the *American Liberator* story, earlier this week, supposedly showing a screen shot of the message itself." The video overlay faded to the alleged screen capture. It took a second but the audience clearly gasped. "If this is real, then people are being forced to go or lose most of their wealth to an unknown agitator."

The guest-turned-defendant couldn't allow that one to sit.

"Samantha… " he leaned toward the small studio audience. "… the *Liberator*?"

They all laughed nervously. The host smiled, chastised but not feeling belittled.

Donneleigh continued, seeing his opportunity to shape the story for the masses.

"Again," he reached over and took a casual sip of water. "I really don't know if the rumors are true. What we do know is there will be millions of wealthy people, gathering around the world's pressing ills and having the ability to review and step into solutions, maybe for the first time bringing immediate and profound impact on the human condition across the globe."

She let him go for another full two minutes without interrupting. She was as entranced as the rest. And, honestly, she found him quite attractive. Another two sentences and time came to wrap this up. Samantha was getting an earful from her producer about ad breaks they'd already missed. Donneleigh had perfected the timing of these kinds of moments over decades of practice and knew he should press toward a conclusion.

"I can't confirm any of this, because I wasn't invited. Again, there is no absolute confirmation here but seemingly the world's high net worth individuals in the millions of dollars received this message. Oddly, the billionaires were left out. That's unusual."

Everyone laughed again.

"I can tell you from informal conversation with those in the same tax bracket as myself that we are more than willing to be part of anything our individual efforts could not achieve. We didn't get asked to the party but we will be waiting outside, anxiously anticipating an opportunity we've all been dreaming about, all of our lives."

Samantha woke to her responsibilities and transitioned, closing and redirecting the interview per requests from the booth.

"Well, thank you again, Matthew, for stepping into unmarked territory this morning with us. Now," she pivoted cleanly. "About that new watch your company is debuting in the first quarter of next year."

She looked directly into the camera.

"We'll get to that when we return."

Lighting on the set dimmed, a brief refuge from the on-air barrage and everyone settled back into their seats. Hair & makeup swarmed Samantha and Matthew, adjusting small areas noted in the first segment. Cables stretched to new shot locations and a handful of techs moved about the small platform, fixing little visual oddities and setting the scene for live again in sixty seconds.

Donneleigh took out his phone and texted his senior assistant.

*Show's producer will never receive a return call again. Clear?*

With that he feigned a corporate emergency, apologizing for the inconvenience and exiting the set just as the pre-count hit *three, two...*

# SIXTEEN

*The river narrowed again.*

**It felt as constricting** as it looked. Only an hour ago the four of them glided down a glassy chute, banks on either side no closer than thirty-five yards. With no foliage directly overhead, the moon—out and full—beamed down upon and softened their passage. While more exposed, the effect was pleasant. And unavoidable. This route provided the only way to their target. Though the water table in the biosfera sprouted innumerable branches, not all of them collapsed again into some grand source. Both the light and threat dimmed now as it became more like traversing a narrow, watery cave. Slower. No, sluggish.

Dalton caught the glow of his smartwatch.

*0130*

"Gotta be close now, right?" he whispered.

A simple nod over his shoulder was all Padre offered.

He'd passed on his turn for rest, back at the only spot it made any sense. Heading down the wide part of the river, he could have enjoyed an hour or so at least, trusting the others to keep them moving in the right direction. Though a smaller man, maybe five-five, you knew from his frame he was in fantastic shape. Not merely skinny, like he struggled getting enough to eat out here. Taught. Wiry but with a purpose and presentation telling you he had strength in reserve. Under control.

Sanchez curled up in a sideways ball, feet against one side of the canoe and head nestled beneath forearms in the other direction. Just behind Padre and in front of Sanchez, Smith's eyes closed as well. Or were they? You never know with spooks.

"So, Padre," Zeb started, matching the man's strokes from the rear of the vessel. "How crazy are we?"

"As loco as they come, Mr. Dalton."

"Well, we'll need to play that card for a little while. Old stories make for good adventures, right? From what I hear, you've seen a few yourself."

No response. Padre was not about to open up to these strangers, even if vouched for by others he trusted. Truth was, he needed the money and playing extreme tour guide for these three would help a lot. The US Government was not his friend. But they did pay well, and in a timely manner.

"What are you two yackin' about now?" Sanchez added, aroused by the conversation flowing past and sitting up in the longboat.

"Well, nothing, apparently," Dalton replied. "Padre's a quiet one. Fair enough."

The sniper stretched her arms and worked the kinks out of her neck, looking around with the steadied eye of a professional.

"Gotta be close, right, LT?"

"Padre says... well actually he nodded, *yes*."

"Good. Pretty much on op schedule. At least so far."

"Sanchez, I been thinking."

She glanced over at him, a dumbfounded expression.

"Well, yeah, kind of what I do. I get that. What I mean is I've been trying to piece things together and..." his voice trailed off, something significant emerging in his mind's eye, something big and not so happy.

"That *World One* thing, right?" she asked.

"Yep. Timing is telling when you're suspicious of everything."

She nodded, prodding him on. "How utterly conspiratorial, Dalton. I assumed you more the cold cynic."

"Well, true on that front, but think this through with me. Each mass death event increased in size along the way. You might surmise a pattern of testing."

"Geez LT, if I'm following your logic here, you've got a massive leap in scale of the event. I mean, how many people are supposed to be going to this thing worldwide?"

"No one knows right now. All quite hush-hush, except for the initial leaks and those have produced very little info. But there are about fourteen million people in the targeted income bracket across the globe."

"Fourteen *million?*" she blurted, loud enough it echoed lightly off the water.

"Yeah, the increase in scale doesn't make much sense at first blush. Assuming the damage is being done by a microscopic bio-entity with a parasitic nature, there's no way enough of any known substance might be produced to that effect. I mean, using an agent like this on a hundred, or even five thousand people is one thing. But, somewhere north of ten million? The probability of achieving this kind of readiness with no one noticing is… "

Her expression this time said *keep the number to yourself, okay?*

"Okay, let's just say extremely, extremely low. And then the question of motive. Which is about as clear at this point as a Seattle January, or February," he offered, referring to the city's famously gray winters.

"Somehow, I think that's not all you're tossing around, right LT?"

"Yep. There's an interesting string to the Caracol story floating around a little in my head too. I got another zipped file of background from the Hendricks before we flew out of Haiti. Did you know the Mayans at Caracol practiced a symbolic egalitarianism?"

Her silence affirmed the answer: no.

"Yeah, Stela 5 from the northern-central quadrant of the dig confirmed it, as well as underground structures found in the early 2000s."

"Okay," Sanchez bit. "A stela is a rock with writing on it. Their history books in public kind of thing. The professors already went over this. What else?"

"Well, for the longest time researchers believed this particular culture had figured out how to spread resources evenly throughout the people, to do it successfully and over hundreds of years. The norm for ancient cultures, well actually most cultures, is always a matter of economic class. But when they uncovered these dwellings, they found a much higher standard of living for whomever lived in these places. Yet, all the public records boasted of their fairness. Until they found Stela 5."

"So?" Sanchez said "They were fooling everybody. Sounds a lot like some 20th Century efforts of our own. Say you're creating utopia while people at the top enjoy more than everyone else."

"Well, no." Zeb stopped her. "Stela 5 showed something completely different. The upper class was in on it. But the lower class, too. They weren't trying to fool each other."

He paused.

"They were trying to fool their gods."

Sanchez scrunched her face and pulled back slightly, clearly indicating more tall-tale than she was willing to take in.

"I know. Weird, right?" Dalton said. "So, here's where things become even more confusing. Two of our events targeted people along the wealthier end of the spectrum. Belize was an investment firm with loads of cash. Montenegro, a group of Central European financiers. If *World One* is anything to worry about, then this fits as well."

He stopped rowing for a second. Letting the boat glide forward.

"But Haiti. That makes no sense. Those people; the poorest of the poor."

Dalton resumed stroking.

"So, all we have is a mortality pattern resembling pictures on rocks an ancient civilization left behind and a story of vengeance between warring nations. Tales about Central American Native People that wanted their gods to think they were fair minded about possessions while secretly continuing business as usual. An unknown micro-parasite that likes to sever humans' spinal columns and then burst out their abdomens while seeking a new host. And the biggest worldwide event ever is unlikely to be related, at least until we access some more data, forming as connective tissue in a theory. How's that sound?"

Padre's hand went up again in the bow. He made a quick move with his oar in the water, pointing them hastily toward the bank.

"Time to get out. Now. Quietly."

**The four transitioned seamlessly** from vessel to muddy shore and then up a few feet of steep, rocky soil to gain their footing again on the jungle path. They all crouched, looking to Padre. He pointed to himself, *I'm in the lead*. Then he posed his pointer and middle fingers toward his eyes and out into the bush.

The other three all knew the op had instantly descended to another level of danger. Instead of taking the subtle but clear pathway, Padre led them up and to the right, a ridge line paralleling the thin, worn patch of dirt stretching out in the distance. They walked above the route as far as possible before dropping back down again. Off it by a foot or so, they awaited their next instruction.

This time Padre's fingers, even using both hands, were not enough.

Twelve soldiers in jungle camo. Each outfitted with a shoulder-slung AK. More than half of them were asleep. It was, after all, still pre-dawn. The men on watch had a nervous presence, giving away their motivations for taking up arms. The image of regular army but their countenance wasn't quite right. Twitchy, undisciplined. Hair trigger in human form. Mercenaries, yes, but those who had only recently discovered the failing of their revolution and now were more practical men. They wanted to be fighting for something but had been burned before by lofty ideals and empty promises. This was simply business. They had traded their virtue for nothing. That would not happen again.

After what seemed like an eternity, Dalton cocked his head, asking for clarity and confirmation from Padre. The return look said it all.

*This is the place. But we're not getting in today, or anytime soon.*

# SEVENTEEN

*The White House Press Room overflowed with lights, handheld recording devices, and laptops. Each device was attached to an eager and inquisitive person, digging for answers.*

**Geoff Bentry** **came off as a natural** from his very first day on the job. Tagged as the new administration's Press Secretary only twenty-four hours after Spurrier was sworn in, he acclimated with seeming ease. A classic *make your way up the ladder* story, the Stanford broadcast journalism grad's path had not always been arrow-straight. Still, when the curves came at him, he read them well. And, to a degree much greater than your best major leaguers, he connected.

"The CDC and WHO are evaluating the tragedy in Haiti but I cannot stress enough to you we have no indication of a threat to Americans at this time. We're investigating all aspects and assisting with arrangements for care of the deceased via our diplomatic corps in-country. Army health units are on site and engaged in data and logistics efforts. Currently, we understand this to be some form of Ebola-like virus. All travel in and out of the island stands halted. No indications of spread from the localized outbreak at the stadium. Not even the villages in closest proximity to the tragedy."

Bentry knew he was handing out half-truths. No original images had seen the light of day. This was a minor miracle. Were people to view the unbelievable destruction of human bodies, far more questions would be asked. And, holding a mere inkling of the two previous events, fear would have spread too quickly to contain. The atoll in Belize disappeared, like it did every year for awhile. Miraculously, Montenegrin leadership agreed to their end of the cover-up as well. Score a couple of points for publicly responsible disinformation? He was glad the topic changed, though this one would require the same deft touch.

"Mandy, yes," he said, inviting the MSNBC pool reporter to go next.

"Mr. Bentry, what is the administration's take on *World One*? Is the president or any of her cabinet attending one of the US sites?"

"I can confirm for you the president's team is working on this currently, assessing the event and forming a response."

Hands shot up again. The woman proceeded with the follow-up anyway.

"So, you can tell us nothing of the president's own status or opinion yet?"

Geoff smiled. Everybody loved his smile. Warm but not over the top.

"Mandy, I will repeat. The administration is working on a formal reaction but I can say there is a general appreciation for this kind of targeted, collaborative action toward solving some of the real problems Americans, and their brothers and sisters across the globe, experience every day."

"So, the president will not be attending any of the US sites, then? According to sources and public records her net worth is well above ten million dollars."

A brief chuckle from the man at the podium, again endearing as ever.

"Mandy, I can not... "

His canned rejoinder was cut short by a staffer stepping up and placing a small 3x5 card at his disposal. He scanned it briefly and looked back up. It was hard to hide his displeasure.

"I have an update from the president's team. I'll read it for you directly."

*Well aware our government has been more secretive than is helpful in recent years, and in the interest of fostering openness and candor, let me brief you of my intentions regarding World One. It is true I received an invitation. It is also true I will be attending. Due to preparations for security, the location will not be disclosed, but, yes, I will be attending World One.*

The flurry of hands was a feeding frenzy. Voices and appendages all vying for attention, to be granted the floor for a moment. Bentry did another fine job, deflecting the inquiries to relatively safe zones and concluding as always with "that is all for now."

Walking away from the lectern, he stepped through the small door to the right, back into the admin center of the west wing. He was immediately joined by a senior staffer, falling into step with the new hire.

"Well done, as always, Geoffrey."

He stopped, sliding back into an open coat closet, indicating the conversation was going to be an honest one.

"Look, Steph," he started. "I can't do that very often and keep the carnivores at bay."

"I know. I know," she insisted. "We all told Spurrier it was a bad idea. She decided. Things are so sensitive right now. She needs a few early wins. You understand, build some trust."

The press secretary took a large breath and then swallowed it, forcing himself to speak deliberately.

"If I am going to have a shot at doing my job, I can't be put in the position of having the president send notes to me while I am trying to redirect the pool. It's a game of how far can they push. Everyone knows that. When they think there's more info, they'll keep pressing. If they think Spurrier is watching from another room and will step in when things get hot, they'll wait it out until mom decides to separate the kids."

He wished he hadn't gone that far.

"I get it, Geoff. She's learning. But trust me, your instincts about her, leading you to take this job? They're not wrong."

---

**"He's pissed."**

"I would be, too," responded the president, leaning back in her oval office desk chair and pointing the end of a Mont Blanc nowhere in particular.

"We need to let that one pass under the bridge for quite some time before doing anything like that again, ma'am."

Stevens was a warrior, but a very prudent one at that. Much of his career accomplishments hinged on moments where he rightly calculated the risk of leadership capital lost, as well as lives on the ground. He would never sacrifice the latter for the former, but he also would not squander the one resource over which he maintained a semblance of control. The adage says *plans disappear once the shooting begins.* Much the same could be said about the slippery slope of influence and trust. Hard to build, easy to lose. And quickly.

"Indeed," Spurrier responded. "I know. In this case, it mattered. I am going to assume for now that whoever is behind these events has the power to scale them to their liking. And I am going to assume that is something on the order of a major escalation and tragedy awaiting not just us but the world also. Lastly, I am going to proceed with the thinking that these things are connected, even that the *Word One* gatherings *are* the ultimate target. Regardless of the truth of any of that, someone like this is watching closely for a geopolitical response, any sense of unsettling or uprising. They've established the rules of the game. We can't give them any hint of our counter moves or we'll lose the few options we have in the first place. The evil behind these deaths needs to think I will be attending, submitting. I don't even care if people frame it as saving my own financial ass. I *will not* let them know what hand we are holding. That's our best shot. It's all we've got for now and we needed to settle the matter before my status created a trigger-finger reaction."

She stopped, knowing all she had just stated was how the general understood it as well.

"Still, I agree. Bentry is a key team member and we'll need him at the top of his game. We don't want to remove deposits from the bank of good will too frequently. Understood."

"Yes, madam president," Stevens nodded. "Is that all for now?"

"Thank you, general. That will be all."

# EIGHTEEN

*"I can get in there. You know I can, LT."*

**He knew it was true.** Still, Dalton hosted a sinking feeling about letting her recon the place alone. Inside, he rebelled against the thought. On the basis of pure data, it remained the only way to obtain any real intel here. He found it far too convenient a circumstance that the very place Padre had led them to start looking for their mysterious parasite was now kept off limits by these armed men.

"Look. Seven bogeys awake," Sanchez said. "Three at the mouth and four around the perimeter. And you know there's another way out, another way through."

Smith appeared confused. Dalton and Padre understood what she was getting at.

Twelve men tasked to this smallish opening in a jungle hillside. Whatever happening inside required a dozen men at its mouth. Still, not the best troops in the world. Maybe disposable in some eyes. Which meant here was not the only place worthy of guarding, and by logical extension, the entrance least worried about by whoever was doing the worrying.

"Yeah," Dalton added. "No one imagined people might be crazy enough to try the route we took." Zeb did his best at a semi-demented expression, his shot at crazy-eye. So poorly executed, it only let everyone else in on how nervous he was about the plan and the idea that Sanchez might head off into the heavily-guarded darkness alone.

"Gonna need some cover at first, gentlemen."

"Alright," Dalton said, coming to terms with it and taking control of the op. "Sanchez, you've got to let us know the moment you're back out. Remember, we're not official guests of the Guatemalan government and we have no idea what's going on inside. No clarity who or what. And no confirmation who's safe or not. Check in every two hours. Secured text only. Signal should work, even at the deepest levels. We'll make our way back out to the airstrip. Once we're clear we can order up some faster transport, right Smith?"

"Yep. Assets in the region and we'll hear rotors within an hour of the call."

"Sanchez, here's the deal: you're on your own for anywhere from 8-10 hours."

No one questioned the timing, though the trip in had eaten up over twelve. Though Dalton was the only one with an actual relational tie to the sergeant, and with all her years of solo field experience, still the team carried a special pressure as her support. Each one had experienced situations in which they'd learned to rely on brothers or sisters in arms. Those moments forged a unique fraternity, bonds formed quickly and deeply. They'd cut the time back to the strip. They must.

**Sanchez looked back,** only the slightest of glances. The commotion buying her entrance was nothing more than the other three creating a bit too much noise heading back where they came from. Immediately at a full sprint, it was unlikely the guards would catch them or see anything requiring further efforts. It worked perfectly. The armed militia pursued the men for about a hundred yards. More than enough.

She was in.

The mouth of the cave proceeded more down than in. While causing her to assume a steep descent early on, it also kept the guards—she'd named them Thing 1 and Thing 2—from peering over the edge. The last few feet outside the opening oozed with bat guano, as did the initial thirty yards of the interior. Slippery was not a good enough term. Sanchez hit it a little too fast and almost went sailing off into the abyss. The guards knew what awaited and they were okay staying out front as far as was practical. They weren't going to come looking anytime soon.

Her next steps became measured but swift. The place reminded her of a national park in Kentucky filled with caves, explored by her family one summer in her pre-teen years. Actually, the exploring was done mostly by her father and herself, as Mom was famously claustrophobic.

"No, I'm fine in the gift shop, Jessica. You and your dad go have fun."

She still remembered the guides handing out old school kerosene lanterns to every few people in the group. Her father signed them up for the pioneers' tour, knowing only the most challenging hike a few hundred feet below the surface would do for his little girl. He knew her so well. She loved him for it.

Moments like this—in a stinky, wet, dark hole in the jungle— flashed her back to these memories. They came easily, if not frequently enough, sending a surge of thankfulness to her soul that she had landed in this particular southwestern American family.

Sanchez was not her birth name.

No record of that name, the one attached to her entrance to this world, was anywhere to be found. Abandoned, left on the stoop of a rural hospital in the hot country of Michoacan, Mexico. Then scooped up into the overjoyed arms of a young Texan and his lovely, dark-haired bride.

"Mr. Sanchez," the adoption officer interrupted, stepping lightly into the immediate connection between this tiny person and her new father. "What name I shall place on the certificate?"

"Jessica," he looked up just long enough for the stranger to see the wetness of his eyes. "My grandmother's name. *Jessica.*"

Both mom and dad were gone now, leaving this earth after more than fifty years together in a quick succession of tragedies, one an auto accident and the other a vulturous cancer. Such a degree of loss lingered, waiting to pounce at any time. But though the pain was sharp and unpredictable, the joy, the deep appreciation of all they planted in her life and heart, remained a constant.

Sanchez looked down. Her wrist GPS sported an altimeter on board. Most versions of the tool measured height above the earth. This one also went in the opposite direction.

-350'

That first hour or so achieved quite a bit of downward progress. Things seemed to be leveling out now. Walls and ceiling closer, that was for sure. After initially hitting an almost foyer-ish area, the hike transitioned to more like walking through a crowded, very long hallway. No encounters to this point with other people. A handful of bats, a weird looking gopher, and a snake den. But no people.

That changed at almost exactly three hours in.

**It loomed, another open space,** this one fitting the term cavernous. Had to be a hundred feet to the closest stalactite formation and those stood at least fifty feet long. Well lit, for being underground. Portable light stanchions did the job, casting a warm glow on the uneven walls. The area beneath her perch carved out into a giant staging and transport hub. Track-fed personnel and cargo carriers proceeded from a series of tunnels to the right, dropped their people or crates, and then returned for more. There was an odd ratio, though, of people to shipping containers. Very few of the former and a constant stream of the latter.

Looking again at the cavern floor, she noted it this time. Automation everywhere. Like a blue-collar worker's worst nightmare. Machines and systems so efficient that the lonely humans employed here must only be technicians, here to keep the robots happy.

*Lovely. The apocalypse has come to the underworld.*

Her spot above the action served fine for an overview but a closer look down these corridors would be required. She relished the thought, always up for another adventure into darkness, hundreds of feet below the earth's surface.

She moved smoothly between outcroppings and down to the main floor, matching the rhythm of human appearances with her progress. Every ten carriers of goods, a person came along with them. The timing stayed perfect, as if set electronically. The whole thing was pretty marvelous to behold, if not for the fact all of this occurred out of view from the watching eyes of the world and therefore likely beheld some nefarious purpose. One more shift and she could move down the long, dark passageway. Folding herself into the natural cleft of the rock and invisible, on the odd chance someone happened to be looking for an intruder. The plan was to catch a ride on the back of one of the transports. They each carried a small set of black bars protruding from the rear, forming a foot and a half wide platform to support something extra, not in the regular bay. Just make sure to hit the next carrier after the human-occupied one.

Four more.

Three.

Two-One.

No lights out front of the line of cargo skiffs. Led by GPS and unmanned, no need for it. The result? Utter darkness. Clinging to the back of her ride, Sanchez' muscles tensed in a grip holding her in place while still allowing for movement once arrived, wherever it was headed.

It took longer than anticipated. At ten minutes into her journey she wondered how long this might go on. And, though not as good at calculations as Zeb, she was no mental slouch, either. A mile and a half. Further than she thought this system went.

Registering these thoughts, a blinding light took over her entire field of vision.

*What the hey?*

Instinctively she rolled right, off the back of the skiff. Two revolutions on the ground and her back slammed into the sidewall, hard. The rock: unforgiving. A few of her vertebrae responded, moving and shifting slightly out of place. Her gut sloshed forward and air forced from her lungs as she came to a stop, head spinning. Looking up to where she leapt off the carrier, she saw it. The vehicle moved through a blackened plastic curtain and into a space where the light shone so pervasive it would have hurt, even if your retina had plenty of time to adjust. The next thing she experienced was the business end of a semi-auto rifle in her chest as her watch glowed, a rapid pinging of visual alarms.

*Crap. Check-in time. Gonna miss this one.*

Sanchez got to her feet, grunting from the impact of the rifle and rubbing a tender spot over her right pectoral. Slowly, her hands went up and behind her head. It's the right thing to do when two men in hazmat suits and UV goggles hold you in the bead of their guns. She let them know there would be no trouble, laying her sidearm down as she stood. They didn't believe her and landed the butt of one of the weapons across her shoulders and back of her skull. The move was not intended to bring unconsciousness, just pain. She stumbled but didn't fall, each careful step forward, into unknown captivity.

# NINETEEN

*"We can't stop now, Dalton. Hey, did you hear me?"*

**Zeb didn't care.** Smith could blather on all he wanted about pace and target zone. Sanchez had failed to check in at the last two scheduled rotations. The woman was as much a regs follower as imaginable. If op expectations existed, she would meet and exceed them every single time. The last secured text Zeb received from her essentially said *pretty dark in here.* No data. No intel. Only sarcasm. He hated and loved it at the same time.

Dalton stepped off the path and began ascending the small hillside covered with creeping vines and loose soil. Each step pressed into the earth with increased gravity. His heart pounded, more out of fear for her current situation than the exertion of getting to higher ground. And that was the idea. Zeb's sat-phone barely functioned in the thick underbrush. Though the crest wasn't more than a hundred feet up, a cleared outcropping persisted, enough real estate to purchase a more direct shot into space. The way he saw it, he could wait until they got back to the airstrip, or take this hill — the only one in sight. The airfield seemed much too distant. Something in him said to make the call, now.

**"Is that all you got?"** Sanchez spat at her tormentor.

He kicked her again, harder this time because his ego lay bruised. The blow landed squarely on her left side, forcing a breath between her lips. She pulled her legs up in a reflexive action but could only coil up so far due to her bonds. Sanchez assumed deep bruising but hadn't felt anything snap. Not yet. Good. The warmth of her skin at the point of impact indicated blood flow, which meant no internal bleeding in the area, likely no organs in peril. These guys didn't seem like seasoned pros at the art of physical persuasion, so she imagined this to be short-lived, more clumsiness than deft probing. But, sometimes the unskilled ones cause the most damage. Focused on body blows, her face, mouth, and eyes remained unmolested, mostly due to the fact they were too lazy to get down to ground level and there were no chairs strewn about the place.

"Stop."

The larger of the two guards recalled his boot, already in motion. The action placed him off balance, a little dance needed to stay upright.

Sanchez made sure he saw her smile.

"Stop," the new voice said again. "This is no longer your concern. Back to the tunnels. Now."

The guard boiled but did as told.

*Yeah, that's right Siegfried,* she thought, having mentally tagged the duo as the famous Las Vegas showmen. *You go ahead and dance back to your stations. Your boss and I have some business to conduct.*

The new guy knelt, a foot or so in front of her.

*Crap. This is worse.*

The man looked her over and peered into her eyes, seeing that last thought and knowing he had a cagey animal on his hands.

"Alright. Let's see. Agency? No, I don't think so. Something about you tells me you're not at all about diplomacy, and that's what the Ivy League is producing these days, right? Current military. No. Not quite right, either. Your countenance is far more inquisitive than that."

Sanchez cocked her head slightly and smiled, but no words.

"Very well, I am a patient man," he stated while calling over another set of guards. "Take our new friend away for now. Two, at all times. I'll let you know when I need her again."

The replacements responded dutifully, stepping over to Sanchez, lifting her off the ground and marching her to her new holding pen. The man in charge used a sat-text system, not unlike the one the team carried into the jungle. He got busy, alerting his superiors to the breach in their operational cloak.

---

**Donneleigh was upset** but you wouldn't know it on face value. He stood from behind his desk and began pacing, making a small raceway between the large windows looking out over Eden and the floor to ceiling bookshelves to his right.

*Peter Stinson* knew better than to speak. He'd seen this hundreds of times—Matthew passing a complex problem through his keen, imaginative brain. A few moments of reflection, usually, and he knew the right thing to do. One of the most intuitive and effective thinkers the world had in this emerging millennium. It was no accident he had gotten this far in the business and technology worlds. Challenges stumping many men, those often requiring the combined efforts of boards filled with the best and brightest, almost always faded after Donneleigh spent some time "walking it out." Almost always. There remained the presenting problems of the globe, which no amount of thinking on his feet had yet solved. But, that too proceeded on the right course now, he believed.

"Peter," the tech leader asked. "Have you ever seen a birthing?"

"Sir?" Stinson stumbled, not quite sure how to answer.

"You know. Life. The moment life emerges from the womb, the egg, the ground, a seed."

He stopped moving now and looked at his trusted lieutenant, calmly, serenely.

"It's always a struggle," he continued. "Almost as if life would rather stay embryonic. But no, that's not what happens. There is always an emerging."

Stinson gave him an attentive look, confirmed that he was tracking, even if the conversation strayed a bit.

"So it is with our mission, my friend. And the life we are helping emerge will have to stand on its own, even as it struggles to come forth. We will do nothing about this woman stumbling into our midst."

He anticipated Stinson's reply and cut him off before responding.

"No, if what we are doing has the rightness of cause I believe it does, then nothing *can* stop it. Our interference at this point will only hamper the true life that is coming. If it has to fight to live, so be it. The new world will only be stronger for the effort."

He returned to his desk and sat, the issue completely settled.

"And besides," he finished. "There is no time to make any real connections here. Our fingerprints are nowhere to be found at the development center. It is extremely unlikely anyone will put the clues together before *World One* goes off without a hitch." His face turned to the garden outside the windows, that last sentence flowing wistfully across his lips.

"No, all will be well."

**Sanchez awoke, alone** in the jungle heat with her head just beginning to clear, to remember. An aching side aided her powers of recall. She sat, loosely bound to a medium-sized palm. The cords came away easily, stretched in the moisture-laden air as she moved her arms, pulling them off.

*What in the world?*

She couldn't imagine why she remained alive. Clearly, something odd was happening deep in the earth, here in the biosfera. Something requiring a significant investment of resources, technology, and secrecy. Activities meant to be kept out of the watchful eyes of the world and backed up by armed force. In this context, her release made no sense at all. No interrogation beyond that second guy. Aside from the clumsy bludgeoning of the lower level types, nothing to keep her from going back in right now and sorting things out, exposing whatever the world they were doing in there.

Weapons? Drugs?

She hadn't been able to obtain clear enough eyes-on to make any sense of it. The slowness of her system signaled the use of a sedative. That made things more confusing, no recollection of anything past the moment the man returned to the small closet they were holding her in. That was all she had. To marshal the resources required for crashing this kind of party in the wilderness, she would need sufficiently more evidence of malfeasance. Right now, all stood as mystery. Maybe even a tragic distraction to their core mission. The veteran sniper tried to force the pieces together. The mass death events. Caracol's hazy history.

*This is crazy. The whole thing is straight up crazy.*

Sanchez kept telling herself this, repeating the mantra as she began her long hike back out. Her GPS unit showed positive numbers for elevation now, as well as the way back to the airstrip. Soon enough she would meet back up with the team. And then what? She wasn't quite sure she had much to offer from her little trip to the dark world.

# TWENTY

*America's first First-Husband held his head in his hands.*

**The last fifteen minutes** had seen his best shot at dissuading his wife from her choice, just made before the entire press corps. Three decades of these kinds of conversations taught him well. His bride would listen. She would consider. She would decide. And that was it. Sometimes his reasoning did the trick. Others, not so much. If keeping track, he'd realize his record was near split, 50-50, indicating a nod to his intelligence and wisdom as much as her ability to collect data and make informed decisions. This one was not going to go his way.

"Gary," she started. "This is how it has to be."

"I know, I know," he relented.

"Look, there's little question in my mind this is the event the other three are leading to. It doesn't take much to see the pattern. Someone wants the world's millionaires together in the same space, albeit in separate locations across the globe simultaneously, there to unleash this thing on them. And whoever is behind this is twisted enough to sacrifice five-thousand lives to throw us off the trail. I am now convinced Haiti was a distraction. A test and misdirection."

She moved closer to him on the couch in the presidential residence.

"No one knows this except a few in the administration and the away team. God alone knows why someone would do this but we can't ignore the trend line of the events and the coinciding emergence of *World One*. Maybe I am wrong here. Maybe this is all completely unrelated and this get-together of the world's wealthy is really what the summons says. A forced-hand kind of thing, sure, but a push toward good, not evil. I am not holding much hope for this possibility. Prudence demands we assume the worst."

"*So*," he almost screamed. "Keep yourself away from this killing field and call them off. You're the president of the United States. Call the damn thing off!"

"I wish I could. But you know that won't work," she reasoned. "If I indicate in any way we are following this lead, the wealth of over 13 million people will vanish instantly from the economic structures of most every nation, certainly the more developed countries of the world. The power of the invitation lies in this ninety-ten proposition. Share too much info and there goes your money. We have to think any sense of meddling by world leaders would trigger the same result, collapsing not only the livelihoods of the rich but the poorer countries as well. Starvation, infestation, looting. Stable economies and governments finding the foundations they relied upon have vanished. Those nations in constant turmoil will only worsen. A new dark age will fall, and this time not limited to the European Continent."

She stopped and leaned in, taking his hands in hers.

"Gary, what if the insane people behind this would take our actions as a cue to broaden their scope—assuming again the target is this group of millionaires—and just decide to not care who the scourge is unleashed on? Right now, it seems to be extremely targeted. A holocaust yes, but not a worldwide extermination. Granted, that's still ridiculously sick but we can't take this kind of a risk. Not yet."

"So, what," he was actually angry this time, "We play along and watch them all die in coliseums and convention centers around the world?"

The truth of the matter resonated, a heavy presence filling the room: millions dead in an instant, hundreds of millions in retaliation, or even more over the course of a few months. That was the horrible, untenable choice.

"No," Spurrier replied. "We play along until we find out who this is, and more importantly, why this is their mission. Assuming the means of delivery will follow the patterns so far we set plans to intersect the agents at *World One* before their bio-bombs go off."

"And then?"

"And then we end this thing."

# TWENTY ONE

*Mort looked the data over one more time. From his safe place in the Vault, deep beneath the public floors of the Pentagon, he whispered in thankfulness he wasn't in the middle of all this. It presented too worrisome a proposition to consider for long.*

**The deep-tech soldier** took an even deeper breath as the triple-wide display on his desk counted down to a secured feed. The monitor pulled up a video link to the White House, a mere three miles across the Potomac, and two separate audio feeds, much farther away in the Amazon basin.

"Go ahead. Transmission locked. You may proceed," came the mechanical voice from yet another location, the hub at NSA where multiple links were centralized and managed. The president spoke first. Stevens stood by, working a late night as well in the Oval Office private room.

"Mort. You have some recent data to add to the emerging picture?"

"Yes, ma'am," Mortensen said. "And it's giving me the crawlies, even from here."

He needed no indication to continue.

"Supplemental labs from Haiti have come in. On-site CDC agents finishing another walk of the field noticed something odd in a side concourse. One of the bodies showed movement, tremors. Thought for a second there might be a survivor but the abdomen had already burst, so seemed strange and unlikely. Observed a pulsing in the lower right leg and approached. Though it worthwhile to take a blood draw and... "

Mort swallowed hard before continuing, knowing the fuller story and trying to hold back his emotions.

"Ah," he forged ahead. "Agent got the sample and the leg burst as well."

"Hazmat, containment?" the president pleaded, hoping protocol had been followed.

"Sorry, ma'am. Wish that were the case. And it gets worse. The agent fell back as the leg erupted, tripped over another body. Rusty handrail behind him. A small opening, nothing requiring so much as a band-aid. But still enough."

A new voice cut in on the retelling.

"What?" Dalton said from deep in the jungle. "How in the world? No protection in place? Walking around a stadium filled with five thousand corpses in a hot biozone?"

"Yeah," Mort stepped back in. "Agent couldn't plunge the syringe with his glove hand. Removed it and took a chance."

Everyone paused, out of respect for the sacrifice but also in horror-filled imagining of the last, few moments of the agent's life.

Mortensen took the cue appropriately and waited.

"Mike," Spurrier prodded the general beside her after a few more seconds. "You will see to it his family receives our best support, correct?"

"Yes, ma'am. I will take that on personally."

Turning back toward the screen, the president needed the rest of the story.

"Mort, please. I am assuming we've been able to recover the sample?"

"Affirmative, madam president. At that point, we sent in a robotic recovery unit."

"Continue."

"So, here's what we know. The active bioagent caught in the sample is a micro-parasite, as suspected. Hundreds of them in the small vial we collected. Though we could observe them in clusters at the on-site lab, we needed way greater magnification to pry down to the level where we could look at them individually. Images went out to D.C. and revealed a tubular body with both pilli and flagellum. The tail-like flagellum aid in movement throughout the blood stream as well as the tiny body hairs. Not so abnormal, at least so far."

"I have a sense this is about to get weirder," Dalton added.

"True that, buddy. Imagery also showed a front-loaded mouth area with a dual-level set of... well, kind of like teeth. But more like two band saws working in conjunction, in contrary motion to one another."

Mort shuddered again and pulled the black and whites up for the president and general.

"The basal ganglia," the president stated.

"Exactly," Mort said. "The shredding of each victim's central nervous system? There's your culprit. Only there's thousands of them working on it at the same time. And Dalton?" Mort continued. "You nailed it, spot on. These things start there, cause total paralysis and move to the abdomen. From there they look for a way out and to another host."

"But wait," Zeb said. "Two things still a little fuzzy here. One, we don't know how they steal into the victim's system. I mean, it can't be that everyone in that stadium had an open wound of some sort and no entry via any other fashion, like directly through an orifice, right? And then, how is this contained so well? Each of the three events has no peripheral hot zones. Normally, we'd note an outward ring of infestation. Diminishing returns, sure, but this is so precise, so clinical."

"Well, thankfully our Haiti team found enough evidence for theories there, too."

Everyone leaned forward.

"We found five cannisters onsite with assumed agents beside them. The bodies closest to the units don't fit the rest of the crowd, so we're going with the probability they were the ones bringing the biothreat into the area. Residues at both Montenegro and Haiti indicate a gel-like substance in the carriers, heated and evaporated on exposure. We are reverse engineering them currently. Quite a nice little system. At the same time, closer eval of the victim-agent revealed tiny, I mean tiny, intrusions of the outer derma."

Dalton took it all in and spoke first.

"A bite."

"What?" the president spoke now. "A bite, Mort?"

"Yes, ma'am. Again, we got lucky on this one. The residue from one cannister wasn't fully evaporated. A little sticky, still. Lab images on a sample showed this… "

The screen changed again in the side office.

Spurrier and Stevens examined the beetle-like creature with equal awe and fear. Same bodily composition. Wings. What stood out as completely different, though, was the proboscis, the tiniest little needle on the front of the head area. They noted the scale indicated at the bottom of the picture.

"You've got to be kidding me," Stevens mouthed.

"Wish I was, sir," Mort came back in. "What you're looking at is the smallest, independent insect known to mankind. Something under a third of a millimeter in length. Smaller than any recently discovered bugs, even *Scydosella Musawasensis*—the feather wing beetle. I grew up in the Midwest and we called insects like this no-see-ums. You'd be enjoying a nice summer evening with your friends in the neighborhood. Smack, your hand goes to your neck, like, *what the crap was that?*"

"Mort?" the general probed gently.

Neither senior official was rude but if this was going to turn into reminiscing about Mort's childhood, they wanted to move on.

"Oh yeah, right sir. So, seems like this little guy is in the cannisters and he's filled with the even smaller parasitic microbe. Poof, goes the lid to the container, the gel keeping them inert vanishes and... "

"And," Zeb cut in again. "There's your delivery profile. These tiny beetle-things essentially wake up from their gel-induced sleep and start looking, literally, for blood."

Spurrier was not squeamish. Still, she backed away from the screen slightly, the level of horror growing with every new discovery. A certain fear accompanies things you can see, can size up with your senses. But a world so small as to go unnoticed every day, suddenly turning against you with a power and lethality thus-far unknown provides an unsettling factor all its own. Add to this the reality that the threat wasn't some random act of nature — no, someone ported its destruction for their own evil intent — and the unthinkable lay on the doorstep.

"Wait," Dalton said. "We still haven't accounted for the controllability of this thing. You'd think with something this virile it would spread rapid and wide."

"That's what makes this thing so perfect, at least in a really creepy sense," Mort finished. "These bugs apparently do themselves in unwittingly. Like, they have one shot at biting their target and flop over dead. Not so much a sting and die scenario, like some species of hornet. We don't know for sure but it's possible there is some chemical toxicity in human blood for them. Weird, but it appears the thing they want is what snuffs them out. Also, we're theorizing a limited kill range after the burst effect takes place. Something like a few feet and a few seconds, and most likely requiring contact with bodily fluids from the deceased. The CDC agent in Haiti fell back, got the cut, panicked, and fell forward again onto the body with the trembling leg. The parasite can't move except for using its flagellum and pilli. Once outside the body it needs to be able to swim in the victim's pooled blood to travel. In every instance other than the CDC agent, the parasites look for a new host but don't find one quick enough to stay alive. Something about hitting the air and they don't last long at all."

**"Well, that's all very interesting,**" a new voice interjected.

"*Sanchez?*" Dalton said, almost reeling upon hearing her voice.

"Yeah, figured I'd let Mort do his thing and listen in for now. Sounds like we've got some operational theories shaping up here, at least far as the question of how this thing is occurring."

Zeb had not known she was on the line. The conversation unfolded so quickly no one bothered to set the table for all the listeners. This sat-call from a hilltop in the middle of the jungle on his way back out to the airstrip was initially an emergency hail of local resources, a means of getting people in play to find her. That his first call had been interrupted by this second group conversation was not out of the ordinary. Significant advances in real-time operations often require immediate connection and action. He was so thankful they had cut in. This was the first he'd heard from her in over sixteen hours, having lost the rhythm of text check-ins while in the cave complex. Hearing her now, alive and seemingly well, caused him to breathe in deeply. For her part, Sanchez had made it back out to a clearing, enough space overhead to receive the call. Though still a bit dazed from the events of the last half-day, she rapidly regained her usual clarity of mind and action in the field.

"Sergeant," the president offered. "Sounds like you have quite a story as well."

"Madam president, I wish I had more hard intel at this point. Strange tale, yes, but maybe not so much helpful information to share."

"Well, nevertheless, having just learned of your recent peril, I am also glad to hear you are doing fine."

"Thank you, ma'am. Me, too."

"Sanchez," Stevens jumped in. "We've got your coordinates and assets are in transit. Should be seeing your ride in about forty-five. Dalton, proceed with your team to the airstrip and once you regroup with Sanchez, the four of you will coordinate through the embassy in Panama. Move to a safe house and comms and we'll go from there."

"Wait, sir. *Four* of us?"

"Yes, Dalton. The four of you."

Zeb looked from his vantage point, back down to where Smith and Padre waited impatiently on the path.

"Got it, sir. The four of us."

# TWENTY TWO

*The venue boasted a retro, communist-chic vibe, hearkening back to its Cold War roots.*

**The current owners tried to recapture** the essence of the former German Democratic Republic, not so much in detail but overall look and feel. Dark wood paneling. Low hung chandelier. Deep reds in the carpet and upholstering. Apparently, the irony of this quite capitalistic endeavor taking on the cloak of life behind the iron curtain bothered no one to great extent. It stood as, perhaps, its best selling point.

*Astra Kulturhaus*, named after and sponsored by the beer company of its namesake, occupied a former WW2 railroad repair complex in Berlin's Friedrichshain District. The converted red brick factory building now served as one of the city's most sought after rooms for live music and nightlife. Acts as diverse as Vampire Weekend and Busta Rhymes had recently graced its stage. In demand for touring bands, the wait for bookings could reach well past eighteen months. Those contracts were unbreakable. Until a few weeks ago. Now, Kulturhaus' management and staff readied themselves for a supremely different kind of occasion.

"Yes. I have seen the broadcast specs and we are contracting the best people we know. That's all taken care of. Certainly. No one besides ticketed guests will be allowed in. We'll utilize our normal security measures. They perform quite well... "

Kulturhaus' manager was a veteran of urban show wars. Hiring on as a stagehand in his late teens, he'd ridden the wave of hard work and long hours in performance spaces throughout Berlin. Adding a tech college degree in business gave him the next leg up and onto a career footing in a notoriously transient vocation. He hoped this stop would be his last for some time. So, he worried slightly at breaking his first performance agreement ever. Thoughts of his reputation with other performers caused him pause when receiving the call. That is, until they offered more money than he'd make in a year to drop Death Cab and book a local hosting of *World One.*

"I am quite aware of the sensitivity of this event. Yes. We have the catering specs."

The thirty-something man was almost ready to hang up. Dollar signs in his head kept him listening and absorbing treatment like he was a complete greenhorn.

"Yes. Thank you."

He set the phone down on the bar top. The man had a nice office upstairs, away from the main floor, but preferred to do much of his daily work here, in full view of the room itself. The space reminded him of what he was doing and that he wanted to do it well.

Fifteen hundred people. Add in the outer foyer area, as planned with additional video screens and speakers, and there would be closer to two thousand. The satellite hardware would be installed Monday. There would be test runs of the visuals and audio the next day in the afternoon. Specialized stamp readers on the way, the contact had said. Looking like the phasers on Star Trek, they secured entrance for all guests. No one would get in without their QR Code checking off as genuine. No one.

Though he might have surmised as much if thinking about it, Kulturhaus stood on the much smaller end of things as far as locations was concerned. A recent internet "expose", mostly a rundown of current rumors regarding the event, theorized as many as millions, maybe ten million, invites had gone out across the world. Hosting that many people simultaneously would seem at first blush to be a physically impossible task. Until you realized that forty-five football stadiums alone in Germany held capacities over 20,000, totaling near to a million screaming fans with every seat taken. The largest in this city, *Olympiastadion Berlin*, could hold nearly four times that number. Worldwide passion for the game flowed freely and deeply and made for human edifices capable of enormous crowds. Even at that, the need outpaced the supply of these giant fields of play. Thus, another stratum of spaces like this one, ranging somewhere between a thousand and ten thousand seats, would be necessary for the event. They might be a smaller fish, but they were being paid well.

The manager sighed and looked over at his lead bartender, prepping for another night.

"Worth it?"

"Um, yeah. Feels like an overactive nanny most of the time but it's worth it."

"Still all cloak and dagger on the phone?"

"Yep, almost comical. Voice comes on the line, altered to sound like a robot, and then whoever starts going down a page of questions. Won't answer any of mine. Keeps asking until I give assurance all is well."

"Well, robots can't actually engage in conversation, right?" the barkeep laughed.

"I guess you're right."

The manager walked away from the bar area and back up to his office, all the while thinking about finally buying this place, not merely running the gig for someone else. The vision warmed him. Seemed more than possible now. Only a matter of time.

---

**Peter Stinson returned to his call list.** The rigor of details was manageable, but barely. Having formed an administrative team and then chairing much of the work himself, he wanted to make sure of no loose ends. And no loose lips. To this point, all proceeded as planned. The larger venues, more experienced with events of this scale, needed less hand holding. This last call, to Kulturhaus, represented the level of oversight necessary for the others. The intimate assistant to Matthew Donneleigh shuffled a stack of papers and set them aside. He paused, struck by thoughts kept relatively safe, tucked away somewhere they couldn't bother.

*No.*

Immersed in the world and work of his friend and mentor for too long to even consider these ideas, he stood and made his way from his desk and down one of hundreds of long, brightly lit hallways at Quantech. Had he been more self-aware, he would have noticed them taking longer and longer to dismiss as of late.

# TWENTY THREE

*Dalton stared at the ceiling. Given the pool of sweat forming on his tank top, he wasn't surprised to see strips of paint peeling away from the finished surface en masse.*

**He couldn't sleep.** Rolling over didn't help, only spread sticky wet perspiration across more of his torso. A window mount AC unit in his room seemed to be circulating the current temp of the space more than anything else. Zeb tried hard to calm his mind and body. The stress of the previous few days in the jungle had taken their toll and he needed to regroup physically and mentally. With each new piece of evidence, every increased data stream, his fertile brain played out scenarios. None of them ended well.

Sitting up and to the edge of the bed, he paused for a moment. He had known large-scale killers before. Had summed up their tactics and motives. Most times these things came down to a bid for power or revenge. But even at that, the flame of justice often faded to a lust for control and wealth. But this, this made no sense at all. Spurrier was convinced all of this was a lead up to *World One*. He was inclined to agree. For the moment, that's all he had. In his mind's eye the scenarios flew by like a lightning fast parade of timestamps, data dumps, and connective intelligence. No less than eight separate but plausible outcomes. The problem was, as always, he couldn't narrow the field to one. Couldn't determine which scenario would play itself out for the millions of people directly affected, and the hundreds of millions held captive in its wake. Control. He'd learned to let that one go in Seattle, a few years back. Well, maybe not completely. But he was gaining an awkward acceptance of the fact that, though he could perceive and calculate to a much finer and greater degree than the average human, he had no more ability to arrange those circumstances than any others.

Dalton stood and walked down the short hallway of the safe house. Unsurprised a light was on in the kitchen, he was even less taken back by whom he encountered at this dark hour.

"Hey," came the soft greeting from across the smallish oval table.

"Sanchez, you look like I feel."

"Now *that* is how you charm a lady, Dalton."

He grinned. Their banter made him seem at home somehow.

Zeb noted the coffee pot's red light and made his way over to pour some of the still warm liquid for himself.

"How're the beans, sarge?"

"Well," she looked down forlornly. "Not gonna challenge the stuff from your little hole in the wall cafe back home."

The mention took Dalton back, flooding him with fond remembrances of the former fur trapper's warehouse, his getaway in the midst of Seattle's urban crush.

"Yeah, wouldn't mind some quiet mornings by a window seat about now. That's for sure."

"But," she added. "Given we have some unknown actor bent on literal genocide and the resulting collapse of the modern economies of the world, we should keep on task here."

"Well, when you put it that way, sure."

The glow of the laptop invited Dalton to peer into her work.

"That looks like a very nice spreadsheet, Sanchez. I like the way you've used color highlighting and cell borders."

"Shut up, LT," came back, though softened with a slight smile. "You think you're the only one who can use numbers?"

"Alright, alright. What you working through?"

Reluctantly, she turned the unit and allowed him a better look. It took him a sum total of thirty seconds to master what was surely hours of work, but he was impressed.

"Okay," he rubbed his chin while responding. "You got it. I see where you're going. Makes a whole lot of sense."

"One to a thousand. We have to assume the ratio at this point," the explanation unnecessary. "The last event had five agents and five thousand victims. By the time we move to the big show it could be less but certainly won't be more. No reason to factor a decrease in potency. It's all too linear, in terms of a testing progression, to go there."

"So," Dalton jumped in. "We cover every venue with as many shooters."

"Yep. Spurrier is convinced we hang this one out until the very last minute. I agree. Any indication we are tracking the bad guys and everything blows up. The rumors of the 90-10 threat are still largely unsubstantiated. We know differently because she got an invite."

"And the bad guy — or guys," Dalton said. "They have to assume leaking but they also know they hold the ultimate checkmate. If they presume nervous nation states are formulating an attack, their finger is on the keyboard, waiting to eviscerate the wealth making the world go 'round."

"So, we plan and we train. But we play this little game out until either we find out who to go after... or we move into place and hope we can make the shots when needed."

"Phew," Zeb whistled, looking at her numbers again. "A lot of assets to manage stealthily. But, I guess when you break it down, it just makes sense."

"Sure. For instance, take a soccer stadium with a seating capacity of 50,000. Fifty agents with their little cannisters. Average time for a solid kill from à hidden perch means each sniper can only tag three bogeys before all Hades breaks loose and they start releasing their tiny hordes on the unsuspecting crowds."

"So, somewhere near eighteen shooters for a site holding 50,000?" Zeb surmised, moving back toward the counter for more coffee. "More doable when you think of it that way."

A simple electronic beep and Dalton's attention turned again to the screen, pulled back by the sound and the appearance of a three by four-inch subnet window popping up out of nowhere.

He froze.

Sanchez caught the moment and stared back, trying to help unlock him with her eyes. No words. Merely recognition between them that the last time this kind of coding app appeared, it had carried the gravest of consequences, the weight of millions of lives hanging on his actions. The incapacity broke, this time much quicker than before. He shook his head and gave Jessica a look of strength, returning to the present.

She typed a response.

*Correct. Numbers and training confirmed.*

Only seconds required for the sender to place more green text on the dark, black background.

*Excellent. Concur on this end as well. Proceed to prep site. Sanchez lead.*

The veteran sniper sat back. Though asked to draw up some initial plans for training and releasing the small army of shooters, the fact she was handed the reigns surprised her. Dalton, for his part, caught the look in her face — whether she was the right person for the job. He leaned over the keyboard, slightly brushing her in the process. His response was unequivocal and spoke volumes.

*Understood. Agreed, ZD. No one else for the role.*

After hitting send, the two of them stayed close. Though not peering into each other's eyes, neither pulled away.

**"Well. What's up, you two?** Early strategy session?"

Smith's voice was followed by his untimely presence in the small kitchen area. Dalton stood and stepped back from the table.

"Yeah, something like that," Sanchez said.

"So, what's the next step?" the agency man queried.

"Eight hours," Jessica replied as she shut the lid of the computer, the predawn darkening even more around them. "Get yourself some rest if you can but we are due at the commercial airstrip north of the city. From there we don't know yet. Secured text will give us the location for Training Phase A."

"Alright. About time we got this thing rolling."

Zeb interrupted Smith. "Yep, you guys have a great time."

For a second Sanchez felt like Dalton was abandoning the team.

"Oh," he assured her, sensing the unspoken words. "I need to keep pressing on the trail of evidence here. If there's any chance of figuring out who we're dealing with and how to take them out, I need some more time with the Caracol angle. It's this odd string, attached to the events but not in any helpful way right now. The rest of you should keep the plan moving. I'll go see our new researcher friends. Hopefully, some more conversation will bust something loose we don't yet understand."

"Dalton," Smith interjected. "Does it make sense for you to head out on your own at this point?"

Zeb's stomach sank. He didn't like Smith. Nothing personal. Just the last time he was assigned someone "official", it didn't work out so great.

"You're right, Smits," Dalton relented. "Teamwork is always better. And seeing someone among us holds intimate experience of the geography and cultures in question... "

He paused to take another sip of coffee and looked at both of them.

"I'll take Padre."

# TWENTY FOUR

*The meeting this time was hosted in the dining center closest to the professors' offices. Efforts had been made at creating a less sterile, institutionalized place to enjoy a midday meal. They failed, miserably.*

**Dalton kept looking for something** not satisfying his entire week's allocation of sodium. He settled for a salad. He wanted the pizza. It wouldn't be Blondie's but called to him, nonetheless.

"Constance can't join us?"

"No, son. She's at her sister's for the weekend. Poor thing fell off her stoop. Not especially fragile, but sure took a wallop to her left temple. They're watching for signs of concussion. Better for her to have some help and a little company."

"Wow, I'm so sorry to hear that, Dr. Hendricks. But great they maintain such a tight, caring relationship."

"Please, please, call me Martin," the older man replied. "And, by the way, they can't stand each other."

Dalton seemed surprised by the openness of the comment.

"See this, right here?" Martin said, pointing to himself like a game show prize hostess. "*This* is what they split over." He winked. "Constance won that contest hands down." His voice trailed off as he grabbed a bag of chips, added to the bounty on his tray. "Best thing ever to happen to me. No question. Now, why is it a strong, smart young man like yourself doesn't... "

"Yeah," Dalton interjected. "So, thank you for making time for me again, uh, Martin."

"Oh, not a problem at all. Let's sit by the windows. My favorite spot."

"Sure."

"Now, Mr. Dalton," the researcher began. "How can I help you? I am imagining your continued interest in our studies means your reasons for being here will remain secretive. And they bear on a certain incident in Haiti?"

"Correct, Doctor... um, Martin. That is all I can say at this point."

"Understood, young man. Virology is certainly not my strong suit but the story of an Ebola strain didn't sit all that well either."

Zeb swallowed another forkful of greens.

"I have been reading the materials you suggested and I'm still a bit unclear about the writing on Stela Fifteen. They seem to indicate an occurrence with major implications, but time lines are missing and the location of the piece is no help either."

"Good. Very good, Zeb. May I call you Zeb?"

Dalton nodded and smiled. "Of course."

"Well then, you are referring to phrase, '*And thus was Caracol's Cleansing*', are you not?"

"Yes. I've noted it listed under some other reference as well. Mostly, though I've seen the topic dismissed as having much historic value. Shows up on alt Mayan sites more than the professional literature."

"Again, very good. I teach final year graduate students with less drive."

"Well, thank you. If I might ask: what are your thoughts on the topic. I noticed your published works mention it rarely as well."

"That would be because no one I know of believes they understand what it means. Or if they do, that it really matters. You've done the reading, the stream of thought, correct?"

"I think so. I mean, the stelae indicate some form of "reset" in their culture, something of enormous impact, maybe even leading to the end of their civilization at Caracol. Some think it refers to an act of their gods. A vengeance play for fooling them about the whole fake egalitarianism thing. I read a few authors going as far as to say the fire in 900AD was *the cleansing* itself, the gods were no longer willing to tolerate what had become of their society."

"Well then, conspiracies always make for a fun adventure, right? But the facts are we simply do not yet understand what this event, if it even happened, was all about."

"Okay. Sure. So, string out for me the craziest scenario you might draw up. What would that be?"

Martin set his spoon down and lit up.

"I like this game. Digging around in the dirt is fun and all but I'll tell you a secret." He leaned in a little more for emphasis. "It's rarely like Indiana Jones. Scratch that. It's *never* like Indiana Jones."

They both laughed a second, clearly enjoying the company and conversation.

"Alright then, son. Let me take my Ph.D. hat off and replace it with tin foil. Here's what I would say."

Dalton couldn't wait. He'd turned these ideas over and over in his head since starting down this road. He wanted this man to go with him, too.

"Tikal and Caracol are enemies but their warring comes to a head with the Star War event of the 600s AD. The Tikal King's legs are brought back to Caracol, where they stay in a mummified, inert state. A health crisis wipes out up to half of Caracol's population around 750 AD. Finally, a massive fire envelops the ancient city. Soon after, their flourishing, advanced ways vanish from the face of the earth."

He looked at Zeb.

"Here's the wild pitch. The health crisis wiping out half the population in 750? Some kind of biological entity, placed into the King's decaying flesh and set as a time bomb for a later revenge against an enemy who thoroughly humiliated Tikal. It goes off. The people see this as warning number one from the gods and repent. This is where the symbolic egalitarianism comes forward. It's a sacrifice, an appeasing of sorts. But all a sham. Everyone's in on it, rich and poor alike because they don't want another scourge to ravage their nation. Fast forward to the fire in 900AD... "

"And," Zeb added. "There you have your *cleansing*."

"Correct, my boy. The gods only put up with so much. Seeing their human charges as irredeemable, they instead must be destroyed. Judgment Day. The Cleansing. So, Mr. Dalton," he summed up. "Take us home."

Zeb breathed deeply.

"The legs are still alive, so to speak. This *cleansing* happened in 900AD but there's someone out there, someone who stumbled upon this bio-agent and thinks another act of judgment—a reset for humanity—is about due. And it still has to do with money. This time, on a much grander scale."

Martin tilted his head, gave Dalton a look saying, *Okay, how far are you going with this?*

"Yeah, I know, Martin. Super out there with no ledge at all. But it seems to me we need to start here and work backward into any kind of sanity. As counterintuitive as it may be, we are required to eliminate the cuckoo to find our way to something more reasonable. And," he finished. "God help us all if cuckoo becomes the truth. Because someone with this reach and these kinds of beliefs presents a powerful foe."

The professor looked like he wanted to say something but was holding back.

"Martin?"

"Well, I just wanted to know if you were going to finish up those black olives. Love those things."

"Got it. Knock yourself out, Martin. Please, give my regards to Constance, will you?"

**Nine hours later** Zeb leaned back in the hotel room across the street from the University. His eyelids were getting heavy and he was about to give in for the day. His head, as usual, was having trouble shutting down but at least a weight of direction now anchored his mental deliberations. Things had gone from too many scenarios to count — for most people, that is — to only a few contenders. Still, the outcomes all seemed rather grim. Hearing the slight buzz of a text message, he turned and reached for his phone on the nightstand.

*9:30 earliest for check-in tomorrow. Have other things early.*

He sat back again.

*Padre, what in the world could you have scheduled in the morning in Tampa, Florida? You live in the jungle, man.*

# TWENTY FIVE

*"No. I believe I've made myself quite clear."*

**Anthony learned to trust** this great leader over the course of three decades. There came a moment in each new R&D cycle, and then again in marketing and roll out, when faced with the choice of following conventional wisdom or the savvy of this man. At every turn, this innovator was right. No exceptions. It didn't matter how high a mountain of experts piled up against him. In the end, Matthew Donneleigh had proved all detractors wrong.

This moment seemed different.

Facing more than the success or failure of some new technology, Dr. Bartollo found himself internalizing his icon's choices with a strength of conviction not dissipating easily. It burned inside him. The vision was planted so firmly, lit so bright, he could almost behold the dawn rising in his imagination. A new day. Not merely some product. Donneleigh's magnetism was tied intrinsically to an underlying premise: their gadgets were always about more than simple convenience or consumption. To be sure, every item in their ever-expanding line carried underpinnings of a moral good. At least they were presented as such. Eco-conscious, people-conscious, animal-conscious. Quantech tapped into a reservoir of humanity left untouched by the vast majority of approaches to development and manufacturing. It was almost as if their production lines scratched at a deep, abiding sense of purposefulness. Maybe even identity. Donneleigh's work unearthed something long dormant in the broader public, however it might be channeled.

So, the senior scientist felt the slightest betrayal from the one in whom he had placed so much of his own trust.

"Matthew. Please, stop for a moment. Think of all we are going to do in such short order." It sounded silly coming from his own lips. Of course, Donneleigh understood what was at stake. That's what made his choices as of late all the more confusing.

"Forgive me, sir," Bartollo backed up. "I don't understand. Help me understand." His eyes began pleading. "The intrusion to the cave is no accident. We have it on reliable intel. This woman is part of a team, tasked specifically to investigate the prior death events. We also know they hold some initial background on the Caracol site and its origins—why they made it to the complex in the first place. Clearly, their leads and data are muddled at best. But why would we take any chances, so close to achieving our... our calling."

Donneleigh looked down, no change in expression. He wasn't mad. Seemed empathetic, even. Picking up the single page laid before him, he studied the faces of Dalton and Sanchez.

"These two are confirmed, Peter?"

Stinson had been in the room, but to this point the silent part of the trio. He'd been weighing the emotional and intellectual momentum in the room. His own thoughts vacillated from Bartollo's side of the spectrum to a place he would not admit openly, and then back again. Stinson's feelings were anything but resolute. It was far too early to allow his heart to settle in any one place. Not yet.

"Yes, they are," he responded. "The woman has not been seen the last twenty-four hours but the man, this former Army Lieutenant, was tracked to the researchers at their university offices. We have no information regarding their actual conversations but must assume some piecing together of the data, however minimal at this point."

"You see, Matthew," Bartollo was gaining steam, possibly crossing the line of propriety. "This is no regular police action, not even at the federal level with all their resources. This is a secret. They are playing this exactly the same way we are. Keep moving forward, ignoring the possibility of opposite covert action, trusting all will be well." His voice had risen enough to require a response.

"Stop," Donneleigh said, though more gently than would be expected in the face of insubordination. "My mind is made up, gentlemen. We will proceed as stated."

The leader started a new line of conversation, doubly signaling this one was finished.

"Now, good doctor, how does our readiness stand at this hour?"

It took a second for Bartollo to shift from impassioned speech to recitation of facts.

"Well, we are on track," he finally got out. "The testing phases confirm a maximum yield of a thousand to one. Efficacy rates fall sharply after this point."

"Good thing we have enough carriers. That will work fine. The control factor?"

"Recent advances in the lab here removed the variable causing us some concern. We are assured of the cannister system and its dependability. Get enough people on site and the delivery mechanisms will work. That is for certain."

"And Peter," Donneleigh turned. "Preparations at all sites?"

"In motion and on schedule."

"Well done, my friends. All the right pressure in all the right places. In keeping a shadow over the events in Belize and Haiti, they stem the tide of panic but also allow us to proceed. This is the dance I imagined. Our every step being countered silently. We turn to the left and they follow suit. Be assured we are in the lead here. The music will end abruptly while they are still considering what is next."

Bartollo couldn't hide his doubts.

Donneleigh caught it.

"*Anthony*. My dear brother, Anthony. Peter and I have already had this talk. I admire—no, I cherish—your passion and commitment to the greatest good this world will ever see. A good that is long overdue. But there is a right and just way to go about it. I will not sacrifice the rightness of our cause to the vagaries of the moment. Indeed, if this is the restart of everything true and beautiful, then no evil may befall it. No forces will prevail against that which is truly just."

He looked at Stinson, including him in the invocation by simply turning his face toward the man.

"Seven days, my friends. A mere seven days," he leaned back and swiveled toward the large glass overlook of his private garden. "And, if God did his work in that amount of time, even accounting for a full day of rest," he smiled. "Certainly we can remake this world in the same."

———————————

**The man finger-drummed aimlessly** on the steering wheel of the 2015 Ford Focus. The nondescript small sedan had been parked for an hour across the street from the mid-grade Tampa hotel. With a steadied, patient eye he watched and waited. The screen of his phone lit and the message notification caused it to wiggle across the upholstered front passenger seat. Picking it up, the man tapped the icon and read the brief instructions.

*Objectives changed. Authority to dispatch upon critical mass of discovery or seventy-two hours, whichever comes first.*

The man smiled as he acknowledged the message, feeling now his very best work could be done. He set the phone back down on the seat beside him. When he looked up, Zeb exited the hotel lobby and turned up the street on foot.

———————————

**Bartollo put his phone down, too.** He wasn't quite sure what to feel. Partly he was shamed. But there was also in his soul a greater sense of obligation than merely to his longtime friend and mentor. He was dearly hoping this failsafe would not be used too soon. But make no mistake, he had crossed the line. Whether or not his boss ever found out, their cause would indeed shine like the noontime sun.

# TWENTY SIX

*"Air support confirmed. Charlie Echo Five. Keep your heads down."*

**He couldn't run any faster.** His lungs, seared with a fire-glazed iron, seemed ready to burst any moment. Still a good hundred yards from the ridge line, the jungle canopy and undergrowth reached up at every step, vying to drag him to a dead stop. The orders in his headset willed him forward, though every ounce of normal strength lay spent, left behind on the barely-marked trail.

*Keep moving. Keep moving.*

Fists pounded in front of him as if pulling the air, using the unseen to catapult his body ahead.

Almost there.

Ten more steps, as large a gate as manageable, and he emerged over the hilltop.

What he witnessed stopped him, suddenly, more quickly than he imagined possible. The motion of his body hung in mid-air though both feet were firmly planted on opposing sides of the peak. A wash of heat. He fell back, shaking his head violently and trying to pass off the effects of the concussion wave while leaning into the event as far as possible.

Too late.

Exploding into vain shouts of the powerless, the agony of his cries all but absorbed the sounds of death, even from this distance.

**Padre returned to the present** and peered into the clear, plastic cup. His right hand trembled as he raised the juice drink to his lips. The cool, thickened liquid helped a little. O for it to be a cure, that he would never have to relive the moment again. He swallowed, knowing better — that the pain was real; as much a part of him as anything else etched into the pages of his story. It did no good to deny it. Still, a full acceptance was a ways off. For now, an uneasy truce with his soul would have to suffice.

"Hey, so how was the early start this morning?"

Dalton's greeting helped some, too.

"Ah, you know. Would rather be back where you found me. What is this stuff, anyways?" he tilted the glass for Zeb to observe. "People drink this crap on a regular basis?"

"Umm, yeah. I think you nailed it," Dalton replied, wincing at the grayish mass. "I am absolutely convinced we'll find out a thousand years from now the all-natural stuff is what did us in as a species. Some alien race will be like, 'What in the world were they thinking.'"

Padre laughed lightly.

"For me," Dalton continued. "Just coffee. All I need. And you can get quality beans most everywhere you go. That should say something."

"You do realize tea is more prevalent worldwide, don't you?"

"Of course, but that doesn't make it right," Dalton shrugged his shoulders. "Savages."

Zeb waved over the cafe staff and asked for their best dark roast. It would be a few minutes, the young woman let him know. A single serve pour-over, his drink would have to be prepared, as opposed to simply slopping it into a mug. He could wait.

"So, what's the black book?" Dalton noted. The small, simply bound volume sat at a slight counter-clockwise angle in front of Padre, indicating he was right-handed. No title. Thin burgundy ribbon for a tie. A basic leather cover and handmade stitch bind added mystery.

"Nothing much. A way to think on paper, instead of out loud."

"Diary? Deepest, darkest secrets?" Dalton wished he'd kept that one to himself, immediately realizing the potential benefit of Padre's little black book and feeling he overstepped with the largely unknown partner.

"Mostly a way to slow things down a little."

"Every day?" Zeb asked more respectfully, this time realizing he'd met this guy in the middle of the jungle and so maybe he did have some things to hide, or at least keep private.

"Nope. When I feel like it. Today I felt like it. Writing down the words from an ancient song this morning."

Padre took one more sip, as if this were the gray sludge's last chance to impress him. He set it aside dismissively. Rising from his seat, the man made a beeline for the door marked *men*. Dalton deduced the mash had hit Padre's system hard and watched him pass the corner to the bathroom. Then, curiosity got the better of him. He tried to fight it off, but the little book was so tempting and the man such an enigma. Dalton slid it over, opened it enough to see the current entry.

*Why do you boast of evil, you mighty hero?*

*Why do you boast all day long, you who are a disgrace in the eyes of God?*

*You who practice deceit, your tongue plots destruction; it is like a sharpened razor.*

*You love evil rather than good, falsehood rather than speaking the truth.*

*You love every harmful word, you deceitful tongue!*

**"We ready?"**

Padre's voice startled him. Nowhere to hide. Caught.

Gently, the man swiveled his own property toward himself, closed it, and placed it in his shoulder-slung bag.

Dalton's face flushed, a slight red.

"Yep," he waved the now to-go cup of coffee. "All good."

---

**Reston, as he was known** to his contracted employers, had been in the business for nearly fifteen years. A certain sense of routine settled about his work, much the same way an outdoorsman knows his marks. There was an understood range of parameters in which this kind of stalking, assessment, and if necessary, termination, was done. Indeed, human behavior is complex, but not so much as to create outright chaos. If the human creature is unpredictable, it is at least reasonable in its variance. The rhythms of men follow a schedule: largely sleep, food, and the generally consistent activities of the everyday. Patterns emerge if you looked long and hard enough. Reston was a hunter of humans. He was patient and he was efficient. He knew how to measure risk and reward, and for all the dangers of his chosen field he was not one to overstep the moment. Which is why he waited a moment before continuing. A key variable had changed.

On this second day of tracking Dalton, Reston somehow missed that he had partnered up. While a distracting event, this was not a game changer upon initial observation. Dalton was not an imposing physical presence. This newcomer, even less so. Maybe 5'5". Thinning hair, salt and peppered. Wiry, which in certain cases could be trouble. But there was something about the way he walked, without much intentionality or force, that gave away he was ambling a bit through life. Reston read this as unlikely to have the kind of internal convictions leading to immediate, unequivocal action.

Dalton, on the other hand, provided much more challenge, he assumed. Not in the sense that the stalked might overpower the stalker—that remained laughable—but that he was aware enough of his surroundings to rarely be taken by surprise. There was an obvious field sense to the man. You could see it, even from a distance. This prey remained wary at all times, but still clever enough to veil the internal, ongoing evaluations of threat and scenario churning in his head. Yes, this shaped up to be an interesting assignment; one taking an extra share of work to bring to conclusion. But that's what made the chase so very worthy.

---

**"So, Padre,** how does the retelling of my last interview with the Hendricks settle on you?"

"Sounds about right to me."

Dalton was looking for more of a reason for easy dismissal than that.

"C'mon. You've got to be kidding me."

"No. Not really. Makes imperfect but compelling sense if you think about it."

"How exactly did you arrive at this conclusion?"

Zeb's question was slightly disingenuous. This same reasoning resonated in his head the last few hours. He just wanted to hear another angle on it. And maybe an actual, real person saying the same things he currently kept to himself.

"Look, Dalton. Could the glyphs and stelae at Caracol be a coincidence? Merely some weird happenstance paralleling current events? Sure, but why not try and tie them together? Seems you may get farther down the road by making that assumption, instead of waiting around for some kind of irrefutable data."

Dalton had what he wanted.

"You're right, Padre. That's what I'm thinking, too. We need to push on this door and see where it takes us. Sometimes crazy turns out to be real. In this case, we've got plenty of that to wade through on our way to the truth. Who knows? Maybe I'll find those Mayan King's severed legs and use them myself to vanquish the bad guys."

"Dalton?"

"Yeah, Padre?"

"Back in the jungle I said I thought you were as *loco* as they come."

"Oh yeah, that's right," he chuckled, remembering that moment in the dugout.

"I was joking then."

"And?"

"You just settled that one for me."

# TWENTY SEVEN

*The last few steps were over cobbled stone, set in place only a year ago as yet another effort at making new appear old.*

**The East Village of Des Moines, Iowa** was your typical urban comeback kid. Gentrification remained an issue but, for the most part, the newer shops and clubs and invigorated business district and nightlife were warmly welcomed. Significant investment in urban residency and a climate fostering startups — particularly new tech and media — had transformed this once sleepy center of all things insurance into one of the fastest growing urban spaces in America. Long viewed as merely the biggest, most boring city in the heart of flyover country, the DSM was on the rise. This shabby-chic bookstore remained no exception.

The clink of a small metal bell signaled someone crossing the front door threshold. A wisp of fall air blew gently at the thumbtacked papers on the locals only board. The bell clanged again as the door shut.

"Mylon."

The man-bun twenty-something behind the counter knew most of his regulars by first name.

"What can I do ya for," he asked the customer.

"Hey, you got those new DC graphic novels in yet?"

"Ughh, Mylon, Mylon, Mylon. How many times do I have to tell you? DC sucks. Nothing good comes out of any universe except Marvel's."

"Yeah, I know, I know. But c'mon, bruh. Two words: Supergirl and Wonder Woman."

"You do have a point, my man. That's actually three words but... straight back and turn left. Should be about midway down the aisle."

The young man made his way back, turned, and found the copy. A few more steps and he relaxed at a lone chair next to an emergency exit. Out of the way. Perfect. He removed his tablet from the light brown, corduroy shoulder bag. Once powered on, the iPad Pro recognized the wifi immediately. He pulled up his email.

There it was.

Nondescript. As much like junk mail as the other hundreds of pieces deleted, most weeks. Yet, this message he expected. No, more than that. Anticipated. Longed for. With as much curiosity and interest many young men would apply to the DC novel, he clicked *open*. His heart raced. Might it really be? His entire life pointed in this direction. As convinced of this as anything—ever—he read and embraced the on-screen directive.

*WF green light*
*Entry secured... QR Code to come via cell fifteen minutes before start*
*Package location and site map once inside*

**"Hey, Mylon."**

The voice came down the shallow aisle, not fifteen feet away. Surprised, the young man hit the home button on his tablet and tried to set his face in a neutral expression. The screen reset to a picture of mountains and a sunset. He found it more difficult to reset his countenance. How does one quickly douse emotions raised by such hope, such fulfillment? He feared it was still obvious.

Man-bun rounded the corner.

"Oh, there you are. Yeah, you get that DC okay? Just got another batch in, literally the last minute. UPS guy must have known you were here, right?"

"Umm, sure. Ha, yeah. Super weird."

"You good, Myles? Look a little flushed. Heater on back here or something?" The worker pounded the radiator a few times in quick succession. "Shouldn't be. Jeez, never turns on when it's butt cold outside but now when we see a great fall day it runs non-stop?"

Mylon knew he had to look him in the face. It took an extra reserve of control to appear nonchalant. He raised his head and smiled. "No, heat's fine, man."

"Sure? Alright then. You want to snatch a look at these? I'll hold 'em at the counter until we enter them in the system."

"Thanks."

The bookstore staff took a few steps and then turned back, holding the books out and gesturing with them.

"Must be your lucky day or somethin', right?"

A simple nod sufficed this time. Then the young man, as true believer as there was, sat back and closed his eyes, imagining what he considered the greatest investment he could ever make to this world. Filled with peace and purpose, Mylon woke his tablet and gazed again at the directive. His focus blurred as he looked into the distance beyond the screen, imagining. But not the momentary chaos of what he was committed to doing in the next number of days. No, his mind filled instead with the glorious outcomes to follow, for what he presumed to be an eternity.

A quiet system alert indicated he had no need to delete the message. It was already gone.

———————————————

**For his part, Peter Stinson** was happy to be sending updates and checking off states and nations, one by one. Overseeing a large team of administrators would be more efficient, but also more prone to leaks. The automation sequences developed under wraps at Quantech worked fine. Things were moving along well. At least, he kept telling himself this.

He took a moment, too, envisioning the events of next week. In particular, he focused on the group he had recently finished. Before working on *World One* he would never guess that more than 60,000 high net worth individuals lived in the State of Iowa. Never. Weren't they all hog farmers? Still, the details of even this smallish state proved a doable task, given no interference along the way. If it was only numbers, they had all the capacity they needed in just three venues. Wells Fargo Arena in downtown Des Moines would host 16,000. The UNIDome at the University of Northern Iowa would hold the same. Then, finally, the basketball arena at Iowa State University seated another 15k. While that left a small smattering to be accounted for, there would be no challenge in getting these people into contained spaces and with the broadcast capabilities required. Hilton Arena, the ISU venue, was home of "Hilton Magic", an ominous vibe for visiting teams more often than not providing some measure of extra pixie dust, thus leading to a win for the home squad.

Peter let his mind wander to glimpses of a not so pleasant essence hovering in the room instead. He'd seen the images. Belize, Montenegro, and Haiti. At the time, he had been able to set the gruesome happenings aside. Now, more and more, it stayed with him. Haunted him. Called out to his conscience that, whatever he had been led or allowed himself to believe, this simply could not be right. No cause justified this act. No vision of a remade creation. No matter how hard a look at the human condition and all its failings—this could not be right and good.

In that moment, he woke up from what seemed a very bad, very long dream.

"God," he cried out in his private workspace. "How could I? What kind of man have I become?"

Tears made their way off his face and onto the floor, passing through fingers that had just typed instructions for a holocaust.

---

**Mylon gathered his things and left.** The bell clanged twice, again. It was a beautiful day. The combined colors of maples and other deciduous flora burst all around, tinting the air as he walked down the slight hillside to his car. A large pile lay in his path and he pushed right through, enjoying the crunch of boot soles on leaves.

It struck him.

This, too, was a sign. A dying, but a necessary one. A brief intermission before a restored blooming to come. It was always true. Season after season after season.

His face flushed, hot. Blood vessels pulsated, filling his lungs with what seemed especially pure oxygen. He felt strong. He felt noble.

And he recalled his bookstore friend's last words.

*Lucky day? If only you knew...*

# TWENTY EIGHT

*Reston waited patiently in the hotel lounge, his observation post.*

**The half-folded *USA Today*** did its job. Though most people were accessing content on either a smartphone or a tablet of some sort, the old school newspaper still fit in among the light evening crowd. The small bar hosted two or three road weary travelers, enough that a lone person sitting at the gathered couches wouldn't seem too out of place. He didn't care that his vision lay largely obscured. All he needed were his peripherals. Besides, the angle to the lobby cameras shut off most of his facial features from here. All in all, he carried little concern of being placed at the scene. His work would be finished soon and he would disappear.

His orders had changed, once again. Based upon his report of the morning's meet at the coffee shop, both Zeb and Padre were officially slated for an early exit from this world. This was now the final stage of an elimination op, which often requires inordinate amounts of waiting and a few, brief flashes of action. Reston's communique to Bartollo had been to the point: Dalton's interview with the researcher led him to a line of inquiry far too close to the truth. Time to remove this possible x-factor, especially given only a few days left in their timetable. Padre, of course, sat in the cross hairs as well. The researchers? Be it either some vague sense of collegiality or maybe another calculation of risk, they were to be left alone. Bartollo had a hard time imagining they could do much damage to the cause at this point.

The newspaper came down. Reston turned his body away from the cameras and toward the hallway. A slow, leisurely pace. At a dozen steps down the thinly carpeted corridor, the man took an abrupt left. Laundry. Ice machine. Stairwell. Dalton's room was on the top floor. Reston needed immediate access and egress, something the elevators could not provide with any sensed of surety. His heart rate increased but only barely, enough to send a bit more oxygen to his mind and extremities. That would be helpful in the next few minutes. One more landing and the heavy fire door opened by itself.

"Good evening," a middle-aged man offered while keeping his young son headed in the right direction toward the pool downstairs. The contrast of an enjoyable family scene to what the man had planned was inescapable. No matter. He had a job to do. Everyone has their place in this world. His was just different than taking junior for an evening swim before bedtime.

"Yes, good evening," Reston returned. The chance encounter required an expedited speed and efficiency of his actions now. A single person in an empty space always draws more attention in the memories of potential witnesses. Regardless of how matter of fact their interaction, it would register as a more defined moment at a later date. This would have to move along. His steps became more fluid — if that was even possible — and his body transformed into something more along the lines of a masterful system or machine. Each component part focused and functioning as a whole. One purpose. All energies allocated and every sense at full alert status.

Through the stairwell door and to the right.

306.

310.

312.

318 — all the way down the hall. Reston made sure he got there first.

The assassin manipulated the lock with a universal keycard and slipped inside.

**Dalton rode the elevators** with a group of ten others.

"Same flight, right?" Zeb asked Padre as they stepped through the powered door and onto the third floor. The others quickly filtered to their respective rooms, anticipating a very regular evening and paying little attention to those not in their family or group.

"Same flight," the older man confirmed.

"Already called the shuttle. Should be plenty of time for security and getting to the gate."

"Got it. Sounds good."

"Hey Padre," Zeb offered, stopping for a second in the middle of the corridor. "You sure about heading back into the biosfera? Have to say, it's been great having you along, even if you are a little mysterious. And, given my other option was Smith... well, let's just say I got the upgrade this time around."

Padre paused, genuinely thankful for the sentiment, but also settled in the fact he needed to retreat to the quiet and simplicity of the jungle as soon as feasible. He had some outstanding debts — doesn't everyone? — and joining the team satisfied those ledgers for now. He'd been cleared. Once they reported back, he could be on his way, traipsing off into the mists of the Central American wilderness.

Zeb saw the answer in his face and understood it to be no personal offense. "Alright. Well, see you in the morning, then."

Padre stopped one door short of Zeb and slipped inside. The soft sound of the closing door settled quickly in the hallway.

Dalton's slid his card through the magnetic reader.

Red.

Red.

*Come on. Really? Gonna make me head down to the desk to get a new card?*

One more swipe.

*Green,* and a click as the door lifted its latch.

The room was fairly standard for the money. About two feet of entryway with a coat closet to the right and a bathroom to the left. A single queen bed with nondescript coverings. Cheap, laser-printed artwork and a small sitting area with a not so inviting chair. Dalton eased in and past the half-closed restroom door. One more step and he was at the foot of the bed.

And struggling for his life.

The smooth latex cord didn't so much cut flesh as place a crushing pressure atop his windpipe. Without any warning to inhale deeply, Zeb's lungs were only half-filled and now protesting that fact. The burning is familiar to anyone finding themselves further underwater than they'd thought, fighting for the surface while trying to ignore the race of time versus oxygen. The body rebels, sends signals throughout the central nervous system that a grave imbalance is in play.

Dalton shot his hands up, back and then to the side, to no avail. His attacker had positioned himself out of the way of these attempts at release. Leverage became a major factor. The assailant carried a significant advantage in height and weight. Zeb couldn't pull him to the ground. Nor could he push to the rear with enough force to topple them both in that direction. His eyes glazed and the room began to spin. In one last effort, and with about half his normal strength, Dalton horse-kicked his right leg backward.

It wasn't a loud sound but the connection of heel to shin made an impact, enough to create the smallest give in the cord encircling his neck. Dalton shot his hand into the opening, forcing even more of a slackening. With the slightest of physical momentum, he rotated, twisting the hands behind his head at the wrist in an awkward face to face confrontation.

Reston reared his head back and slung it forward, completely ignoring the pain of impact. His grip on the cord now lost, he let it fall to the side. Dalton lay on his back, in between the bed and a side table, rolling over slowly from the concussive blow and loss of breath. The attacker pulled a six-inch blade from alongside his left calf and made a large, graceful arc downward. Mid-strike, the arm stopped. An order from the near the doorway.

Padre entered the chaos of the melee, demanding his presence, and the change in odds, be recognized. Reston did just that, pivoting as cleanly as Dalton had ever seen and sending the blade at Padre's head. Zeb's partner ducked to the left and into the bathroom. A dull thunk — drywall receiving the hardened projectile — signaled a miss.

The next image was fuzzy for Dalton, still trying to catch his breath. It seemed as if the unknown man leaped over him, out to the balcony and directly over the railing some three stories up. The truth was somewhat less magical. Having rolled over the rail, Reston grabbed twin fir trees only two feet from there and clambered down to the parking lot. Ever cautious, the man had reconned this option as an egress and now used it to perfection. Within ten steps he was folded into the streetside evening crowd and on his way to regroup.

**Fifteen minutes later** Zeb tapped out a secured text message to Stevens while Padre taxied them nowhere in particular.

*Trail turned deadly. Expediting return to DC for report.*

The reply came quickly.

*Negative. Reroute to training base. Details to come.*

"Well, Padre," Zeb still having trouble with his vocal cords. "Have to say you are only becoming more and more valuable these days. Sure you won't reconsider?"

The older man looked over slightly. "Two more days. That's it. By then you should be able to keep from getting yourself killed."

"Well, not sure if that's so true," Dalton replied. "But I'll take what I can get."

# TWENTY NINE

*Their faces bore pain unequal to their short years on the planet.*

**Donneleigh stumbled upon the folder** on his hard drive, clicked the first image, and then let the slideshow function run. Every three seconds a new set of eyes. Another village. Another shot of him and his team laboring among people who through no fault of their own fell into circumstance and opportunities so unlike his.

Housing projects. Education and micro-loan centers. Health clinics. In every way possible, Donneleigh's resources and people, and yes, his heart, given to the possibility that things could improve in this seemingly god-forsaken patch of dirt. Real change. A difference painting a much better picture for these people and the generations after them.

At first, that was indeed the story. Gains not seen for a hundred years flowing into the lives and economies of the forsaken. But all was cut short by night raids and privations. The daily encumbrance of armed militants, forcing his team to halt their efforts and strangle the distribution of goods and services, almost as if they took a giant leap backward in a tenth the time taken to build them up. So, the philanthropist turned to darker works, positing he could remove the evil and begin restoring again. But this proved even more difficult than his previous efforts. Almost as if an understudy for local dictator waited in the wings of every needy community. An unlimited supply. In the end, this became folly as well. Maybe not folly, but certainly not effective. And so it was that Matthew Donneleigh, one of the brightest stars Western thought had produced in the last few decades, left behind the foundation of reason and stepped willingly into the ancient past for a solution, something he felt would hold him and his failing world upright. Extreme? Yes, but necessary. This parade of faces only caused him to double down. The man was not a monster. Madness, without question. But even in the deepest recesses of his mind this stood as an attempt to cure, however ill-positioned.

**Matthew placed his phone system on do not disturb,** walked from his desk to the floor-to-ceiling oak shelves and pulled out a side drawer, beneath the counter space. Removing a multicolored waist sash and head covering, he fastened them both into place, took two steps to the left and then knelt on the hardened wood floors. Though the stone head icon garnered much attention from visitors, it held an entirely different attraction for Matthew. It was a focal point for his belief system. Though some would argue it was an idol, he would be quick to describe it as a stand-in for an actual deity, or rather a raft of them. The statuette was only stone. But that the figure had been fashioned from something both natural and strong symbolized the nature of his gods.

Donneleigh began intoning long-forgotten names. Asking for help. Seeking strength to carry through with his given mission. His heart was not after blood per se. Neither did he imagine the recipients of his prayers now delighting in the same. While the streams his beliefs flowed from occasionally dabbled in human sacrifice, Donneleigh's approach now was not one of appeasement. It instead became an act of contrition on behalf of an errant world. More cooperation than propitiation, he fully believed to be setting the stage for what the gods always intended for humankind. Again, the familiar ease washed over his mind, bringing a glow to his being and setting him at peace.

---

**At thirty-five-thousand feet** a certain clarity sets in, a prioritizing lost in the multi-threaded nature of life on the ground. Dalton let it do its work. A momentary peacefulness not regularly encountered in his soul.

The immense cargo carrier he and Padre had boarded sported fewer windows than a commercial jet. Still, Zeb positioned himself to catch as much as possible of what flew by outside. Leaning back into the jump seat netting and shoulder straps, he craned his neck to get a decent view.

The order on the ground was a beautiful thing. He'd often noted that from this elevated vantage point the middle of the country seemed much more organized than other regions. Dependable. Consistent. Predictable. How he longed for more of that in his own life and story. So many others below were allowed a regular routine, no idea what loomed on the near horizon. He often wished he didn't know as much he did, hadn't seen as much as he had.

Chaos awaited much of the world in the next few days. The initial death tolls, were they unable to intercept and foil the whole thing, would be the biggest shock wave humanity had experienced since the Flood. The result would be nothing less than worldwide suffering and a complete resetting of cultural norms and strata. The more Dalton considered whomever behind this as following manic religious directives from millennia past, the more scared he became of the potentialities. An ordered approach to human captivity and invasion held a certain known quality. Heinous, but something one could process on a historic or emotional level. This was something completely other. Though following the thought patterns and doing his best to circumvent them, no way existed to even brush the surface of understanding. Nonsensical. Illogical. None of the normal categories applied.

**"Alright, heads up,"** came the tin-metal voice from the cockpit. "We are beginning our descent. Welcome to Beatrice, Nebraska: small town, big missile."

The loop and downward arc of the plane provided Dalton a wide view of the very open plains region. Just as imagined. Empty.

"Hey," the voice over comms surprised him, followed by a slight startling that someone had sidled up to him in the cargo bay.

"Padre," Dalton replied. "You gotta stop that stuff. Sanchez is bad enough. I don't need two people who can sneak up on me at every second of the day, okay?"

"Sure. I'll make a habit to announce myself. You read up on this?" he pointed out the window.

"Yep, everything I ever wanted to know about cold war missile installations in the middle of nowhere. Equally unsettling and interesting."

"Imagine," Padre probed. "Men down there, given the responsibility to push the button when ordered, sending a huge rocket with a destructive force unknown to mankind toward other humans a few thousand miles away. Of course, it was assumed we would be responding to their missiles already headed toward us. So you got that going for ya."

"What? Some kind of insane vengeance play?" Zeb opined. "Seen enough of that up close, my friend. Enough to last a lifetime."

"Well, not sure about that, Dalton. Maybe the very best intentions on both sides were more a protective instinct. A noble cause, albeit one with the direst of outcomes."

"I think you give people, especially leaders, too much credit, Padre. And wait a second," he turned and continued. "Why do I sense your whole disappearing into the bush act has been a reaction to the nationalistic use of force anyway?"

Padre paused before responding, looking Zeb directly in the eye.

"No, no. Not completely. I've seen too many people control, try to *own* others, to dismiss the means needed to halt bad actors in their tracks. So, yeah, practically speaking there has to be a way to stop, to protect in those cases. I'm just not so sure how you get to the rightness of cause anymore. And I don't trust anyone, least of all myself, to get it right every time."

It signaled a rare openness for Padre. Dalton understood it as such and received the honesty with respect, as if something precious had been unloaded in his presence.

"Well, old timer, you and me both on that one."

The familiar screech and pull of touchdown brought them from deep places to the present moment. Not too many minutes later they stood side by side on the slim tarmac of a little-used runway and facilities. It was a wonder the pilot stopped them in time, given the bulk and mass of the jet and limited run of pavement. Two hangers, each enough space to support planes the size of the one just exited, sat in the near distance. A temporary barracks and meal tent. A small component of personnel flurried about the buildings as they were ferried by jeep to the nearest one.

"That it?" Dalton asked their driver en route.

"Yes, sir. Well... was. One concrete bunker. Home for a single Atlas rocket carrying her deathly payload to a Soviet location of your choice. Fifty-eight meters of *hello-from-America, you Red Bastards.*"

No one laughed.

"Well, at least that's how we felt about things back in '58," he concluded.

Padre shook his head and refocused to the front of the vehicle. They stopped a few yards outside the smaller office doors, met by a group of three men in Army regulars.

Zeb smiled as he stepped out of the jeep.

"Colonel Meers," he extended his hand, received and shaken with an understanding born of common struggle.

"Lieutenant Dalton. So good to see you again. You're looking well, as long as I dismiss that horrid bruising on your neck."

"Why thank you, Colonel. Nothing a little time and some makeup can't take care of."

Padre gave him the *maybe you'd like to let me in the club, too* look.

"Oh yeah. Padre, meet the indomitable Colonel Meers. He and I spent some quality time together at another training facility before sending me back over the mountains to take on some fifty-thousand Chinese soldiers. And by the way," Zeb looked to Meers. "I never really thanked you properly for that."

"Don't mention it, Lieutenant."

Meers turned and entered the doorway, signaling the two to follow. Once inside the cramped office space, the leader offered them bad coffee — to which Padre said no thanks but Zeb took personal offense — and asked them to be seated. From there he launched into a briefing, much of which the men had previously consumed, in-flight. The summary was rudely broken into by the sounds of a training regimen gone wrong outside the inner door, in the main hangar bay area.

*Taylor. Do you think that rep was anywhere near effective? Because if you do, you can leave right now.*

*No one's perfect? Sorry gentlemen, perfection will be required of us this time around.*

*I am dead serious.*

Dalton turned his head, smirked, and then returned his attention to the colonel.

"Yes, Lieutenant," Meers said, confirming Zeb's recognition of the voice and tone. "Sergeant Sanchez is at work. And doing her usual bang-up job."

# THIRTY

*The long, well-lit hallway passed by in a flurry as Stinson made his way to the lab.*

**The text message** communicated urgency. He and Dr. Bartollo occupied the rank of equals, both key lieutenants in Donneleigh's grand plans. No orders would be issued between them, compelling him to leave his own heavy schedule behind to make his way down to the labs beneath Quantech headquarters and work as partners. Yet, they were colleagues as well. This close to *World One* any number of things may go wrong. An ever widening slit in his soul told him that might not be a bad thing.

"Peter, thank you for coming down. I needed to show you something. Something very important."

While Stinson heard the familiar voice, his eyes fixed on the ten large screens encircling the lab floor. Each one showed parasitic ravages in process. The mutilations were unbelievable. Some shots close-up. Others, group images. Belize. Montenegro. Haiti. He found it difficult to turn away, yet making him sick to his stomach at the same time.

"Anthony?"

"Yes, Peter. Reviewing some of the trial footage. Comparing it to the numbers. Want to make sure I am not missing anything. We're so close. It would be a shame if some unforeseen anomaly ruined the yield."

"Certainly." Stinson broadcast as much confidence as he could, though in the moment weaker than ever.

"Peter, do you know what I see, from a broader perspective?"

Stinson received this as more statement than questioning and let it settle, waiting for Bartollo to continue.

"I think back to the way in which we became invited to this mission. Think of it. We had no intentions of anything like this. The opposite, in fact. An ancient story leads us to the deepest jungle regions of Central America. We literally stumble upon this wonder of nature, perfectly preserved for a time and purpose unknown to anyone before we went in search of cures. Oh, Peter. Think of the ways in which this exact solution was set apart for us. For us! As a man of science, I cannot discount its beauty, its design. Though I am lost to explain in any measurable way the sequence of events bringing us to this place, neither can I dismiss the certainty we are taking steps laid out for us by a force greater than ourselves."

Bartollo got quiet before speaking again.

"Matthew is not the only one to carry within himself the devastations of this present world and its systems. Who do you think was in those tents in every village, desperate to apply medicine, research. Longing to heal, only as progress, real gains become shoved rudely to the side, time and time again, as humanity foiled its own best opportunities at something different, something better."

Another pause.

"Which is why I am concerned, my friend. And why we needed to talk."

"Certainly, Anthony."

"I am especially troubled by this," Bartollo stated, pointing to a group of four bodies on the nearest screen to his left. "In placing some aspects of scale over the image, you can see what happens when we lose control of the spacing of victims."

Numbers and hash marks appeared. A few lines from tips of extremities to the torsos of others nearby. It was all quite clinical, though the scene was as humanly repulsive as anything Peter had been forced to view in his life.

"Now," the scientist continued. "Seating in major arenas is fairly normative across the globe. Most attendees will be within the effective target zone for the initial strike via the carriers. Many, likely most, will fall a foot or less of where they are seated. But that is mere extrapolation, my friend. Our real data has a ceiling of five-thousand victims. Beyond that, we own no idea as to what kind of timing and chaos effects we are looking at. At a gross yield of fifty thousand or more, what happens then? True, they are tightly managed initially but what about a longer than tested strike and incubation? If larger groups of people fall farther than the optimal distances away from one another, we may observe a significantly different outcome. Something lesser than the cleansing we are hoping—no, we are *called*—to bring about."

"That seems highly unlikely, Anthony. Doesn't it seem that the larger numbers will only increase effectiveness?"

"Of course, my friend," Bartollo assured him. "That is, unless," he turned to his desk and spoke softly, "... unless they knew what was coming. Imagine an arena filled with people, sent into unmanageable motion. No way to predict their wild, survival instinct movements."

The statement hung in the air as the accusation it was meant to be. Neither man moved. This was a moment of understanding, not of words.

"I attempted to bring these concerns to Matthew," Bartollo said. "Did my best to help him consider the effect of a Judas in the works. He dismisses the idea, both as a matter of principle as well as a seeming inability to believe those closest to him could be capable of such traitorism."

Bartollo turned again, facing Peter fully.

"Anthony!" Stinson got out. "Whatever you are thinking, this is utter foolishness. We have been a team since the beginning. Trusted allies and servants of a great man and a great cause. Please, tell me you are not saying what I think you are. This very morning I made final preparations across the globe for our triumphal event. You must be joking."

The researcher cocked his head sideways, peering deeper into Stinson's face.

"Peter, I am not sure what lingers in your eyes. I am a scientist, not a mind-reader. Though Matthew is unwilling to take action, I must admit I am somewhat uncertain of your further commitments. I have no proof. Only observations which, again, as a scientist I will collect, organize, and interpret as necessary. There can be no other way forward."

"*Doctor* Bartollo," the formality of the title landed as intended. "You are seeing things where nothing exists to be seen. Maybe your own anxiousness is clouding your normally clear judgments?"

Bartollo reached up, placing his open hand slightly over his lips, a gesture of skeptical consideration.

"I doubt that is the case, Peter. Still, I have no evidence, just a feeling."

"How unscientific of you, Anthony."

"Yes, true. But in matters this important, something more may beg consideration than simply factual evidences?"

"Are we finished, Anthony?"

The senior researcher refused to answer that one.

Stinson left and Bartollo returned to his work. Of special focus this day: a status report on cannister readiness from his supervisor at the cave complex. He was pleased. An email and accompanying spreadsheet now populated his inbox. The scientist opened the file and ran his eyes across the figures.

*Yes, good.*

Then he skipped down to some bullet points. One in particular caught his attention. "Final production run underway this afternoon with first shipments already in process."

*Indeed. This is all very good.*

----

**The UPS Hub in Memphis** was always a busy place. Unsurprisingly, that was the singular aim of the international shipping giant. Lots of packages, all the time. At a gross revenue of 58.3 billion dollars annually, they had managed to hone in on the human desire to send things to one another over long distances. They'd gained fame for innovations making real bottom line improvements, including things like the counterintuitive 2004 directive to make more right turns than left in vehicular traffic, bringing an annual fuel savings of thirty-five million. The state of the art facility outside this southern city never stopped. Never.

A ubiquitous brown-clad worker approached the captain, one last check of the cargo and release documentation.

"Well, let's see, cap. Europe again? Get your wings, travel the world, right sir?"

"Yeah, something like that," the pilot voiced matter of factly, looking over the manifest. "So, high-risk medical on the list today? You got that under control back there, son?"

"Absolutely, sir. FDA and CDC regs on this one. Ready to go."

"Fine, wouldn't want anything bad happening, now would we?"

"Indeed. Gotta keep it moving, sir."

"Any idea what we are taking with us?"

"No sir," came the simple reply. "They just tell us how to handle it, not what's in it. Miracle cure for some nasty disease? I like to think we might be a small part of something like that."

"Yep, with you on that. We'll get it there — whatever it is — on time and intact."

Ten minutes later the plane was wheels up, ascending smoothly into the low hung clouds.

---

**At that very moment** Bartollo sensed something. Though a man of science, he was learning to give credence to a more intuitive, non-rational awareness of his world. He could not quantify in any way the feelings washing over him as he stood at his station, yet he felt deeply that something had gone right, some significant step for their greater good. For many years now he had followed Donneleigh's lead. Mostly, he believed in the man while remaining skeptical of the ideas driving him. Maybe this was changing, too.

# THIRTY ONE

*The end of the tunnel was not the end of the tunnel.*

**Emilio Escoban** knew these dark, dank places better than anyone. The forty-three-year-old Belizean had been a part-time tour guide at the Caracol historical site for the last decade. He also served as the trusted caretaker for the Hendricks' research team during the off-dig season, primarily the wetter portion of the calendar year when transportation and heavy equipment ground to a halt. While the road leading to the dig had received a more formal, drivable entry in latter years, the majority of the ongoing plots were a bit more challenging as muds remained deep and wet weeks persisted.

On a routine watch, with particular awareness of the cave systems located below major attractions, Emilio was surveying for weakness in the walls and ceilings when he stumbled onto it. Literally. His toe caught the edge of something not made of earth. Reaching down, he brushed away a layer of dust and found a latch in the process. Now, he stood over a portal to who knew where, and wondering what he should do.

**"Emilio, you were** right to call us."

The reassuring sound of *Mr. Doctor's* voice on the other end was a help.

"Emilio, I have no doubt you are telling me the truth. I just am a bit wordless here. You say you're at the termination of tunnel K8? Okay, yes. I know. Supposedly nothing lay below that level. That's what's surprising. Deep-resonant imaging from two years ago showed nothing but dirt and rock. Nothing to pursue, so we focused elsewhere."

Escoban took another couple of photos with his phone pointed down into the hole and hit send.

"Yes, I see," Dr. Hendricks replied. "Emilio, could I ask you to take a look?"

The flurrying mix of native tongue and Spanish made sure the answer was received as intended.

"No, this is not part of your job. I realize that." The doctor scurried in reply. "Yes, you have a fine family and I would want them to receive you home today as well. How about this then: you just leave things where you found them and we can get to it when we arrive on site again in a few weeks?"

That option worked for everyone.

**After saying goodbye** to his trusted co-laborer, Dr. Martin Hendricks leaned back in his creaky office chair. Constance was present, too, catching the gist of the conversation.

"Mart? What in world is going on?"

"Well, my dearest, I am not quite sure. Smugglers, drugs, local rebels. Could be any one of those options. Neither is good for us and our work, that's for certain."

Martin looked past her a second. Something more remained.

"What is it, Mart? Something else is troubling you."

"Constance, you know me so well, my dear," he breathed out. "Emilio called me earlier today, when he first found the hatch. I got some initial information from him and asked him to take some measurements and photos. Waiting for him, I had this strong feeling

I should call that Dalton fellow as well. I didn't tell you this but his investigation is leading him to push further into the Caracol myths. Deeper into the unsubstantiated, on the theory that the other events are tied somehow to the mists of the past, appropriated now toward some evil ends."

"Oh, my. That sounds pretty far-fetched, dear."

"Yes, true. The shocking thing is I agree with him. The patterns and timing are too convenient. Too closely related. And now this."

"Okay, so what did he say. What is he going to do about it?"

"I have no idea."

"He seemed a nice man, Martin. Why wouldn't he confide in you after all you've done to help him?"

"No," he replied. "That's not it; not at all. I called the secured number he gave me after our last conversation."

"And?" she led on.

"And, a pleasant mechanical voice told me the number was no longer in use."

# THIRTY TWO

*Seventy-five yards. Clean shot. No obstructions.*

**"Engage targets."**

The simple command carried a weight disproportionate to its form, a reverberation that would have been shocking were it not for the combined experience of the twelve men and women currently on rotation at the remote Nebraska location. Each sniper fired five times. Each rifled projectile met its intended target.

Terminal dispatch. With authority.

A loud, insistent buzzing filled the space and the lights came back on. The dozen rose from prone positions and removed visual gear and comms. Relief and accomplishment is a fine pairing. These committed men and women savored the moment, even as they prepared themselves for the real thing, always more difficult, always more uncontrollable factors. Still, for now, this was a fine run.

The massive hangar had been set up to resemble the seating and infrastructure of an indoor arena, in this case *Madison Square Garden*. The well-known fixture in midtown Manhattan had been in operation for over fifty years now. Recognized world over for hosting the upper echelons of sporting and entertainment, the hand-lettered signage in this pole-building mirrored her layout and passageways inelegantly but effectively.

"Nice work, Freeman."

"Ma'am," was all the young woman could express, in awe of someone who had largely been the reason she pursued this career path in the first place.

Sanchez caught it and worked quickly to diffuse the moment, to fix the focus back where it belonged.

"Freeman, tell me about your shots."

"Yes, ma'am. Positioned across the floor and above the Madison Suites. Though we are presuming no one will be allowed to attend in the private spaces, we have to be able to penetrate the angles presented, just in case. This rotation I had a bogey placed outside the glass and above the interior seating area. Not a problem."

"If assailants break the glass in order to reach targets in the suites?"

"Well, trickier but still doable, ma'am. Timing is key there. And acquisition. But I know the possibles. I can make it happen."

Sanchez knew it was true. First encountering Freeman at the Army's sniper prelim school, she forecast she would be good. Maybe even better than herself, one day. Still, much ground existed between talented but green and matured enough to make tough calls in the field. This factor alone had been why Freeman had been turned down for accompanying Dalton's return trek through the mountains and into Seattle a few years back. Devastated she would have to sit that one out, nonetheless she kept at it. Waiting. Her patience and diligence were now paying off.

"Surfaces?" Sanchez probed.

"A little dicey, sergeant. Everything's hard in the place."

"Except?"

"Except the target," she finished, intoning a long-held sniper's mantra.

"Freeman. Excellent work. As always."

Dismissed to further debrief and then a meal, the young woman took the comment to heart.

**Thirty minutes later,** Dalton and Padre grabbed a seat in the hangar's office area.

"Colonel Meers, from what I've seen so far," Zeb started. "We're doing all we can to cover on-site contingencies. Training is coming along here and I assume everywhere else needed. Mind-boggling really, but impressive at the same time."

A new voice startled him.

"I'll take that as a compliment."

*Crap. She did it again.*

Dalton's head snapped around in his cheap chair. As did Padre's. That was even more telling. Probably settled on her as payback for him catching her approach in the jungle.

"I *shut* that door," Dalton said.

"Yeah, you did," Sanchez replied with a smile. She sauntered over to the empty couch in the corner and sat down with a satisfied air. Padre held a look of respect and cocked his head toward Dalton.

"Don't worry, Padre. You get used to it. Some kind of weird game for her."

"Maybe," the older man said. "Also one helluva advantage for our side, no matter how you draw it up."

Jessica nodded in thankfulness and gave Zeb a lecturing glance at the same time. *Never heard that from you* was the basic interpretation.

"Hey, here's another question," Zeb said, ignoring the scold. "Smith? Last time I saw you guys he was with you all. Alive."

He moved his eyes to Sanchez.

"Hmmm?"

"Oh, trust me, Dalton. I for sure wanted to punch his ticket. The real story is much less exciting."

"Okay, team," Meers offered. "We need to focus here. We are only slightly plus forty-eight hours out and it's time to get serious. Yes, Dalton, Mr. Smith was recalled to Langley for some debriefing the spook factory thought better handled there. No drama. You may or may not see him again on this op. We don't control the intel side of the house." The colonel had been around enough soldiers and operators in his career to know banter was often teamsmanship in disguise. Still, characters like these need redirection at times. He continued.

"Sanchez, all indications are your specs here and abroad are doing a fine job of op prep. The rotations are showing a greater grasp of the challenges at every turn. Initial gaps in overall skills between legit snipers and the new-hires are becoming less noticeable by the hour. Your focal points have been a tremendous kick start."

"Wait a second," Dalton said. "Colonel? What, we pulling rookie cops and FBI desk jockeys for this duty?"

"Hardly," Meers said. "Do the numbers, Dalton. That's you're thing, right?"

To which Zeb did exactly that. He held some long-reserved data from Defense and Justice Departments, easily recalled in a moment such as this.

"Okay," he agreed after a second or two. "So, field agents, best in class across the agencies and services. Got it. Extrapolated internationally, the numbers check out as well. An all-star squad for target rich environments. Some of them will perform their work where elite athletes regularly show off their stuff. Nice. Kind of poetic."

"Like you'd know anything beyond a salty limerick or two?" came from the couch.

Dalton let that one go.

"People," Meers reminded them. "We are on the clock, not after hours at some local pool hall where you can shoot the bull. Let's bring it back in, shall we?"

Dalton and Sanchez relented. Padre sat there thinking this was why he liked the quiet of the jungle so much. The conversation came to a halt at the single beep of Meers' laptop and ensuing white noise, almost like an old school modem establishing connection. The truth was not too far removed. A video window popped up and Meers turned the screen so all could see the vision of Mort as he chewed at a fingernail nib on his right thumb.

"Oh, come on, Mort," Dalton groaned.

"Crap," the tech let out. "Didn't realize we had lock. Gotta get someone to program a better alert."

Another potential distraction. Meers was not about to let things go this far off the rails.

"Mortensen."

"Sir," the apt reply.

"The principals are here. What do you have for us today?"

"Colonel, this is just in on our end but seems very good, sir. Very good. So, we've been running our systems non-stop on both scenarios for you. We've got refined calculations now on the active shooter scenes, with a much better level of detail for each team. Sending those out in the hour to add to the regimen already in place."

He paused.

"Mort," Meers plied. "Why is it you appear anxious to tell me something else? Like a fifteen-year-old on his first date, about equally ready to leap for joy and vomit at the same time?"

Dalton snickered. That was pretty good, actually.

Mort's puppy dog face wasn't enough to keep them all from pressing in.

"Correct, sir, I do have something additional" he replied, mildly chastened this time. "Sanchez?"

She turned a bit more toward the laptop in response.

"This familiar?" the PO3 asked.

Jessica sat up straighter this time. "Those are my shots."

"Yes, they are. As of the last check in from your little cave adventure we had about thirty images uploaded from your phone via secure text dump."

"The auto-loader."

"You got it. We've been passing them through both electronic and human eval. Funny, machines missed this one."

"What? Missed what?"

"Picked up by some guy in a backroom office at NSA. Here, let me zoom in for you."

A wide view of the larger cave space. Jessica had seen this same view from her perch. Zoom down to ten feet, focusing on the automation equipment itself. Closer in still, to a few inches surrounding one of the support legs of the machinery. Dirt and a small scrap of paper—crumpled and torn, but at the right angle. A work order with just enough text left on it. Everyone in the small hangar office had it settle on them at the same time.

Quantech...

**"Seems sloppy to me,"** Sanchez offered after the line elapsed to their partner at the Vault.

"On first blush," Meers replied. "But Mort's explanation holds up reasonably well when considered."

"True," Dalton chimed in. "Relative light is a key component of electronic image filtering. The paper didn't register enough to flag the computer protocol for a further look. We should be glad the NSA geek is one curious dude."

"So, we go with it?" Sanchez asked.

Meers nodded. "Our clearest piece of intel yet, as best we can tell. If there's a chance Quantech, and then likely their CEO, is involved, we need to run this down, and fast."

"Agreed," Dalton said. "Their headquarters. North of San Jose, right? Basic Silicon Valley set up with free smoothies and a game room for every department?"

"Something like that," Meers responded, clearly pulled from the conversation to something on his laptop screen.

"What? Something wrong, colonel?"

"Well, Dalton. Not sure," he said. "Only one way to find out, though." He turned the laptop so Zeb could see the just-appeared messaging window.

*Private, secured comm waiting.*

*Eyes only: Z. Dalton.*

# THIRTY THREE

*Everyone else left the room. Protocol. Had they known the source and matter at hand, it also would have been a sign of basic human decency.*

**Zeb sat at the bare metal desk,** awaiting confirmation of the secured connection.

*Dalton, Zebulon Mordecai.*

Authentication in process...

**Dalton gasped** as the screen filled with the image from a remote location. A simple room. Light pink paint on the walls and a vertical wainscoting. The camera angle sat slightly off axis, most likely a laptop or tablet placed on the bedside table. A few vases. About half the flowers needing to be tossed. There, in the left middle of the screen, lay *Claire Dalton,* clearly failing and far worse than he had last seen her only a few weeks ago.

"Mom?" The single word, sticking midway in his throat.

She breathed unevenly, laboring with each rise and fall of her chest. The oxygen feed to her nose made a sucking sound, obscuring attempts at speaking. She so wanted to exchange words with her son, the urgency of life's end pushing her through the discomfort.

"Zeb," she smiled, her eyes the only thing lighting up her countenance.

"I'm here, Mom."

It was all he could get out before tears fell freely. Dalton knew immediately this was the last time he would speak with his mother this side of the grave. Given his current state of understanding about any kind of life beyond this one, it may well be the last time forever, he thought. One thing became clear, sitting in this small, temporary shack of a training center: someone had been alerted of his mom's condition and owned enough clout to put this transmission through, protocols be damned. Someone caring about him and his situation intimately.

*Stevens.*

Zeb understood and was thankful. The crusty, old general was both the hardest man he had ever met and the most generous. Chiding from the guy only meant he cared about you, saw some untapped potential needing a stern lecture or a swift kick in the ass — whichever was appropriate to the moment. He'd let you spin out into the repercussions of your own choices, all the while rooting you on to make better ones. He never gave up on those he believed in. Never. Dalton so wished he were here.

"Zeb," she tried again. "My son... so proud... "

The coughing fit overtook her voice. Though cancer spread far and wide throughout her body, the weakness in her vocal chords was more byproduct of lack of sleep and intubation when she had begun struggling between breaths. The tube was out now but that served as more harbinger than blessing.

"Don't... " his own chest heaving. "It's okay, Mom. Really. I know. Believe me, I know."

Peace washed across her face. Still, there was something. Something else needing to be done. Claire waved her hand off-screen. Another arm reached across Dalton's view. She took a dry-erase board in her frail hands and began to write. The act appeared almost as much struggle as talking. Finished, she nodded to whoever handed her the board, likely a nurse. The extra arm entered the camera frame again and turned the surface toward the lens.

"No," Zeb said, not so much in defiance but weakness.

Claire would have none of it. Even in this state, she was the mom here. Garnering what strength remained she poked a finger at the board again. And again. And again.

"You can't ask that. It's just not possible."

She pointed again and pled her case with her eyes.

Dalton's head sank to his chest, his heart breaking. He had nothing left. His rock, his entire world was exiting this life. Their family crumbled. She remained his center. When his young faith and worldview became one more casualty of someone else's greed and self-centeredness, she stood immovable. Coming home from his first tour in Afghanistan, freshly baptized in the horrors of combat and the seemingly endless bloodthirst he encountered on both sides, she welcomed him back home—safe. And, eight years and multiple tours later, when he walked in a broken shell of a man, her presence held promise that healing, eventually, might come.

Claire pointed to the scribbles one more time.

With no idea how he would follow through, Dalton acquiesced.

She closed her eyes. The linens covering her settled for longer and longer periods of time upon her chest. Soon, the fabric lay motionless.

Dalton sobbed; giant heaves lying dormant in every man surprising even the closest of friends and family upon surfacing. After a few moments he peered up again, one last glance. She did look peaceful. The frailty of her body, the skin and bones, proclaimed more victory than defeat.

The words remained emblazoned, the board now set against a vase on the side table:

*Your father.*


**The comm link ended,** abruptly and without warning.

"Zeb?"

Jessica could be incredibly empathetic at times. She merely kept it under wraps until someone earned that kind of closeness. Not in a controlling manner. She believed relationships were worth something, that people were important. So, no lip service. No fake feelings, only loyalty and commitment. Everyone, she figured, had a limited amount of care they could dish out. Better to make it count.

"Zeb. I am so sorry. Your mom... she was an incredible woman."

Dalton nodded in thanks, knowing she meant it. The one or two times he'd seen them in the same room it struck him they were of a similar mold. No wonder a quick cordiality formed between them. He gathered himself as best he could, forcing back enough emotion to talk, albeit minimally.

"We... " He cleared his throat again. "Umm, we can't take time to..."

"Zeb. Of course we can. It's your family we're talking about here."

"No, we *can't.*"

She knew he was right.

"Look," he continued. "I'll be okay."

At this point, he was saying what he needed to say, not so sure of how to move forward but knowing he should.

"Zeb," she changed tack, wagering that action might be a helpful first step in mourning. "We both know your mom was amazing. As good as they come. Well, there are some not so great ones out there, too. Right now, we're about two days from finding out just how bad. We've finally got a lead. A solid lead. So, what do you say we go find out if the bad guys live in Cali. If they do, we'll blow their plans up in honor of people like her."

Dalton appreciated the call to action. His mom always stood for what was right, even in the harshest of circumstances.

*Okay. When this is over, we'll remember. We'll celebrate you.*

Somehow, he knew she agreed with the plan.


**Meers and Padre walked in,** care and sorrow etched across both their faces. Sanchez looked up, searching Meers for official approval of what she had already promised.

"I guess it makes about as much sense as anything else. The training regimens are almost complete, so the teams are mostly on local control at this point. We will need a replacement on your assigned site, though. What do you think? Is Freeman ready?"

"Exactly my thinking, colonel. I believe she is good to go."

"So then," Zeb said. "The three of us. Let's get our heads together on this thing and... "

"No," Padre said quietly. "I gave you an extra two days, Dalton. Been fun and all but it's time for me to go." The way he said it made arguing pointless.

Zeb and Sanchez looked over to Meers.

"I am sorry to hear that, Padre. I really am. Your service has again been appreciated and valued by a grateful nation and especially its commander in chief. But yes, we have no means of detaining you any longer. Godspeed, Padre."

Just like that, the man walked away and out the door, onto the tarmac, and out of view.

"He gonna hike back to Guatemala?" Zeb asked.

"Nah," Meers replied. "Transport plane waiting. We had this talk an hour ago."

Dalton thought out loud regarding their brief but important intersection. "That is one mysterious cat."

"Oh, if you only knew, Dalton. American foreign policy in the 80s. Central American revolutionaries. An armed wing of the Catholic Church."

"*What?*" Dalton questioned.

"Yeah, that one will take more than a few beers and some lingering sunsets to unravel. Would make one incredible book, though. Maybe you'll get the chance someday to ask him yourself."

# THIRTY FOUR

Thursday PM, 48 hours prior to *World One*

*Evening light faded, softening on the low hills and open lands of the Virginia countryside.*

**General Stevens enjoyed the quiet.** Still, he stood operationally readied for the clandestine meet. The message came across urgently, passed through trusted channels at NSA. He wasn't about to pass up the opportunity. Two hours now into the drive, the Triton V8 engine running his decade-old Ford Super Duty 350 performed its job quite nicely. Though the crew cab extra seating mostly ferried grandkids these days, it remained one very nice, very large truck. On this misty November night, the back bench held a car seat, occupied most weekends by the youngest of his daughter's kids. It sat right next to the loaded M4. Just in case things got dicey.

Over the Potomac and west on I-66 for much of the trek, he recently had turned south toward Chester Gap, not far from the northern edge of Shenandoah National Park. Now heading down a single lane, unpaved road, he forced himself to focus, to be attentive to his surroundings. While likely a legitimate opportunity, there were surely those who would like to remove him forcefully from his new position of influence in the Spurrier Administration. A lifetime of military service poses certain threats. Politics is a whole other level of risk. More shadowy and uncertain. Lesser honor, and therefore less predictable.

Gravel popped beneath the truck's wheels and Stevens came to a stop, thirty-five yards from the old farmhouse. It had been a while since she'd hosted a family. Yet, the mid-nineteenth century workmanship held its own against the ravages of weather and time. Sure, paint peeled and roofing lay at odd angles, but that was all superficial. Everything that mattered stood in place and on duty. Stevens sat in the cab for a full five minutes before approaching. Patience. Wait and watch. Subtly, appearing so briefly as to be imagined, the smallest blue wash of light emanated from the upper floor west window.

The general exited his vehicle and stepped across the leaf-strewn circular drive. Three paces from the front door he patted his left side holster, pulled the Beretta M9 out and held it alongside his right waistline. His right hand probed the doorway, opening the heavier wooden door and gaining the first few feet of vision into the space. The swift, practiced move from side to full ready position accompanied the rest of the door opening as he stepped into the hall. Both hands up, head cocked and left eye closed. Stevens swept the room: left, right, and back to center again. Fifteen steps up to the landing, back against the wall and body to the opened space above. He arced across the narrow upstairs hallway as well. Three more quick moves and he paused outside the main bedroom, as flat against the sidewall as possible. His contact at NSA had been clear. An initial visual signal and then upstairs to wait, exactly where he was now. A second signal would confirm all was well.

Stevens breathed as lightly as he could, trying to be patient.

Nothing.

*Ten seconds more. That's all. If this op is busted I am not hanging around to find out why.*

Finally, Stevens pushed on the base of the door with his right boot, forcing it back on its hinges. This one creaked, so might as well throw it completely open. He did, edging inside left of the frame, putting himself offline of anyone in the room. Sliding through, he swept the space again, this time more vigorously. He didn't catch it until coming back to center, his eyes landing at the foot of the bed. An arm, laid across the covers and toward the headboard, cell phone dangling in a slackened grip. Stevens rushed backside of the bed to see the thirty-something male on his face, a growing pool of blood beneath his drooping head. The rag doll impression left by the angle and disposition of the body broadcast little, if any, time remaining for this man. Moving in and checking for a pulse, Stevens recoiled when the almost-corpse let out a sudden breath.

"Don't try to move. I'll get help to you. Just don't move, at all."

"No," the man gasped, his voice a mixture of blood and air. "You... " he coughed again, his voice so soft the general cupped his ears to get any sense of what he was saying.

"Not now," Stevens ordered. "Stay still."

In a final, courageous act, the man somehow pulled his arm off the bed and flopped over, against the side table.

"Look at me. Listen."

The man was trading his only hope of survival for a chance to finish what he came here to do. Stevens leaned in.

"Quantech. Labs under Quantech. Donneleigh."

The general watched the man's eyes glaze over. His chest stopped moving. Stevens turned away from the body and saw the bullet hole in the window.

*How did I not hear that? Must've been suppressed.*

This much was true. But as Stevens looked harder he noted the glass had already been compromised; spider veins at the edges of the pane, too far from the point of impact to be a result of the shot. Or this man was much, much braver than he appeared, even now. Fatally hit and still got off one signal? That scenario would have required at least five to seven minutes of heavy bleeding and excruciating pain, as it would have preceded Steven's entrance to the home. It also meant the general himself had walked in cross hairs from vehicle to front door.

Stevens looked at the body. A wave of respect came over him.

*Thank you, whoever you are.*

**Reston clambered down** from his perch and kitted up. Thirty seconds more and he was on his way, into the now-darkened Shenandoah National Park, heading to his car on the other side of the forest. The stand of sturdy oaks at the extent of the property provided an immediate operational edge. He had no problem with close-quarter work. It was just that distance often supplies advantage, in terms of dispatch as well as ex-fil. The dirt path through the woods seemed fairly well maintained. Which meant he couldn't use it. Chances were he would run across a biker or jogger, out for a last bit of mind-clearing exercise before bed. The man couldn't chance an encounter; no desire to leave another body. No morality issue here. Simply trying to make an efficient footprint. He had come for one reason, at least on the scorecard that mattered. Two setups. Two failures. This had never happened before. Reston ran a brief replay in his head again, wanting to be certain before he reported back, especially given that his customers would not be pleased.

Target sighted from his tree limb hide.

Truck enters circular drive as target in upper room moves to foot of bed, achieving perfect angle of acquisition.

Trigger pulled. Hit. Down. Body falls out of range, beside bed.

Awaiting next target to enter room.

Blue wash from cell phone tells him target one has survived, at least enough to signal.

Watching intently for two shots through window, finish the job.

Target two moves out of range and over behind bed.

No shot.

Reston caught the dying man's words over the super sensitive field mic. Time to go. The Quantech connection had been established and he needed to report in as soon as feasible. Dangling in a tree would not be his best operational footing when a scared, or angry, man came back out of that house. The natural camo of springtime was a very different thing than open limbs dropping their last foliage. Seven months from now he would have taken another shot. Mid-November only left him exposed, unable to move.

The man now paused atop a small knoll over the parking lot. Having tread through the underbrush, he wanted to make a similarly unseen entrance here. The only challenge awaiting him was a high school couple, finding the darkened place to be perfect for this portion of their evening. Thankfully, they were engaged enough with the few feet around them that his emergence didn't register. Reston walked briskly to the rental car and threw his kit in the backseat. Though a man with a long-ish duffel bag stepping out of the woods didn't catch their attention, his turning over the engine did. The couple's heads lurched up from both surprise. The young man performed an evade and exit maneuver with his dad's Bimmer that would have impressed the best of the Secret Service Presidential Detail. The teens may have noticed the general look of Reston's car. It was highly unlikely they took down the tags. They weren't looking for data to recall later. They just didn't want to get caught.

Alone now in the lightly lit space, Reston began an initial contact via secure text.

*Target one down, fatal.*
*Minimal but crucial intel shared.*
*Quantech and Donneleigh implicated but no details.*
*Expect pressure soon.*

Finished, he set the phone aside and put his hand on the wheel. Time to reassess. And then clean up this mess for good.

# THIRTY FIVE

Friday early AM, 36 hours prior to *World One*

*"Zeb, I am so sorry."*

**"Madam President,** I appreciate that very much. More than you know. But I would rather not talk about it. At least not until this is all over."

Dalton felt his emotions on the rise, reaching a state where he may not think and act as clear as he should. Though completely natural, these were the kind of factors throwing operations into the crap pile faster than you could imagine.

Spurrier understood.

"General," Zeb turned his attention to Stevens. "Words cannot express my appreciation for you setting up the video feed when you did. She did not have much time and I would have always hated myself for not being there at the end. I assume you broke all sorts of regs but... "

"No idea what you're talking about, LT," Stevens bluffed.

Deniability. Simply a part of life now for the soldier turned political appointee.

"Well, be that as it may," Dalton replied. "We're about six hours out from Quantech now. Working on the intel from your meet. Some kind of not so obvious space beneath the regularly publicized floors is where we'll need to take a look around."

"So cliche," Sanchez added.

"True," Zeb said. "We do seem to keep running into bad people and surprising things underground."

"Just once," she continued. "Just once I'd like an evil genius to do his dirty work on a first-floor walkup. Is this too much to ask? Maybe a nice three-bedroom ranch-style? I mean really. Save us all a whole lot of skulking around, right?"

No one on the call flinched. Dark humor has a long and varied history in the face of dire circumstances.

"Mort, you got anything new for us?" Dalton redirected.

"Nope, not currently. We reran all the images from Sanchez' time in the cave complex. That shot was the only one bearing anything actionable. And it would remain a slim lead had we not gotten those last words from Stevens' meet last night."

"We got lucky," the general observed. "Pretty sure the way our contact was dispatched confirms we are on the right track. And also why the two of you need to exercise extreme caution in your next steps. We own no element of surprise. Someone on the inside chose to leak the connection to Quantech. Someone else tried to erase the lead and is now assumedly looking for a follow-up."

"That would be us," Zeb said solemnly.

"Indeed, that would be the two of you, lieutenant," Spurrier interjected. "So, let's be clear. We are only a day out now. If a link is to be found you need to find it quickly. Any hope of shutting down this event from the inside, before it happens: we need to apply every resource possible toward that end. If you fail or are too late, our teams are already in transit to each location. I would much rather we contain this thing now. I am sure you would as well. It seems unnecessary to press the precarious nature of this event any further, am I correct?"

"Yes, ma'am. We are crystal on the objectives and the challenges," Sanchez summed up.

"Very well, then," the president left it. "Let's take care of business, shall we?"

# THIRTY SIX

*Every seat lay darkened, all lighting and focus forward, to the man possessing the upstage position in Quantech's auditorium.*

**Donneleigh continued the mid-morning session,** with eight hundred live and likely millions more via streaming broadcast giving him rapt attention. Already through the front-end vision "imagine with me for a moment" pitch, he now dwelt in the lands of detailed specifications. The people watching stayed with him. Every step. This was the world they lived in. Technological possibilities that fifty years prior would have been solely reserved for things like sending humans into space and back again were now dwarfed by the enhancements he described. In the end, it was merely a wristband, even though the power harnessed in this sleek band stood as truly incredible. Which made it even more noteworthy they were impressed but not floored with this particular update. They'd come to expect so much. This time around provided some nice feature gains. Enough to keep bloggers and tech writers at their keys for a few hours this afternoon, but not much more than that. Matthew was never in danger of losing a crowd. No matter how mediocre the topic or rollout. He knew how to capture them. Had understood early on that what he did was never about capacitors or silicon. There lurked a hunger for something out there. As much as a sophisticated world would deny it, they longed for a taste of things beyond the pale of their modernistic existence. These kinds of technologies were nothing if not a way through that curtain and into something unexplainable. For sure, there were people who understood the science of what they held in their hands, stuffed into their Eddie Bauer shoulder bags, and wore on their wrists. A slim, almost non-existent minority. The rest of them received the gifts as something outside their powers. Something transcendent. Maybe even sacred.

**A fader switch from the broadcast booth** split the feed in two directions. While scores online continued to view the previously taped tech session, the live audience and another 12,000 or so across the globe moved to a quite different kind of engagement with the billionaire leader.

All channels clear. Proceed.

Donneleigh received the green light from the producer. With a visible shift in body language, he took on a more urgent, yet still calmed tone.

"Thank you," he began humbly and honestly. "I have remarks prepared but now that we are all here, they seem somehow insufficient."

He stopped himself from tearing up. The flush of blood to his face came through regardless. The crowd responded in kind, feelings of euphoric purposefulness flooding them as well.

"So," he took a deep breath. "I don't need to say much, right? I mean, we all lie on the cusp of one of the great adjustments of our race. All that is required now is for us to follow through. We've been handed the moment, and the means. Years, maybe decades or centuries from now, as much clarity will rise in the broader population as you presently carry in your hearts and minds. If the history of mankind has taught us anything, it is that major shifts are always a shock to the system, a glorious upsetting that allows for a stronger, more robust emergence."

"And you," he couldn't stop the tears this time, words caught in the back of his throat. "You are of a mind that counts your place among others as one of the whole. That the sacrifices of a single life could and should be measured on the scale of our ongoing communion and goodness."

A full twenty seconds of silence. Aside from minor shufflings in place, even their collective breathing patterns forged a unison.

"So then, my friends. No—my *brothers and sisters*. Your efforts are now outlined in a secured transmission to your devices. There's nothing more to say. Nothing more to be asked."

Donneleigh stepped back from the stage wash lighting and turned, silently. Three steps more and he disappeared backstage. The timing of the dual broadcasts had been perfect. No one would ever know about the conversation between Matthew and his believers. At least, until their work had been finished and discovered after the fact.

---

**No way to know.** They looked like every other business traveler. Settled into economy class seats, lap belts secured, pulling out in-flight magazine to peruse any number of deals on gadgets or reading brief travelogues of their destinations. No signs of nervousness, other than the norm for jetting above the earth at 30,000 feet. More bored than anything else. Most of these clandestine warriors took advantage of the deep meditation service Quantech provided for its employees, learning to reject the natural inclinations of their nervous and respiratory systems. Control, at least outwardly, played across their faces and bodies. Hundreds of them boarded at SFO, an easy BART ride from Quantech headquarters. Many more split off to flights out of San Jose. Across the world, they literally flowed onto trains, planes, and automobiles en route to their ultimate step-off points, local expressions of *World One*. Only a day and a half now. Enough margin to do the work.

None of them doubted. Not one.

Though seemingly hard to comprehend from an outsider view, the numbers were not out of the norm. For a few thousand people to commit themselves and others to death had been seen over and again in the annals of religions, movements, and kingdoms. Jonestown. ISIS. Every generation. Just different names and claims.

With a present human population of somewhere near 7.5 billion, that a number slightly greater than ten thousand of them would follow through on such a vision did not surprise. Not ten percent. Not a single percent. 0.000176% to be exact. Less than inconsequential. Nonexistent, in a purely mathematical sense. Except for the fact that their actions would soon end life for north of thirteen million others. Still, if this expected impact was shocking, the sheer quantity of men and women committed to this cause was not, historically speaking. Previous attempts at culling the race in one way or another employed something more on the order of hundreds of thousands. Warring, in the traditional sense, carries a much higher cost. This time, the aggressors were simply being more efficient. And so, what began with a single zealot on an impermanent, sandy, tropical beach, now lay staged for its ultimate ends.

No one flinched. No one thought anything of it, other than the heady clarity of mind they carried while looking outside the windows of their particular mode of transport. Some eight hours after receiving final word from Donneleigh all 13,174 of them moved into action across the globe, not terribly unlike the everyday crowds headed to family, friends, and business.

---

**Matthew rose from his kneeling position** one last time. This office, once thought of only in terms of his work, became a sanctuary. These last few minutes: as blissful as could be. No warning signs in his soul. Long past that point now. Caution flags removed as the searing of his humanity allowed him no compunction. Convinced. So convinced he had no need of assurance, at least in any metaphysical sense. Yet, he would take one more look out the back windows and into his private garden, not to steady himself but in a moment of great joy. Had there been a real place like this once? A brief instant of perfection for man, one including a seamless interaction with the gods, or God, or whatever higher order existed out there?

Donneleigh thought of the words inscribed on the long-forgotten scripts. Though giving them enough credence to act on his calling, he held no idealism about them being the one true words transferred to humankind. True? Undoubtedly. A singular revelation, to be received as fundamentally superior to all others? No, he was not of that mindset. These instructions came to him, through this specific mode of communication. While worthy of his very life, he nonetheless could not bring himself to consider them universal holy writ. The universe was far too complicated to think in this fashion. No, he considered looking through the glass and admiring some of the rarest flora known. A literal garden, likely not. Something akin to a clean start for his species, yes. And now, just like all biological streams, a redirection was required. This particular seed – people – had grown far too unwieldy, a rash of contaminants and imperfections that could no longer survive, much less thrive as intended.

With a solemnity and quietness, he activated a scrubbing sequence for his files at Quantech and shut the laptop down. An hour later, he too boarded a flight, his private jet. Peering outward and seeing the ground grow further and further away, he closed his eyes and breathed satisfyingly. Matthew was not headed to a mountaintop where he would await the carnage's settling and then come down again as conquering king. No, he was headed to his own death as well. Committed to the uprising of the lowly, he had every intention of this taking place outside of his future influence. He had done his part. The rest would be up to others.

Words from the cockpit didn't disturb this peace. They instead fell into line perfectly.

"Mr. Donneleigh... we are en route and on time for our destination outside Belize City. Total flight duration is just under six hours and local weather is about 76 degrees with slightly overcast skies. Should be a very smooth ride from here, no heavy air for us at this point."

*Indeed. As it should be.*

# THIRTY SEVEN

*The trek from plane to car to campus had all been fairly straightforward. Now, they required clearer direction.*

**Mort's triple screen monitor layout** buzzed, a fast-flowing stream of digits. Top to bottom, cascading like a waterfall disgorging springtime snowmelt, the data was unrecognizable. For most people. Mortensen had been doing this a long time. Arguably top-tier in this specialization, he knew what to look for.

"There you go. There you go, now."

The PO3 paused the screen and clicked on the comm connection to the team on the ground.

"Yeah, Mort. Was waiting for your call."

The snippy response came from a large common area, outside Quantech's senior leadership building. Crowds of workers passed by in the gentle, warm sunshine as Dalton awaited further intel from the Vault, on the other side of the country. He kept his ear to the phone, not unlike so many others traversing the red-bricked square.

"Well, just another second. Let's not get ahead of ourselves here, okay?" Mort shot back. "So, here's what I've got. Two buildings are your probables. Turn east of your position. Four-story, glass and

steel. Three sets of double doors out front. Got it? Now focus north
and through the narrow walkway. Physical plant. Grey, Basic. Kinda
ugly now that I look at it. Anyways, of the rest of the campus, these
two sites rank in your 85th percentile as likely. Everything else falls
off at the less than 50 mark."

"Alright. I like the numbers, Mort. What kind of breach are we
looking at for either?"

"Totally different on the surface, LT. You got way more front door
problems with the first one but who knows? Most secret labs are not
generously opening their doors these days."

"Got it."

Zeb put the phone away and looked at both again, considering the
approach.

"Decision?" Sanchez asked.

"Decided," he replied. "Always a sucker for modern architecture."

**ID supplied by the pros at Langley** moved them through the first layer
without a hitch. Sanchez smiled, catching the young security guard's
attention. Dalton smirked. He understood exactly what she was
doing. The man's mental imprint of her would be much stronger from
her lingering a second while passing through the line. Never over the
top. Enough to burn her presence into his memory. In the event of an
incident, she wanted Dalton's face and body to be the fuzzier
recollection. The seconds this bought might be the slimmest margin
of escape or survival. Zeb remembered the last time she had to do
this. Building 25 at Microsoft. Chinese soldiers with much larger
weapons. Worked then. It worked again. Always did.

The schematics Mort supplied suggested a likely route and location
for this secretive lab. Topography and sediment layers pointed to the
flat center of the space. Everywhere else the foundation touched
much heavier rock. For some odd reason, a substantial soft spot lay
at the core of this building's placement on the site. Engineers are
practical people. Made sense to use the natural contours of the area
to such an end. And now, standing in the four-story atrium, Zeb saw

even more of what drew him to this conclusion. Like the hub of a wheel with spokes extruded from its center, a main tubular passageway spread, out to adjoining floors. At each level above them, skyways jutted to workspaces taking up the rest of the building. People went into the tube and exited over their heads, gliding along glass pathways to their offices and duties. It was quite beautiful.

*I guess this is what you do with more money than you could spend in a thousand lifetimes.*

Dalton gave Sanchez the agreed upon signal. Both headed for the stairwells, albeit from opposite approach vectors. Once in, the obvious choice led downward. At each lower level, fewer and fewer people milled about. A good thing for the most part. It also made their presence more conspicuous, were someone actually supposed to be there not recognizing them. Three more floors. Only two others passing them on the way and headed up. Zeb arrived first. No more doors. The corridor ended under the stairwell with a lonely "break glass in case of emergency" box mounted to the right of the door.

"Hey."

Dalton caught himself before responding too loudly, sending a strange echo up the imminently reverberant surfaces. She'd done it again. No footsteps whatsoever.

"Starting to think you really enjoy that, Sanchez."

"What can I say, LT? Use it or lose it, right?"

"Ha. Sure. Okay, let's see what's behind door number one, shall we?"

Their transit to this point had been so uneventful and what they sought after so momentous, the whole thing seemed a bit odd. Still, the next step, through this door, may be the one challenged by force. Steeling themselves and taking an over-under posture, Dalton pulled the handle.

The door came open without much effort. A long hallway, reasonably well lit. No security. At least not yet. Three visible windows over quite normal looking entries. They'd be trying all three. One and two opened easily via keycard. Nothing. Thirty seconds each. End of the hall. One more door. Still, undiscovered in such unauthorized spaces. Dalton looked over, both carrying a greater measure of anticipation this time. Might be lucky number three.

Swipe. Open. Step inside.

Only more nothing. Boxes. Dust.

They both had the same thought.

"I know, I know, Sanchez. Physical Plant Building. Let's hope we didn't burn up all our stealth points for nothing."

---

**Bartollo hovered over** his crumpled colleague. Stinson paled by the minute. Death waited, but not patiently, for the man's body to succumb.

"I knew better than to trust you, Peter. My instincts proved right. Matthew is a great leader but he is also a bit foolish. Peter, *Peter*," the scientist lamented. "How could you?"

"How... could I?"

"Come, come now, my dear compatriot. You are weak. Your mind, and now your body, has failed you."

How convenient of the man to neglect the part where he had aimed and fired the bullet now destroying Stinson's insides.

"Not much time left but I fear you may have, shall we say, wounded, our efforts."

All Peter could do was hold his side and try to breathe. The immense pain fired every fiber of his consciousness, like nothing he had ever felt. He coughed up blood onto his pant leg, doubled over on himself, and fell where he had been struck.

"Now. You have caused me undue concern. For that, I should leave you to suffer. But we have been through much together, have we not? I am a man of honor – unlike you."

Bartollo stood up fully, pausing and then pointing the handgun at Stinson again, this time close enough to ensure a headshot.

"Goodbye, Peter. I am sorry you were not... "

The senior researcher twisted in an ungainly fashion, rotating backward and then falling beside Stinson. His eyes fixed upward, a face showing utter surprise on the front side of a head now missing half its shape. Peter recoiled, both from the concussive sound of the event and the aftermath lying next to him.

**Sanchez approached first.** She knew even as she pulled the trigger that her mark was dead on arrival. Not so much from hubris. More a practiced sense of situational confidence. There were times when things simply lined up. She placed her fingertips along Stinson's carotid artery. His eyes glassed.

Dalton kneeled beside the two of them now.

"Anything?"

"Don't think so, LT. If only we'd gotten here a minute earlier."

The sounds, unexpected, were harsh; unintelligible for the most part.

Dalton, as surprised as Sanchez, leaned in close, doing his best to listen and understand. Stinson tried again. No movement except the briefest parting of his lips and then nothing more.

Sanchez searched Zeb's face for confirmation.

"Yeah, that's what I got, too," he said. "Matthew. *Caracol*."

---

**Seventy-five minutes** after Zeb and Sanchez had departed Quantech's campus, Reston reviewed the physical evidence. Bartollo and Stinson's positions and wounds told him all he needed to know. Powder burns identified Bartollo as the initial shooter. Stinson's grime confirmed it. But the scientist's head wound came from thirty or so feet away and over by the entrance to the lab. That, combined with the two incapacitated men outside, filled in the picture. An intruder. Stepping into Bartollo's moment, the second shooter took action. All it would take now was a replay of the security footage.

*Well, well. Zeb Dalton, Army Signal Corps, retired. Thought I'd run into you again along the way. How's your neck?*

Reston watched the last thirty seconds again, this time with emphasis on Dalton's partner. She immediately brought more concern. Confidently physical. Clearly comfortable with what just occurred. A bearing that bode well for fieldwork. One more rewind. There. Both Dalton and this unknown woman leaned in toward Stinson. Stepping back, a sense of direction and purpose grew across their countenances.

They knew where to go next.

Well, good thing, so did he.

# THIRTY EIGHT

*More than seven hours had passed since Bartollo and Stinson last checked in. Though Donneleigh assumed they lay dead, he wasn't worried. Their sacrifice just meant the leader would have to assume control from here.*

**Plan A triggered certain aspects** of *World One* from both locations, Quantech headquarters and Caracol. Silence from the researcher and aide changed the plan, placing double-duty onto Donneleigh's shoulders. That was fine. Everything was set. It just meant he would need to use more automatic sequencing than preferred. A truly worldwide, simultaneous happening required an enormous amount of asset management. Though not occurring in every single time zone around the globe, this was almost the case. Room for variance existed. Not much. Certainly not enough to allow for emergency police or military intervention at any of the almost fifteen-hundred spaces where high net worth individuals would gather in little more than a day now.

Donneleigh set these concerns and the men's deaths aside, turning to the last reports from his now-silent partners.

Only a handful of invitees had challenged the call to *World One*. This pleased him. The fools were now sufficiently less wealthy and the news—that the invites held no empty threats—had spread rapidly. Surely, some were glad to come anyway, appreciative of the opportunity to divest themselves and invest in greater humanity's trials. Most, of course, came under pressure of losing everything they owned. Or nearly everything. Living on a mere ten percent of their resources seemed impossible. Untenable. So, yes, they would come. They would hear the pitch and give in accordance with the need. Walking out with only half their net worth intact parlayed a much better bargain than ninety being snatched with no recourse whatsoever.

Matthew was not naive. Some of the world's best financial investigators and tech malcontents had been employed to break his system, reveal who lay behind this whole thing and bring it crashing down into nothingness. That's why he had spent the better part of a decade prepping the groundwork, perfecting the multiple, disconnected rings of security keeping his plan safe. Everyone likes to think technology is penetrable, given the right tools. They were wrong. Matthew understood this and so gave himself fully to this cause, this moment.

The means of removing excess wealth was already in place. It was time to prepare for redistribution as well. It would do no good if the end of all this only brought down the haughty. By necessity, there would have to also be a mechanism through which these billions found their way into the hands of others—ones appreciating the gifts of an unknown benefactor. It had not been easy, like everything else Matthew planned, but the code now sat readied. Once unleashed, hundreds of millions of immediate electronic transfers would be processed across every continent. Untraceable. Impossible to reverse.

At one time, early on, he imagined the transfer of resources to be enough. That forcing the acts of the wealthy, bringing them low while raising the rest of humanity, would be sufficient. Time changed his mind. Enough of it elapsed in the development of his systems and planning that he discovered a more fundamental festering than merely who had how much. Then, he stumbled upon the answer, an ancient precursor, in the jungles of Central America. A revelation. A moment of complete freeing, bringing him to a solution not yet considered; one aimed at the deeper problem. A spiritual problem. Move the money around? It wouldn't matter. In the end, those lording over their human kin would do it again. Their malevolent presence assured a prevailing sickness. Now, the cure was at hand. The noxious weed would be pulled by the root. All he needed were the gardeners. In time, these faithful workers had been provided as well.

———————————————

**Stevens' face came across** the secured video feed, clear even to the remotest teams engaging tomorrow's op. He had finished going over the comms protocols and rules of engagement and was wrapping their time together. This conference was critical. ROE meant everything in cases like this. Regardless of how it's played in the movies, the vast majority of soldiers want to follow orders. Few, if any, cowboys exist in the real world of field operations. Though the standing joke was what kind of ROI the shooters got from their ROE, their ass sat on the line if things went off the rails. They were willing to take the heat but only when absolutely necessary. Only with team members or innocents safety compromised. They viewed their own lives as negotiable. But others? No, that would not happen.

The general moved the time to clarifying questions. Odd. Almost like a gruesome call-in show. Soldiers, facing one of the most difficult operations of their lives, typed in requests on their tablets and phones. A major at NSA collected and categorized them, forwarding the most common and cogent of the bunch.

*Do we have targeting authority, outside the universal green light from command?*

*Yes,* answered Stevens. Given the intelligence of the last twenty-four hours, this was almost certainly a large-scale kill event. While efforts remained in play to frustrate the source of opposition control, it was too late to call everything off, even supposing full cooperation from various national and local authorities. Such a defensive move would trigger the ninety-ten forced collection of assets and, with it, the financial downfall of much of the Western and Asian economies, with possible reach into developing systems as well. What they knew must stay secreted. The precarious balance they all faced was to take out the source of control or the agents without any of the broader mechanisms kicking in. So yes, if connection with central command faltered, another level of ROE applied. This one, at least in theory, was simple enough to act on without compunction. Confirmed sighting of the cannisters was enough, whether or not operators were left on their own.

*Civilian casualties? Acceptable loss ratios?*

This one proved a little more difficult to answer. But, *yes* as well. If the question begged authority to take out attendees in order to eliminate an enemy agent, they would be expected to do so. No one liked this question. Unintended or civilian casualty is the ever-present bane of an operator's life. But it was always a reality. Those who believed otherwise had never held their finger to the trigger. Or they worked from an ideological netherworld creating such confusion and timidity that one wondered why force would ever be authorized, at any level. Armed conflict can never be as surgical and precise as our better angels desire. To engage, an uneasy acceptance of these grim realities is required. This case would prove no different.

A few more lines of questioning, but none as heavy.

Another forty-five minutes. Time to call it. Stevens took the moment for what it was: sending his people, good people, into harm's way again. He didn't know all of them. Actually, he didn't know a good many of them. But he knew their kind. He knew their character. And he was taken back again by the weight they would carry, both in the next number of hours and for decades to come.

"Ladies and gentlemen. It is an honor to work alongside you. You will receive no further communication until ninety minutes before the opening of *World One*. I realize this will be early for some of you and quite late for others. Get on site. Get in position. We'll talk soon. Godspeed."

**Spurrier stood by,** the entire time. She never really questioned Stevens' fitness for the post. The last hour and a had half sealed the deal.

"General," she opened. "Fine work. I imagine this kind of prep and planning has never been done before and you have once again brought a commensurate measure of leadership and thinking to the moment. When this is all over, I wish I could say we might find a way to officially appreciate your efforts. I doubt we'll be given that latitude. So, let me say it again now: you're the right man. For the right job. Right now."

Stevens understood the nature and depth of these remarks, considering she was facing her own mortality as well.

"Ma'am. The honor is all mine. Let's just make sure the American people, and the world, are given a chance to see your work over the next eight or so years, alright?"

"I'll settle for a few more days first, general. We'll take it from there, okay? Now, I imagine we both have some important things to do in the next few hours. As you are scheduled for some quality time in the cramped spaces of the Vault along with one Petty Officer Third Class Craig Mortensen, I may be getting the better end of the deal." She reached for his hand. "Mike, glad to serve with one of the good guys."

Stevens met her grip. Then he took a step back, hand snapping to the corner of his right brow. A crisp turn on heel and toe, and he exited the room.

# THIRTY NINE

*Wheels down came after sunset.*

**Sanchez and Dalton waved off the pilot** and walked to the edge of the tarmac. Though dark out the single, obviously reinforced SUV made more of an appearance than the duo desired. The sergeant couldn't believe such carelessness. Probably some embassy rental guys. *Can't they figure this stuff out? I mean, who thinks it's a good idea to sit off the runway like this, lights on and engine running.*

Two last steps and they opened the heavy doors simultaneously, Sanchez to the front and Dalton to the back.

"Hey, great to see you two. Getting the band back together?"

Smith.

A collective groan—all that was needed.

Of course, it was Smith.

The agent let them get seated and put the car into drive. Leaving the airstrip behind, he turned onto the highway in a southwesterly direction. The first hour and a half would be the more southerly advance of the trek. Another two hours and change transited them in and through the Mountain Pine Ridge Forest Reserve. The last 16 km would be on Caracol Road, leading to the ancient site, a touch off the Guatemalan/Belizean border.

Dalton and Sanchez had been in enough hot zones to acquire that strangest but necessary of warrior skill sets: the ability to fall asleep when needed and only for a span of time advantageous to the operation. The flight from the Bay area to Belize had been long enough for some shut eye but they were too preoccupied with operational readiness and last-minute intel to close their eyes. Needless to say, neither had been to these ruins before. If Donneleigh was hiding there, running this sick form of event management from somewhere among the stelae, tunnels, and tombs, it might not be that easy to find him. They'd need to take every advantage of the time they had, hitting the ground — literally — running. In this case, the almost four hours between pickup and arrival would be their only opportunity for rest. And, starting right away meant less small talk with Smith.

Win-win.

In all honesty, the guy hadn't been a huge detraction to their work. A decent enough pilot and now chauffeur. Simply not enough help to justify adding another team member. His former presence and now reappearance had more to do with politics than anything else. Summing it all up as hand holding by career diplomats and lifers in the intel community, they hoped that soon enough Spurrier would have her own people in place. Not much time for housecleaning when you get handed a worldwide crisis in your first week in the job.

*Fine,* Sanchez settled in her mind as she drifted off. *Just make sure you know how and when to use that weapon, Smitty.*

**The dream was a new one for Zeb.** A large, stone and gated entrance loomed up and beyond his field of vision. Something kept him from seeing over, like his head weighed down, unable to lift. The simple door in the middle of the wall opened and a buzzing sound signaled he should proceed. Stepping through: a long, empty hallway. The sides of the walls met the floor in more of a curved fashion than a normal ninety-degree angle. It threw his balance off and he found himself having to work hard to stay in the center of the hall. After seemingly far more steps than the distance traveled, he turned to face a room, closed off by bars but more luminous than expected for a place of incarceration. A man sat still, inside, his back turned to Zeb. Dalton looked up. Above the space:

*Walla Walla State Penitentiary, Prisoner 452308*

Zeb turned vigorously away, to the left. He knew that number. Hated that number. It had been on every single unopened letter from his father over the last one and a half decades. From the moment the verdict had been read in that lonely King County courtroom, Dalton swore he would never come here. Ever. Turned to the side, he tried to run. Not two heavy steps forward a desk appeared, filling in details the way dreams do as they unfold. The figure, Zeb assumed to be the guard on duty, looked down. Not so much in boredom or attention to some reading, or more entertaining material. No, this head hung from sadness. Brokenness.

The realization stopped him in his tracks.

Claire.

Dalton's mom glanced up, eyes pleading him to go back, to make an attempt at the cell door.

Zeb didn't know how and instead fell to his knees, exhausted.

**His moan,** or cry, or whatever it was in the real world came out sufficiently loud in the car to both pull him from sleep, as well as give pause to Smith and Sanchez.

Usually, Sanchez would seize the opening, inserting the required amount of sarcasm to keep their relationship on equal footing. Not now. Not in the wake of his recent loss. Snark was like glue for them but limits apply, even to the unhealthy boundaries in which their partnership normally existed. Keeping her thoughts instead to herself, she gave him a look that said, *I'm right here. Not going anywhere.*

It was useless to try and sleep again. They'd made about three-quarters of their run, so not too bad. It was also the least developed part of the route, save for the last few kilometers that had been paved to the ruins, so they'd slept through the bumps for the most part.

For people accustomed to northern climates, the noise of the night is a shock when first encountering jungle regions. It doesn't seem right. At home, sun goes down, everyone shuts up. Here, and the three experienced this again while stepping out of the SUV, nighttime is anything but solemn. Howler monkeys. Oro Pendula birds. Lizards. Lots of other sounds they couldn't identify but surely came attached with stingers, claws, and teeth.

Standing at the edge of the site, it was anyone's guess as to where they should start the search. Dalton often wished their quarry would post a big sign overhead, make it simple, and proceed with the confrontation. It all ended up that way. The intermediate steps seemed so unnecessary.

The road deposited them near the South Acropolis, adjacent the A series of buildings, arranged in a small village style, complete with ancient ballcourt. Dalton recalled the largest formations to be further north, the B grouping, with those designated B19 as the most significant underground finds to date. Heading there made as much sense as anything else. If he were a bad guy, somewhere deep beneath the surface might not be such a bad spot for an evil lair.

"Alright, let's stay closer to the treeline and make our way up to the B group. There's more to search, so we might as well concentrate in that area. It's also a better match for the legends. That's supposedly where the Tikal King's legs were stored."

Smith gave Dalton an incredulous look.

"Hey, we jumped ship from reason a long time ago on this one, buddy. Might as well strap yourself in on the last train to crazy town and enjoy the ride."

"You're the boss."

"Yes. Why, yes, I am."

The trio made their way past structures older than their country. Far older. Equal parts breathtaking and sobering. Such advances, so long ago. And yet, in the end, this didn't last either. *Same old story,* Dalton thought. *Human ingenuity aside, nothing we build seems to last for long.*

"Babel," Sanchez mouthed.

"What?"

"You know, LT, Babel. As in the *tower of...* "

Zeb waved his hand dismissively. He recognized the reference.

**Five minutes later they stalled,** dropped to the ground suddenly by a rustling not previously heard in the bushes. This was no creature, slithering or otherwise. Dalton and Smith held position. Sanchez moved up and behind from where the sound emanated. The two men stayed low but kept eyes forward, peering through waist high grasses. In one slippery move, the sniper emerged and stood, pulling a man up with her, steely sharp blade to his neck.

"No, no, no trouble!"

Sanchez moved to cover his mouth but the stranger got a few more words out.

"No, *Mr. Doctor*. Mr. Doctor send you?"

"Wait," Dalton took a chance. "Mr. Doctor. Doctor Hendricks? Martin Hendricks?"

"Si," the man was terrified.

Sanchez began reading this guy wasn't here to hurt them and let up a little on his neck.

"Sanchez," Dalton said in hushed tones. "Let him talk."

Turning his attention more directly to the man. "Why would Mr. Doctor send us to you, um... " Zeb probed for a name and some greater sense of the situation they'd stumbled upon.

"Emilio," he got out through shaking teeth. "Mr. Doctor told you about the hatch, the underground. You come to see?"

Sanchez let go.

202 WAYNE C STEWART

"*Emilio*," Dalton tred softly, following the unexpected lead. "Yes, *we are* here to see the underground. Mr. Doctor is my good friend also."

The caretaker realized all would be okay. He had seen more men around the B structures in the last few days, all heavily armed. Staying away until hearing the team's approach this evening and watching them for over an hour now, he could tell they were here to help.

"This way, Mr. Doctor's friend. This way."

"Ah, Zeb will do fine, Emilio."

Dalton caught Sanchez' expression as they followed the middle-aged man into the densest portion of the ruins.

"Looks like we got lucky," she said. "Or..." drawing her knife across and out from her neck in a mock killing.

# FORTY

*The darkness of the underground world lay thicker than you would expect. A musty curtain held the air in place as each step probed forward onto uneven ground.*

**Jessica took point.** Zeb knew enough about his partner to yield any speck of pride to her greater awareness and fieldcraft. Dalton was no slouch at this kind of thing but she remained the true professional here. Although no hard data, a good guess was that her lead grew their chances of survival many times over. Emilio followed close behind Zeb, with Smith completing their little formation at the rear. So far, the company man had been the one to stumble and make the most noise. More bureaucrat than agent, apparently. Truth be told, Dalton would have left him back in the driver's seat of the SUV given the choice. Steven's didn't like it. Neither did Spurrier, though finally relenting to the strong call from the political side of the administration for some measure of accountability. Smith would accompany them throughout the op. That was settled at the highest levels.

Forty minutes in. For the most part, their eyes had adjusted. They'd left the areas where work lights aided some time ago. Though not as clear as daylight vision, the human ability to make sense of shapes and shadows and the brain's reckoning of the looser data into meaningful input, worked quite well. Except for the ground. The uneven surface remained their greatest challenge at moving forward stealthily. The team relied on a soft shuffling to keep them headed forward while brushing away loosened material. Small rocks and patches of stubborn clay made every few feet of progress a challenge. It was a noisier approach than any of them wanted but given the circumstances, the best they could manage. Sanchez' normally silent ways announced more presently as well. Not much, but certainly not up to her standards. Another fifteen minutes and they peered down into a whole other state of blackness.

"Emilio," Dalton whispered. "This is not supposed to be here, right?"

A simple nod of the head sufficed. The caretaker was well beyond frightened and wanted no part of the extended expedition.

"You've been a great help, Emilio. Couldn't have gotten here without you. It's time for you to head back out. Time to go home, friend."

He needed no more than that. The man was very ready to leave. Still, grave concern played across his face, the slightest hesitancy.

"Go, Emilio," Sanchez stepped in. "We've got this. Take care of your family, okay?"

The man nodded again, a finality in the gesture this time. Reversing his steps, he headed into the dark and blending to black in seconds.

"We got this?" Zeb turned to Sanchez, more affirmation than questioning.

"Absolutely," she responded. "I mean, what might be so bad down there that the two... uh, the *three* of us can't handle?"

Dalton swiveled. The over-wide whites of Smith's eyes beamed back at him.

"Only one way to find out."

**The wooden slat came up easily.** Meant to be hidden, it was also fashioned to swing open with minimal effort. Heavy enough to work the necessary motion repeatedly without falling apart. Smooth enough to cause minimal noise and concern in dark, empty spaces. A nice piece of engineering and construction. Whoever put it in place intended it to work for some time. This was no temporary solution to a drug runner's immediate needs. This was planned, designed, trusted.

Sanchez sat down, pulling a small mirror from her pocket. Dangling her right arm under the opening's edge, she probed the ceiling and first few yards of the lower corridor. Sweeping it in as clean an arc as possible, she looked for something, anything to give her a sense of what they were stepping into, or who might be waiting. The surface reflected nothing in the immediate area, the few feet left or right of where they would enter. Finishing, she pulled her arm back up and moved to her knees. Wordlessly, the woman indicated her conclusion with a simple shrug of the shoulders.

Dalton and Smith caught it and prepared for the unknown as well.

A single finger, pointing to her chest. Then a tap on her left wrist, as if she wore a watch, and then three more fingers. The men acknowledged the timing signal with equal nods. Then, with no more hesitation, she launched herself over and down into the darkened void. Landing in a cat-crouch, Sanchez flowed to the right and against the cave wall. Dalton followed, a similar result. *Not bad,* she thought, watching his descent and impact. *Not too bad at all.* Besides falling the last inch into the other side wall while standing, the announcement of their presence had been minimal. So far.

Unfortunately, Smith came next. And Smith was just Smith.

Underestimating the distance, he came out of his crouch too soon. Pulled off center of body mass, he tumbled to the left, that hand grasping wildly for something not there. You can't cheat gravity. Barter with it, maybe. But, cheat? No. The muffled grunt played plenty loud. The other two shot their heads around, realizing their pace and approach was blown. This well-honed operational sense became confirmed as the ceiling began moving. Footsteps from the level above, where they had just traveled, shook dirt down upon them. The tunnel was newer construction, hadn't achieved the kind of settling coming only with time. The footsteps continued, an increased and ominous presence. Though the approacher wasn't yet upon them, they held no margin to discuss which way to go. Any weighing of left or right was completely moot. No longer carrying the advantage of stalker, they were now reduced to fleeing, searching for shelter or strategic cover at every turn or twist of the subterranean system.

Sanchez leapt forward, into escape mode There was nothing chaotic in her form, even given the forceful nature of the act. Dalton followed, again knowing she would be the best one to lead. No need to look back. Smith had screwed up. No time for penance.


**Reston raised the slat and flung himself** downward into, for him, completely unknown territory as well. He didn't care. At this point, he was wrapping up loose ends, anything tying him to his last week of work. But there was also a new, although smaller motivating factor, in his languid motions. The man had been employed in the darker arts for a long time. He'd built a reputation that commanded fear and, honestly, a very good price for his services. Until this last few days he had never experienced failure. Not once. Failure in his line of work ended careers and lives prematurely. While he was on the verge of possibly aging out, settling into a different season of life altogether in some out of the way villa, he could not stomach the idea of leaving the game on a loss. Much less two. This operation now had a tinge of vengeance to it. Mostly business. He was, after all, a professional. But some small, inescapable component of this had moved to the personal side of the ledger.

The man proved surprisingly agile, floating down and out of the drop in ready position. He sensed the chase, almost smelling and feeling it out front of him. No need to actually think, only react and move. The passage formed a considerably more constrained path than the level above. Though Reston almost stooped, it didn't keep him from moving forward. Brushing the sidewalls, his strides ate the distance quickly, through a series of turns and breakouts. Again, he let instinct guide and began to hear the faintest of echoes confirm his gut.

Closer now. Left.

**The burial chamber was larger** than others previously discovered at the site. High, finely carved walls met a floor set in stone and jewel. The contrast from the tunnels was shocking, only underscoring the preeminence of whomever lay in rest here. Or whomever had been laid to rest, before grave robbers made their play at some point in the distant past. Washing basins surrounded, like a trough, waist high. The water had stopped flowing sometime ago but their purpose remained clear. It was a holy space, all who approached bound to care and reverence. At the far end of the room, an arched opening awaited, beyond the raised tomb. The crypt's stone cover lay askew, shifted enough to remove whatever had been inside, its massive weight the lone impediment to casting it off fully.

Reston spied the edge of the opening and caught Smith's last step, out of the way and around the corner. With a slim target lined up — the man's left side and no more — the killer brandished his weapon, firing twice in rapid succession. Chances of a meaningful penetration were slim. Still, any hit, even a grazing was a positive. It didn't matter. He merely wanted to get things started, creating chaos into which he might bring the finality of death.

# FORTY ONE

*In what passed for as close to normal life between them as might be afforded, the president looked over her shoulder at her husband, on his back in their bedroom in the residential wing of the White House.*

**He couldn't sleep.** Far from it, his eyes fixed intensely on the ceiling. No words. None were needed. All had been said in the last hour, a brief but wonderful respite from a world gone mad and the constant stress and pull of the presidency. But more than that, an unspoken understanding lingered: this could be the last time he saw her.

Karen Spurrier began to sit up but was immediately drawn back into her husband's embrace. She gave him the required *Babe, I gotta go* body language but they both knew it wasn't honest. With his nose against the nape of her neck, he kissed her again. The peck carried the combined weight of some thirty-odd years of marriage, kids, and careers. No less than eight moves from very different places. One teenage angst season that went farther than many and an almost bankruptcy. Like a wax seal on a proclamation from some medieval kingdom, the briefest impression of his lips left no question as to the fidelity and strength of their bond—an official, unbreakable statement.

She had not initially been impressed. Called out by the TA in their Stanford freshman chem lab for a dangerous frivolity, Karen lost track of him for another year. It was likely she would have moved on without much thought, were it not for the insistence of a sorority sister talking up some guy taking the Chem Eng school by storm. Turned out the mixtures he toyed with in their previous class were more advanced substances than understood or imagined by the vast majority of the school's current Ph.D. candidates. He swung by one beautiful Spring evening, not for her. Her house sister — his planned but unannounced date — wasn't there. Instead, the two ended up talking on the front porch of the elegant old home, and then at a small cafe until the early hours. He was brilliant, that much was sure. Karen required nothing less, so it was good he could keep up. But something more lay beneath the sparkling eyes and genuinely handsome features. A deference for others. Not a stepping back in false modesty. More like he wanted everyone else to be their best, to find out what they could be and become. Karen had things to do in this life, a trajectory that was part upbringing in a famous family and part natural inclinations. Things requiring long hours and difficult decisions. She did not need a relational anchor causing her struggle upstream with every new venture. She also had no desire to carry a token male along for the ride. *Gary Spurrier* was exactly the man for her to partner with. She'd seen it then. Those deeper impressions had never faded, only holding true across these three and some decades.

The president stood from their bedside and glanced down again. Her husband was not one to cry. He wasn't emotionally constipated, just didn't express himself in this particular fashion. Probably a good thing. The weight of such a moment could easily overwhelm. His look said he understood. All part of the same deal. Their relationship was all encompassing. Every aspect a unity, including the ways they served their community and country. To love each other more by sidestepping their roles beyond this bedroom? As foreign a thought as possible. Their connection to one another stayed stronger because they served. Their service flourished in their intimacy and loyalty.

Thirty minutes later her head of detail knocked on the door.

**"Madam President.** Time for us to leave."

She opened the door and stepped out, agents flanking her as usual to the front and rear. Her brisk pace carried her through the older portions of the White House and out to the green spaces separating the mansion from the bustling streets of DC. Marine One awaited, spun up and completing their last round of preflight checks. Once inside and seated, the pilot reached up, engaging flight controls and guiding the large rotorcraft gently off the turf.

"Marine One has lift. *Cabernet* is in motion. Flight time is seventy-three minutes."

The Marine Major had a steeled look, knowing the privilege and responsibility he held, literally, in his hands. With practiced fingertips on the controls, he joined with the other almost eight-hundred men and women tasked to the duties of Marine Helicopter Squadron One, also referred to as the HMX-1 Nighthawks. Flying the "white" version of the UH60 attack chopper, this specialized airwing not only ferried the president but numerous other government and foreign diplomatic officials. And as he began the initial ascent up and out of the White House complex, five identical whitehawks rose as well. Known as the presidential shell game, these decoys would mask Spurrier's eventual touchdown for as long as possible. Such a safety net provided some amount of insurance against bad actors, as well as the general nuisance of an often overzealous media. The classified orders on the major's comm setup listed the fake destinations as well as the real one. Looking down, he caught the location and imagined the flightline in his mind's eye.

39.3549° N, 74.4384° W

Boardwalk Hall — Atlantic City, New Jersey.

---

**Kulturhaus' manager** spied the old clock on the far wall. Despite carrying the latest iPhone in his pocket, he preferred to check the time on this ancient oval with faded hands and an even more faded beer promo. The slow walk of the long, thin hands seemed a better fit. Less pressured and more content to mark time in increments longer than seconds. Passing their turns in a never-varying cycle, unimpressed by the important and urgent.

It was beyond odd to have an empty house at 11pm on a Saturday. In any other scenario, he would be counting the loss of revenue per person against their weekend average. Three staff and a bartender's wages, drink and food stock, lights, and heat weighed against zero Euros being passed to him via cash or card. A deficit no matter how you slice it. In this instance, he sat more than satisfied. Paid in full, as a matter of fact, in advance of the event. Yet another strange aspect of this particular contract.

The hire-in streaming video team performed their last round of gear and signal checks and he walked among the seats, making sure the given specs were followed to the letter. Pulling out a tape measure, the manager did a number of random spot checks. He'd never had a customer so fanatical about the distance between attendees before. More often he had been instructed to accommodate a certain occupancy, whether or not fire codes argued against it. The downloaded directives were far more specific than that.

*Why in the world would you want your guests that close to each other? We have enough room. Plenty to spread out a little more.*

*Oh well,* he relented. The cash told him to ignore the oddities and do what he had been told.

The old beer clock announced another three hours before the "show" went off. Though another of the particulars of this event, it made sense. No one on the shadowy other end had confirmed Kulturhaus as a location for the event everyone was talking about. Still, he surmised as much. Upon receiving the contract and putting two and two together, he looked for info on the internet. Little hard data. An abundance of conspiracy theories. The only thing he was fairly sure of was that this place would fill in a little over three hours with some extremely rich Germans. Likely. And while it was not unusual for the venue to be filled at 2am on a Sunday, it was usually occupied at that point by those far overextended in drink, money, and time. Surely not accustomed to clubbing into the wee hours, this new group would nonetheless take their seats, not so long from now.

The video guys made the last physical connection and engaged the software control. A large, seamless visual wall came to life, brushing aside test patterns and color bars. Now, it was official.

*World One: Sat Feed HN130.67: time to lock: 02:57:16.*

# FORTY TWO

*Chaos.*

**The report of gunfire** echoed mercilessly in the restricted space. Dalton covered his ears, tried to assess the moment through muffled impact resonances while keeping his head down and away from the line of fire. He looked over. Sanchez screamed, grabbing her lower leg. Though the full force of her voice lay muted, her face portrayed the agony just the same.

Dalton caught a better look.

Compound fracture. Bone snapped, piercing the outer derma.

While both had slid downward from the burial chamber into the altar room, she must have hit something hard as their pursuer commenced his deadly intentions. The arched opening seemed inviting from the middle of the outer chamber. Ushered quickly to its edge by the surprise of the attack, they both hung out over the space before giving in to the drop, their only next move. Able to control the first few feet alone, it all became a bit of a tumble, uncontrollable, leaving them vulnerable to whomever was fast approaching.

Grasping now at her distorted shin with her left hand, she kept firing back up the incline until no more bullets remained in her magazine. Mostly an attempt at cover fire, she held no position from which to gain a good angle. The only propitious part of her fall and injury was that she landed on the other side of an ancient stone and mortar table. Her forward motion stopped against a wall, enough behind the table as to give her a moment of reprieve. In an odd moment of prescience, Sanchez noted the platform and its likely purposes, steeling herself with the vow she would not be its next sacrifice.

Zeb's gaze traveled from Jessica and to his weapon, stripped from his hands on the tumble down. He could see it now, sitting silent and only a few feet away. Moving would bring him out in the open, into the direct line of fire. Their pursuer owned the high ground. "Fish in a barrel" didn't begin to capture the untenable scenario properly.

Zeb's mind went into overdrive.

87-13.

*Well, I'd like a little better odds than that but... here goes.*

Sliding forward onto one knee, Zeb grabbed at the dirt floor as if this could get him there faster. Bullets pinged the ground around him and the walls behind. If not for the odd shape of the room, he might think their pursuer was toying with him, making him "dance" like in an old spaghetti western. A series of quick shuffles and he was almost within reach.

Almost.

The last six inches.

There. More exposed than he wanted, still, he clutched the gun, the reassurance of stippled grip in his palm as he moved back to safety. On the return trip, he caught Jessica's face. She'd stopped yelling at her leg and focused her words instead at him. Everything was so loud, yet her message was crystal clear: *get back NOW!*

Without warning, Dalton felt two impacts. First, the force of air and shattered rock behind and to the right of his head. Second, the glancing blow of a bullet, ricocheting and tearing a line of flesh from his skull cap. He fell back listlessly against the ancient stone wall.

**Reston waited thirty seconds** before transitioning down to the scene.

By then the cordite stench from gunfire had settled mid-air, no place to go. The haze, a mix of expulsion gasses and chipped stone, filled the small, formerly holy space. While death came repeatedly here, it had been under quite different circumstances centuries ago — at least for the former Mayan faithful. It was unthinkable. The contracted nature of Reston's acts would have appalled whoever lingered over this altar in the past. No honor. No virtue. Removal of impediments to a desired outcome as well as a minimal mix of vengeance. The taking of life in exchange for a paycheck. But then again, stripped of the veneer of spirituality, wasn't it all the same thing anyway?

This moral haze was equaled by Dalton's literal visual distortions as he sprawled against the cold, stony wall. On the edge of consciousness, the room and sequence of events focused in and out every few seconds. Zeb felt the hard surface against his back, so the spinning of the room must be a mental appropriation, his body doing its best to access available data while working with a sensory web only half functioning. So, it was a bit oddly — with an underwater sensation, hearing muted and his thinking dulled — that he watched Smith come from around the only corner in their small environs, a cutout serving some important purpose but now emptied. Dalton's inner voice cried out for the agent to act, to move. At least a warning shout, but no, his lips would not respond. His mind raced in anger and concern while his body froze, immobile, not even the simple raising of his arms in outstretched gestures of imminent danger.

Reston's shoulders swiveled, already in a rock-solid firing position, to meet Smith's aim head to head, maybe ten feet between them. The men sized up the standoff and the pause became exaggerated in Zeb's distorted mental space. Both men's stares shared a mixture of intensity and anxiousness. This would not last long. The moment Dalton presumed to be the final one before dueling commenced, a shot rang out from behind, somewhere unseen. The blow impacted the killer's high neck and right shoulder area. He lurched forward slightly, registering the energy of the projectile as it spun and burrowed into his flesh. Oddly, Zeb thought he viewed entrance and exit wounds open in slow motion and the man fell left, the natural response of his body to the angle of attack.

Smith's head turned left, toward the sound and origin of the unknown bullet, releasing his eyes from the danger in front of him.

It was only a second.

Reston's muscle memory, imprinted over decades, told his hands what to do even as his body leaned away from the target. He fired twice in quick succession. Each bullet found its place in the soft tissue of Smith's center body mass. One caught his right pectoral region, tearing through ribs and exploding inside his right lung. The second burrowed into the aortic passageway, effectively sealing off the flow of oxygenated blood to the rest of his system. It was a final, fatal blow. But Smith would not perish from bleeding out on this dusty cave floor. He would simply languish as organs shut down and his brain ceased to function. Thankfully, the lung would collapse, speeding the time of his death.

The distant realization of what was happening caused Dalton to scream inside his own head. To no avail, he remained in place, as still as the stone walls and furnishings around him. A shadowed figure approached, came across his left peripheral vision and then beyond where he lay. Two more longish strides and an arm extended toward Reston, now lying on his side and unable to move. A muzzle flash. The contracted man's body moved slightly up and down, autonomic nerve function and nothing more. Two final breaths and he lay still and silent.

Zeb waited for the unknown figure to turn toward him. Looking at Sanchez, he pleaded silently for her safety. Maybe he was praying, he wasn't sure. There was unfinished business here and he was not the one in control. Try as he might, his vision and thinking would clear no more than this. Awaiting his own end, a warming sensation flooded his head, beginning at the outer edges of his face and moving inward.

Soon, all was dark and quiet.

# FORTY THREE

*Dalton's head felt like someone had placed a fifty-pound lead weight on top of him. Soon enough, this general dullness morphed into the realization of jaggedly sharp pain and a sticky wetness coating the back of his skull and down his left shoulder.*

**Vision clearing,** the pieces fell into place. Zeb tried his voice again. This time it worked, albeit a bit strained.

"Donneleigh. Matthew *Donneleigh.*"

"Mr. Dalton. I must say, you have been a little more trouble to dispatch than imagined."

"Yeah, well I'm like that sometimes," Zeb shot back, stretching his neck to check for range of motion. "Kind of my thing, you know, not wanting to die and all."

The tech guru returned to his station, a simple laptop on a clean, orderly surface, without responding. The conversation ended abruptly. A broad silence.

"Sanchez," Dalton demanded. "*Where's* Sanchez?"

Again, no reply.

It was in this act of verbal valor and its accompanying effort to move toward wherever she was that Zeb realized his hands and feet were bound securely. He sat stationary again, just like in the last place he remembered — the altar room, but this time his mind was in full gear, at capacity. Donneleigh had no idea who he was matched up against. Zeb's thoughts raced, multiple concurrent data streams all doing their best work. His head, though aching, cast a wide view throughout the darkened space.

Dirt floor. Walls fashioned of small stones, stacked in ancient masonry patterns. The ceiling stood only about six feet high, giving the room a claustrophobic feel on that dimension. But the square footage spread out for some thirty or more to his right and left. It reminded Zeb of the creepy confines of the attic in his childhood Seattle home. But instead of heirlooms and old cardboard boxes, this place hosted a single metal table and enough light to barely illuminate the edges of the space, a sharp angle rising inward from floor to the low center peak of the room.

To his left, Dalton cast his focus on a small antechamber carved into the stone, like a closet space except without a set of doors. The covering and structure presented as anything but old. Plexiglass. Sharpening his gaze, he shook his pain-filled head to make sure he saw correctly.

"You've got to be kidding me," Zeb half-mumbled.

No response, still, from the only other person in the room.

Sure enough, squinting this time, reality only became more bizarre with each passing second.

"Is that... a leg? I mean, *the* leg?"

Still, no reply, as Donneleigh typed in a few line commands and watched over a screen filled with video feeds from around the world.

"Hey, I'm gonna need a little more than that." Though Dalton had no advantage whatsoever to play, his voice came across more insistently this time,

Donneleigh turned reluctantly, sighing in concert with the squeak of his chair.

"Mr. Dalton, as you can see I am quite busy but, yes, it is the appendage you are thinking of."

Zeb's mind whirred. Recalling the data from the research team interviews and the onsite visit, a picture began to emerge. Finally, the pieces fell into place. Odds and ends forging into a singular whole, a necessary front-runner of the multiple possible storylines.

*Caracol's Cleansing.*

The stelae at Site 8. The fire sending the ancient metropolis into its death spiral wasn't the tragedy, it was an attempt to stop one. The theories were all wrong. A millennia ago a nation state bustling with life and commerce took drastic measures to keep something from spreading beyond their jungle city. Something so horrific that only the ravages of flame could abey it. A thing so aggressive and violent these people chose to kill themselves rather than allow the rest of their known world to suffer. *The Cleansing*, as the stones of testimony named it, was a last act of mass self-sacrifice for a people reputed to take others' lives in acts of devotion.

"I see you are putting it all together now, Mr. Dalton."

"You sick, *son of a...* "

"On the contrary," he inserted before Zeb could finish the epithet. "I am not a man of ill mind. Neither am I an evil person."

"You can't be serious, Donneleigh," Dalton's voice rose. "Why now? Why this drastic?"

Silence settled in again, followed by the realization this intruder would not rest, disallowing him the sanctity of the moment he had planned these last number of years.

"Please. Be quiet, Mr. Dalton. Your vain imaginings of this being some kind of madman's last moments and de riguer monologue is beginning to annoy me."

Zeb could sense his opening. His brilliant mind was not his only weapon. The other? A famed presence as a massive pain in the ass. Dalton could needle his way under most people's skin quite nicely, creating just enough tension to garner a reaction. It might be all he had but he had to keep pushing, somehow dividing Donneleigh's attention, waiting for the opportunity to act.

"You've got to admit, this is pretty crazy, right? I mean, I'm not really sure you've thought this thing through." Zeb waited a beat, making sure he had the man's ear before plunging deeply into his psyche.

"The way I see it," he concluded challengingly. "It's a severely flawed plan."

---

Washington, D.C.

**Mort had eyes-on** as the shooters made their way into position.

With nearly two thousand concurrent sites, it was impossible to observe their progress in realtime. Each operator bore a headcam and sent live video feeds to their national and regional supervisory networks. But for one person to keep track of all those subnets would be vain effort. Instead, a world map spread across the triple-screen setup in front of Mort with a simple orange, green, or red dot declaring the ready state of the teams on the ground. Orange was the ready state. Green: confirmed clearing of the threat.

Red. The color they all feared.

The assaults had to be scheduled down to the second. An operator revealing him or herself too soon would trigger the still unknown central command of this sick kill event. Believers would be sent into motion, releasing their tubes of death upon the unsuspecting crowds before the operators could stop them. It was a dance in which timing and coordination amounted to the lives of millions and the ensuing collapse and devastation of the world's economic and social structures.

From only six miles away, General Stevens waited, anxiously watching the clock in the White House situation complex some three hundred feet below the surface and praying for success. Having made final checks with Mort in the Vault personally, he was now managing all assets from here.

---

**Zeb had his attention now.** Enough hubris remained still in the man for the accusation to turn his head.

"*Flawed?*"

"Yep. Terribly so," Dalton replied.

"You have no idea what you're talking about."

"Well, okay," he pushed. "Let's start with the obvious. Why only the millionaires? Surely the people with a big old "B" at the bottom of their asset sheet account for more of the problem. Why weren't they invited to your worldwide parasite party?"

Donneleigh tried hard to maintain composure while focusing on the screen, turning toward it every few seconds.

"Fine," he assented. "All of this will be finished soon anyway, so we might as well dispense with your ill-formed notions."

He spoke sideways, eyes fixed on the laptop. "Mr. Dalton, this is not about economics. That's the problem with your thinking. Those people with B's attached to their names, such as myself, are builders, innovators. They get where they are because they are concerned with achieving something great, contributing to their world and creating gainful opportunities for others to do the same as they partner with them. But *millionaires?* Not so. They are pariah. The vast majority of them got where they are from the toil and ingenuity of others. And then they spend it all on themselves. Enough wealth to be comfortable personally but not enough to become uncomfortable with the ills of their fellow man."

Donneleigh seemed to be warming up now to the "last speech" thing.

"And then the cycle continues," the CEO rambled. "Starvation. Disease. Overpopulation. Irreversible damage to the very ecosystems sustaining us." His eyes glassed over, slightly unfocused and clearly seeing some kind of desirable future. He let his mind go there. "And so, we will set things right again. The vacuum created by these people's absence will be filled by the noble, the ones who take nothing for granted. The ones for whom life has been a constant struggle. They will now rise with a purpose and strength forged in their trials."

"... and figure out ways to commandeer power and control for themselves," Zeb cut in.

"No, Mr. Dalton," Donneleigh retorted. "That is another way in which you are dead wrong. Blessed are the poor. Isn't that a core tenet of one of the world's great religions? We've just never put it into action. The answer was there all the time. We just didn't want to do anything about it."

Awkwardness ensued. Donneleigh had spent his seeming last cache of emotional energy in explaining himself.

"So," Dalton aimed, knowing time was running out. "You're going to trust that, after initiating the greatest single genocide in the history of the world, the folks next in line are going to do any better? That's a whole lot of trust for a race that has consistently shown itself selfish, willing to do whatever it takes to survive."

"No... Mr. Dalton," softer this time. "They are different. They will take their newfound position with a measure of communal concern that is simply not to be found in the hearts of the wealthy."

# FORTY FOUR

*Mort's globe lit up with orange indicators. Ready.*

**"General, we have confirmation** at all sites. On your command."

Spurrier was still running this op, even while currently playing the part of attendee in Atlantic City. She wore a micro earpiece, so deeply into the canal no one would find it other than her ENT doc with his scope. Though she couldn't let on verbally, she was staying abreast of developments, wearing a simple sensory plate on the inside of a ring on her right hand. All that was needed was a tap with her thumb to transmit. The basic nature of the gear left her with only a "yes" for one and "no" for two kind of interaction, but it had to do. Like an on-air talent's divided attention to their script and producer, she would maintain the outward appearance of merely another person in attendance while processing constant intel from the Vault. She would draw no irregular focus. Aside from the presence of her secret service detail, which was standard procedure regardless. Yet the weight she carried was far more than could be summed up in a simple tap of the ring, either yes *or* no.

For the most part, the executives of foreign nations in which these events were being held were blind to the snipers in their midst.

Needing a few more team members than the US could muster on its own, Spurrier reached out to France and the UK. But other than the complement of operators these historic allies provided, everyone else was in the dark. The irony was hard to dismiss. Here she was, only a few years downwind of another American president's actions, ones somehow meant for good but as far afield from sane as anyone could imagine. Now she sat in the same seat of decision, with warriors in play that she would need to account for, succeed or fail. Her goal was to stop a mass extinction event, not start one. Still, the required subterfuge would eventually bring her choices into question on a worldwide scale, same as before.

"Mort. Confirm readiness," Stevens commanded over op comms.

"Confirmed from the Vault," the general stated. "Ma'am?" Stevens asked in a single word.

Spurrier tapped once.

"Confirmed. We are ready. All locations."

---

**Every last seat** of the 80,000 person capacity of AT&T Stadium was filled. The vibe in the Dallas metro arena had been pleasant enough while the parade of top-tier country music acts entered stage left, did their thing, and walked off to wild applause. That was thirty minutes ago. Now, the massive crowd waited somewhat impatiently for the single line of text on the one-hundred-sixty by seventy-two-foot screens to change and officially begin the fleecing they, for the most part, felt compelled to attend.

*World One: Global Transmission Begins Soon.*

While the wealthy in attendance focused on the screens stretching from twenty-yard line to twenty-yard line, a lone eye loomed from its perch in the HVAC intake above Section E13. Steady. The mid-twenties operator ID'd her target zone and anticipated the go from control.

Freeman awaited the call.

Taking Sanchez' place as Dallas lead had freaked her out for a moment or two as orders came down from Col. Meers. Her response was more than respect for her elder female operator. It bordered on sniper fan-girl. Yet, beyond the hype, Freeman also appreciated Sanchez for doing her part in shattering one more hardened glass ceiling. Some uses of that term were superfluous, the younger shooter thought. Not this time. Access to the field itself and not some harder to quantify issues had been brushed aside and opened for this noble protectorship to be more than a boys' club. In this case, the proverbial glass had indeed been breached. Well, more like splintered into a thousand tiny pieces with a 7.62 Match Grade round.

Yeah, she preferred that image.

"Dallas ready," she whispered, barely audible yet still transmitted via throat mic as if using normal voice volume. "Targets either camo'd in crowd or not present. Waiting. Team Dallas, take your time. No margin on this one. We either get this right or a whole lot of people die tonight. And I for one do not like bugs, much less ones small enough to kill you without feeling their creepy little bodies doing their thing."

The thought caused a slight shudder. Good thing it wasn't yet time to take a shot.

---

**Dalton looked over** to the small chamber. It glowed, pulsating with bio-activity. Noting the almost perfectly sustained condition of the leg, he started to piece together the possibilities. It occurred to him that some form of mummification kept the organism alive through the centuries. Looking further into the plexiglass he saw a light brown hue at the edges of the ancient flesh. Amber? Maybe. He'd read some about its embalming properties but no accounts of this kind of thing existed in the Mayan traditions. But what of the fire? The cleansing?

*Yes*, he thought. *That's it.*

How it was released in 900AD, he had no clue. But the suddenness of the scourge must have kept them from investigating its origins. Somehow, the long-dormant parasite had emerged; maybe grave diggers looking for the inevitable gold and jewels placed with the dead. Who knew. Regardless, it must have spread so viciously through the causeways and outer parts of the city that their only recourse was to burn it all to the ground. Zeb imagined for a moment the chaos. 150,000 men, women, and children destroying their very existence in an attempt to stave off further losses. But while flames ceased the outward rampage, the nexus of the killer remained alive, here in this burial chamber.

"How did you know? How in the world did you find it?"

Donneleigh shifted slightly again.

"A fortunate happenstance, Mr. Dalton. The healthcare side of my foundation received word of a miracle cure for the most virulent ailments known to man. We followed the lead into the densely forested area of what is now northern Guatemala. I had almost given up on the hopes of my work bringing about change in the human condition. I considered this my last effort and led the team personally. We did not find what we originally came looking for. Instead, one night around the campfire, an old villager told us of the legend of the legs. He told us all the old people believed Tikal exacted its revenge on Caracol, lying in wait with the killer until the fullness of time would present the opportunity. Though the end of their civilization should have finished the story, many believed the curse still remained, waiting its final and greater moment. We simply traced the evidence no one else paid attention to and found our salvation here, in this room."

Zeb watched in fascination as Donneleigh made his way over to a single, small statuette on the ground. There, he quietly knelt. No words. Breathing slowed. A look of peace in his countenance.

"*What the hell?*" Dalton erupted. "Not only are you the most insane person to ever live, you have some kind of twisted religion going on here as well? Unbelievable; freaking un-believable."

Donneleigh rose and took his seat. Calmly, he spoke again.

"I do not expect you to understand, Mr. Dalton. The writings I discovered with the biosource made it all so clear to me. Yet, you would have to completely remove yourself from your received worldview to see the beauty in what I have been called to. Just when I thought my efforts would die with me in vain, I came to know a new purpose, a new way to make it all matter again."

Zeb had seen enough of the excesses of misplaced faith for a thousand lifetimes. Some of the craziest things in the history of the world had been done in the name of gods of one sort or another. And his own family lay irrevocably torn asunder by the fraudulent brand of religion his father peddled.

His mind raced and a single phrase presented itself, immovable from his thinking.

*... it all comes down to authority, right?*

Those words, spoken by a young man at a pizza joint in Berkeley; so distant yet ever-present. Dalton knew it to be true. Just as he had discovered he was not the ultimate authority when pressed to release American nuclear forces upon the sovereign nation of China, he understood the question now to be one more complicated than that. Establishing he wasn't divine, recognizing that power and attendant responsibility was not in his place, wasn't enough. Donneleigh's folly proved that point, dramatically so.

"Look, Donneleigh. I get you want to make things better, make things right. But let me ask you: how exactly do you know these writings—whatever it is you found—to be reliable? Why is it you've let them shape your entire life... and now, *this?*"

Donneleigh didn't answer.

"Okay, but at least tell me why you killed your henchman back there. He was on your side, right? Seems to me your ancient wisdom comes across as pretty much what you want to do, whenever you want to do it. Wouldn't something from the gods be a bit more reliable? C'mon, Donneleigh. You're out of your mind."

Still, no retort.

Instead, the man punched in a few last commands, watching with satisfaction as the screen changed to live operation mode. Next, he walked to where Dalton was held fast and nonchalantly ran a six-inch blade across his forearm. The sting of severed flesh warmed as blood flowed down and off his wrist. Just as silently, Donneleigh slid the sharpened steel across his own left shoulder. Then he lifted a gun from its place on the desk and fired repeatedly at the chamber's plexiglass cover.

# FORTY FIVE

*Mylon's hands shook uncontrollably.*

**He stayed in the bathroom longer** than intended. The QR Code had indeed gained him entrance to AT&T Stadium, as easily as promised. Wandering and trying his best to fold into the crowds after transitioning through the outer gates, his head jerked up at the incoming text message. Thumbing the icon, a 3D map of the venue appeared, instructions to his cannister a blinking blue set of directives overlaid on the concourse framework. Following the map, he retrieved it from an out of the way storage space, deep enough to hold portable seating stanchions and dark enough to provide for corners of the room where no one would ever go unintentionally.

But then the unforeseen happened.

The man was sixty-eight, skinny, and fit the part perfectly, actually whistling some happy tune when he noticed movement in the storage space. Way back in the corner.

*What in the name of Sam Hill?*

His euphemisms landed as pleasantly as his everyday disposition. His airy musical ramblings an everyday part of the stadium's crew. Now he lay dead, body dragged to the outer recesses of the room, to be discovered at a later date. It had been an ugly fight. Mylon had no idea how to attack someone but gained the advantage from his place in the shadows. He couldn't use the cannister, didn't know it to be sturdy enough to survive a blow to the man's head. So, all he had left were his hands. He shot them up and around the worker's neck and held on as tightly as his shaking arms allowed. The unfortunate soul struggled but succumbed, a series of last gasps and reddened face telling the final, tragic chapter of his story.

His face. Mylon couldn't escape the look. Not just surprise, though that certainly evidenced. More the question of *why?* And even more clearly: *why me?* The equation made no sense to a man living a quiet, circumspect life of hard work and family. Men like him were supposed to pass in bed with loved ones gathered to express their deepest feelings at the moment everyone knows is coming, sooner or later. The injustice of it landed on the young man. That which lived completely in the realm of ideas was now real. And intimate. Though having committed himself to an act of killing in the grand sense, he now knew the chill of causing death, up close. It was far more unsettling than imagined. Mylon stood cautiously, wiped away the stench of bile as best he could. It lingered. As did abject fear of what he was about to do, and had just done.

**Freeman swept the outer concourses,** her scope telling her everything she needed to know. The young woman's eye fixed to the reticle, no time left to move from the mono-focused world between hash marks and the depth and clarity afforded by the human visual field of two eyes on.

A change in music signaled a shift in the program. Freeman made another left to right of her target area. No one knew where the assassins would appear. In her responsibility lay no less than two thousand human beings. If the numbers proved right, she might isolate two targets from that sea of humanity. Two to take out as cleanly as possible before unleashing their hellish micro hordes on these unsuspecting crowds. She rehearsed the other scenario. The one they all balked at in orientation back in Nebraska but still reserved as a distinct possibility. The normal transfer range for the parasite was quite contained. In the three kill events, a tight radius was the norm, what they all expected. But in one single instance, the forensics pros seemed more than a little nervous. They did find one young man, outside the Haitian ball field. Tracing back and using the maximum distances for transfer of the bug, a perfect line of transmission emerged, from him to everyone else on the inside of the gates. He'd jumped it quickly enough or had enough stamina to get another few yards before falling. It opened the door to a theoretical spread beyond these gathered spaces. Highly unlikely. Still, every op has an unintended consequences factor and a resulting *Plan Z*. Freeman's orders for Z were clear. If the cannisters were released, no one would leave the interior of the stadium alive.

No one. Including herself.

**Mylon tried to steady his body,** pacing through the small tunnel of E15 and out toward to main seating. He was very much alone. Everyone else inhabited their seats in the last ten minutes. The massive screen above gave the countdown and they dutifully took or returned to their assigned places. He had to stop thinking and just act. Were he to give in to the mental and moral confusion setting in, he would likely not follow through on all he had come to believe, everything he owned as his destiny and purpose in this world. That was inconceivable. So, convinced of his rightness of cause, an innate, embedded motion took over, tossing aside the bidding of alternate voices. But the voices, be they unclear, only grew louder. A chaotic crescendo mounted within. He no longer could maintain the slow, waiting posture required of his station and duties.

Mylon ran.

Emerging from the concourse tunnel, a raised cannister shone in his right hand.

"Fiat justitia, ruat caelum!"

"Fiat justitia, ruat caelum!"

The phrase was completely lost on those closest to him, partly due to the nature of his surprising appearance just as the formal program began. But as well, the introductory video played loudly enough to render the odd proclamation a secondary focus. Lastly, though many in the crowd came from elite private schooling, their compulsory Latin did them little help, fading not too many weeks after graduation, much less retaining the skill all these years later.

**"Subject has emerged... E15.** Hand in the air. Some kind of verbal statement. Eyes on distribution device. Copy, Team Dallas. Other movements?"

"That's negative, Dallas Lead. No eyes on for our sectors."

"Say again, Team Dallas. No targets in sight?"

"That is correct, Dallas Lead. Seems you scored an early bird. Or the first in line, giving green light to remainder of agents."

---

**Mort ran the audio back** two more times, as quickly as possible. Then he let the Vault's machines churn out a translation. Seconds later he had it transmitted back to Dallas Lead.

---

**Let justice be done,** *though the heavens may fall.*

Freeman bit her lip at the cruel irony.

*How the hell is this justice?*

She needed direction but had no more time. The young man in her sight stopped his speech, took a big breath, and shifted the cannister to a position where his hands could activate an opening sequence. He looked at it again, pausing and glancing up. Though not seeing Freeman from her perch, his face stared back, framed perfectly in her viewfinder. The subtlest of realizations came over him; anxiousness and a sixth sense awareness that he was being watched. He turned the cannister over in his hands and motioned his right thumb toward the upper surface area of the smooth silver cylinder. Mylon's hand closed on the activator.

His thumb moved forward.

She pulled the trigger.

# FORTY SIX

*"We have activity in Dallas. Go. Go. Go! All teams execute. Acquire targets now!"*

**Spurrier responded to Stevens' harried communication** from Washington, knowing a rapid succession of events would follow now that action had been initiated. Her security detail saw her expression and moved to surround, doing their best phalanx move—once she was out of the row—in an attempt to transit her to safety. It caused an understandable reaction. People panicked. A recognizable world leader, quickly removed by security forces. That spells danger. Imminent. Present. Most people won't wait around to see what's next. Understandably, they moved, across and over one another. Civility replaced by raw, primal fear.

And in response to that fear the believers surfaced, assuming their assigned places at the venue in Atlantic City.

---

**Donneleigh's attention** was pulled away from the shattered plexiglass, to the now bustling activity on screen in both Dallas and New Jersey.

"No! Fools!"

In a resolved act of his own, the man set the gun down and turned back to his laptop keys. He entered two sets of simple lines of commands. Now, everyone held a green light. Every event site. *World One* was released to do its own cleansing work.

"Stop!" Dalton cried out. "You can't do this!"

Again, no response.

Donneleigh took the twelve steps forward to the now-opened containment unit and walked in, kneeling and then laying on top of the Tikal King's severed leg—his body a final offering. The swarm encompassed his head and torso, having made its way up from the ground to the tech leader's frame, his recently opened wounds filling with the advancing horde. With head forced back in an unnatural position, full paralysis set in. Thousands of tiny invaders had gnawed away his spinal cord and were now coursing through his vascular system, looking for more flesh to destroy, and then a way out.

---

**The Dallas gathering transitioned** from semi-bored state to outright confusion. Shots rang in the large arena as teams attempted to take out their targets. The crack of single bullets seemed like echoes to the people nearest to their firing positions. In fact, they were just more rounds going off in other parts of the building.

---

**Dalton knew he had** little time left to live.

Flailing against his bonds for a few seconds, the futility of his efforts settled and the retired Army Signal Corpsman stopped fighting. Resolved. Not so much calm but knowing no other options presented. Watching in horror. He was next. Cringing, Zeb leaned away from the sight, trying to anticipate the parasitic expulsion from Donneleigh's cavity.

**"What, you want to stay here** for the full show, young man?'"

Shocked by the voice behind him, Dalton first thought he was hallucinating, dreaming. Maybe this was the kind of thing that happens when your brain knows it's about to be shut off for good?

"I know we've never seen this happen first hand before," the new voice said. "Let's just say for the sake of argument it's the same every time. And we might not want to hang around to confirm our theory?"

"Mart... *Martin!*"

Dr. Hendricks worked Dalton's ties more quickly than would be presumed of a man in his season of life. He pulled again and the last of Zeb's bonds came loose. No one needed to give the duo any instructions. They rose and fled.

Not many steps later, Zeb and Martin both heard it: a sickening rupture of flesh, signaling the parasite's egress from Donneleigh's body. They'd barely made it into the dark causeway outside the cave turned control room. No more time. Keep moving. *Have to keep moving.* The archaeologist progressed with a speed and agility belying his age and they edged further and further away from the threat. As fast as manageable, they headed down a narrow passageway, one Zeb had not experienced while conscious. Mart was in the lead. Dalton was glad to follow. A quick left turn and the two slid through a visual switchback, designed by the ancients to hide the lower levels Donneleigh had come to occupy.

"Zeb, this way! Keep going!"

Sanchez' ever authoritative voice rang out and they quickly came upon her and the other Dr. Hendricks, both crouched against a wall in the altar room. It was the very same place he had last seen her before he passed out from the pain and shock of the flesh wound bullet grazing on the side of his head.

*Donneleigh left her alive, in the same place he killed Reston and took me captive.*

It made no sense. None at all. Yet, even in this moment of hurried flight, he could reckon nothing he'd learned about the man and his warped plans to follow any kind of logic, evil or otherwise. Zeb's best attempt at sense was that the man made no sense at all. That would have to suffice for now. Maybe always.

Martin coaxed them all forward a few more steps, to where he had left a rope ladder in place, back up to the burial chamber. They both helped Jessica, despite her injuries, ascend back up to higher ground. Constance followed, then Zeb, and finally Martin. Pulling the ladder up after them, he glanced over to Zeb.

"Did you see anyone else down there?"

"Not from where I was being held, but can't say for sure. He dragged me there unconscious at some point."

The four of them looked back at Smith's body, knowing they had no time to get him out with them. All four held an unspoken hope they might be able to extract him at a safer moment.

Zeb and Martin formed a human support structure for Sanchez, taking as much pressure off her badly damaged leg as possible. Every step down the darkened, twisting hallways was excruciating. She breathed rhythmically, almost labor and delivery style, keeping the pain at enough of a distance to stay conscious. Blood loss was minimal, mostly stanched now around the place where jagged bone pierced her flesh and the fabric of her pant leg.

The same kind of help was needed for everyone at the exit back up to the previously known tunnels in the system. Their egress was considerably less smooth than when they'd dropped down here only hours ago. All up top now, they closed the lid.

And then everything blew.

The entire underground structure shook violently, chunks of ceiling falling all around. Thousand-year-old dust threatened to choke off the little air existing this far down into the site. Everyone's ears became non-functioning as all moved in slow-motion, yet again.

# FORTY SEVEN

*"Zeb?"*

**Dalton heard his name** but it remained a bit fuzzy at the edges, distant and unreachable.

"Zeb?"

Dalton coughed, thick dust hanging everywhere. Milk jug-sized rocks and clay lay across his lap. Nothing too heavy. Didn't seem to cause injury, at least. He brushed them off and placed the bigger pieces aside. Though his head still hurt, things began to clear and he recognized Jessica's voice. The very sound of it brought a thankfulness that surprised him. Then he turned, looking frantically for the Hendricks, thinking of the researchers' lives as well.

"Constance? Martin?"

"Over here, young man," Mrs. Doctor Hendricks replied.

Sanchez lay arched over her more fragile frame, shielding the bigger pieces of rock from connecting with the older woman. "I am fine. Just a little dust and dirt. Seeing as that has been my life's work, no problems over here. But I am not so sure," she concluded, looking again from Zeb to Sanchez. "This is the best way to secure a girl's attentions."

Jessica smiled. They all laughed.

"Martin," Zeb asked breathlessly. "What? How in the world... "

"Well, you can thank Jessica for that, Mr. Dalton. She left a message indicating you two were looking further into the story of *The Cleansing*. Figured you would be on site at some point and you might need some background and such. We got an alarming call from Emilio, our caretaker..."

"Ah, Emilio," Zeb said. "God bless him."

"Yes, he's the best. He's safe, although he might require a raise in pay to stay on the team. Don't blame him at all."

"No kidding," Sanchez said.

"So, anyway," Martin continued. "We came back a week earlier than our next scheduled digs and things didn't seem right. Thought we'd take a look, assuming you would go down into the uncharted tunnels through the hatch and we found your lady friend here, all busted up."

"For the last time, you guys, I am *not*... " Sanchez began.

"Well," Constance stepped in. "I sent Mart down through that false wall we found in the altar room. Just in case."

"How did you know it was there in the first place?"

"Well, son, we've found five others across the site. Same design, same telltale curvature to the wall that opens to spaces beyond."

"But Dr. Hendricks," Zeb said. "That was incredibly foolish. It was also very brave."

"Ah. Forget about it. Let's just say I've still got a few surprises up my sleeve, young man."

Martin patted the shotgun next to his side.

Dalton had been in such a hurry it escaped him the older man was armed. Zeb wondered if he actually knew how to use it and if he had ever had to fire it at another person. Glancing at Martin, he realized he was about the right age for the tail of Korea or possibly Vietnam. Something in that wordless exchange told him the man had faced his fair share of impossible choices at the end of a barrel, as well. Remembrances laying under deep layers of a good, long life in pursuit of other, better things.

"And the explosion?"

*Not me,* Jessica nodded

Everyone looked at Dalton, trusting he'd fill in some blanks.

"Hmmm. Can't know for sure yet, but best bet is Donneleigh, when you think it through," Zeb surmised. "Didn't want an uncontrolled outbreak of the parasite? As much as he was a madman, his madness didn't extend to the extermination of every single human being on the planet. Makes sense. He had a very targeted goal in mind. Bad idea to let it out to the general public. Blow the place up, seal it forever under deep layers of rock and earth. Maybe in a limited way, he acted in line with the ancient inhabitants of this place?" Dalton queried.

The professors looked puzzled. No clue what was going on. They were completely in the dark as to Dalton's estimation of the Caracol story and Donneleigh's appropriation of it.

"I think I unraveled your myth, Mart. Spending some quality time with one Matthew Donneleigh, it occurred to me the end of this place was an act of self-sacrifice. *The Cleansing* wasn't a random event, the fire everyone assumes. The flames were only their best shot at containing this scourge. He must have found some documents you haven't yet had the chance to evaluate. Referred to them as the revelation behind his self-assumed righteous acts. Gotta say, seems unlikely now that we'll ever retrieve them, though."

Still confused but now intrigued, Mart opened his mouth, a million questions about to emerge.

Dalton looked back assuringly and stopped him before a word came out.

"That's a story better told over a couple of cold ones on your veranda. First things first. Let's see if we can get out of here and to some fresh air and a late evening sky."

# FORTY EIGHT

*The normally cramped spaces of the research compound seemed rather luxurious after being stuck underground for so long.*

**An ordinary kitchen table** with worn formica counters: such a welcomed sight. Though none of the survivors had a chance to shower yet, they had all drank their fill of clean water and been able to wash their faces and hair, removing deep layers of stubborn dirt, helping them feel one step closer to human again. Dalton managed to re-patch the researcher's sat phone and eagerly awaited a clear, secured signal. The line buzzed and then opened.

"Dalton, Zebulon M. Please wait for group call."

Something about the normalcy of the operator's voice intimated success, that the world was not currently falling apart around them. That was likely a hopeful personal projection on Zeb's part. The real effects of something like *World One* would not be felt for at least a few days. Massive wealth pulled from national and transnational economies, not to mention the voids left in businesses, governmental, and non-profit entities. Even if Donneleigh had been correct about these people's relative worthlessness to their companies and other enterprises, the hole would gape on a scale never before experienced by humanity.

"Mr. Dalton. Can you hear me?"

President Spurrier's voice was a beautiful thing to behold.

"Here, madam president. Sanchez as well, although she's got one crazy leg injury. She won't admit it but she's in a ton of pain and needs some top notch medical as soon as we can get it."

"Excellent, and noted," Stevens jumped in from the Vault. "Carrier Group 1 with the Saratoga, is in range. Huey is on the way. Can you handle field dressing until they arrive on station? Meds available locally?"

Sanchez carried that look on her face.

*I got this, Dalton.*

"Yeah, general" he grinned. "We'll do what we can here. Something tells me she's gonna be alright. As usual."

Zeb redirected the conversation, anxious for a sit report, however preliminary.

"Okay. Enough small talk. How did we do?"

The short silence made his heart sink.

"Lieutenant... " Spurrier began.

*Oh no. Using rank is never good news.*

"... we're still accessing reports as you can imagine."

"Ma'am, please. With all due respect. A number. Grade. What have you got?"

"125."

*Thank God.*

"... thousand."

The kick in the gut couldn't have been harsher. No. It couldn't be. *An eighth of a million.* Dead. In the most horrifying manner.

Stevens sensed the reaction on the other end and quickly joined in reassurance if nothing else.

"Dalton. We couldn't stay out front of the action in every location. The worst, of course, was... AT&T Stadium."

"Dallas..." Zeb finished the statement, remembering the chaos overheard from Donneleigh's control station. "Anyone? Anyone at all?" Dalton pleaded.

"No, son. I am afraid not," the general replied. "Had to be. Completely out of control. The chance of transmission outside the arena grew exponentially. Parasites got the vast majority. The few escaping, well... " his voice trailed off.

"Freeman?" Sanchez breathed out, overhearing the report from a few feet away.

No response. None required. Everyone on the call realized the personal hell she had been called upon to endure. Decisions no one ever wants to make. Clearly, anyone fleeing was already infected. Her actions? Necessary in the most basic sense. Their quieted respect honored the young professional. After a moment, Spurrier continued.

"She had local command authority. Her call to engage. We trust people like her to make the right moves on the ground. Served her country and people today with uncommon valor."

"Huh," Zeb let out, eyes fixed somewhere other than the immediate interchange.

Stevens caught it, even from so far away and over the sat line.

"Come again, LT?"

"That word, sir."

"To what particular one are you referring, Dalton?"

"*Authority*, Ma'am," aiming his ramblings toward the president now. "You said she had command authority; the right to act in the moment because we trusted her, because she was a woman of character and loyalties and showed that to be true in her actions, especially her last ones on earth."

"Yes, Mr. Dalton, that is what I said."

"So," he probed out loud. "The reason she was given authority is because she was trustworthy, not the other way around. Or you could say we were able to trust her, which only supported the authority given."

"Zeb?"

He stopped for just a second.

"*Zeb?*" Sanchez pried. "You okay... LT?"

"Oh," Dalton snapped back into the moment. "Yeah. Sure."

"You sure? 'Cause that was a little odd, given we're on the phone with the President of the United States and her chief military adviser."

"Sorry, madam president," he was all back now. "Nothing. Just a line of questioning for my World Religions prof at Berkeley — if I ever get back there. Come to think of it, I may have missed the final."

Sanchez shook her head, noting again the duality of his depth of insight and horrible social timing.

"Ma'am," it struck Dalton now that she had survived her own frightening version of the last few hours as well. "Are you alright?"

"I have a great team, Mr. Dalton. The best. Once the Dallas carrier revealed himself early and Freeman took the shot, they got me out of the venue and to safety before any cannisters released. Kudos to our people there. Every target down. No other casualties besides injuries from rushing crowds."

"I have the outline from your end of things, Dalton," Stevens offered. "We'll expect a complete reporting when you return. For now, if you could stay on site and direct the med crew with Sanchez' ex-fil and the incoming forensics and hazardous materials units, that would be helpful. Given the transit radius and the damage to the ruins, it's unlikely we still have a hot zone there. But we can't be too careful. We'll probably need you there for another forty-eight to seventy-two hours. We will take the proper steps with regards to Smith's next of kin. And, as usual, an unnamed star in Langley's foyer."

"Sir, I hate to be macabre, but… the bodies?"

"Not at all, LT. Reasonable question as there are lots of contacts to be made for next of kin and final disposition of the victims. It's gonna be a bit of wait and see for the next few days. More contained venues like domes and covered stadiums will be sealed up and robotic teams sent in to measure the level of biothreat, if any, remaining. Our initial numbers from Mort are little to none expected. The parasite has a very short life outside the human body, but we can't take a chance here. Worldwide, we have safe zones established around every single venue, so again little to no spread there. We just have to wait and see before we go in with actual personnel. Everyone wants to go in now, get the bodies out and help folks get a grip on what actually took place. Unfortunately, things will be a little less optimal than that."

Dalton's mind began to draw up the ugly scenes, decomposition rates, what they'd have to work with by the time everything was cleared. He shuddered. Then he shut it off. He just chose to not go there. He couldn't.

Martin saw the internal struggle and walked from the fridge to where Zeb and Sanchez sat, four beers in hand, all bearing a frosty glow. Holding one up to Dalton, he gave him a knowing look, a look that had seen a fair share of life's trials as well. A look confirming they lived in a world — if billions of people were right, even including Donneleigh — that was a fractured, distorted shell of what was once intended.

"Okay, general. We got things on this end. If you need me, I'll be here in this little tropical paradise. And thank you again, madame president. Your leadership has borne the weight of many an administration, even in these first months."

The official call ended after another round of congratulations, although of the kind tempered by loss. Zeb closed the line and Dr. Hendricks served his wife the drink first before handing a brown bottle to Jessica and then the last one to Dalton.

"They said you might require some pain management, young lady."

"Doctor's orders, *Dr.* Hendricks?"

"Why yes, that's correct. I *am* a doctor and you should do what I say."

"Can't argue that."

**Their banter,** enjoyable enough to linger in for hours, was rudely cut into by the unmistakable rotor wash of a military grade chopper, closing in on the Caracol site for Sanchez' airlift. She took one last, generous swig and put the half-finished bottle down disappointedly.

"Crap. Well, that'll have to do for now, I guess."

Dalton met the young, heavily suited airman at the door, directing their efforts to transfer Jessica as painlessly as possible. She was tough. The toughest he'd ever worked beside, man or woman, and that said much considering his years in the fray. But something much deeper lay still, beyond that obvious strength. A simplicity and honesty about her, making his life feel like a three-ring circus. Honestly, he longed for more of whatever it was she had going on beneath that super-sniper cloak of hers.

At the edge of the chopper bay door, he needed to shout a little for her to understand.

"So," he cupped his hands in an improvised megaphone. "The last time we did this I was the one all messed up. I got you, Sanchez. You'll be up and at it in no time. And I'll see you real soon, okay? Soon."

Her dark eyes twinkled.

"Counting on it, LT. Counting on it."

**After the sounds of the helicopter faded,** Dalton ambled back into the kitchen. Mart sat there and Constance held a knowing look. Seeing how much Zeb cared for his partner, she walked over and gave him a peck on his right cheek and then cozied up next to her husband of so many years.

"So, Mr. Dalton," Martin redirected. "You said you had an epiphany in the presence of evil down there."

"Well, yeah. Something like that."

"Well then, young man," he pulled a chair out from the small dining table. "Do tell. Do tell. I'm sure this will be good."

# FORTY NINE

*Dalton knocked on the nondescript apartment door. It opened and his stomach sank, confirming that, yes, he was doing this.*

**"Hey, LT.** Not bad. Not bad at all."

Jessica smiled coyly and grabbed her jacket. Tossing it across bare shoulders, the woman stepped outside to meet Zeb in the hallway. Dressed casually in jeans and a sleeveless cotton top, she joined him, heading for the elevators. Displaying a slight limp, it was clear she was still officially in rehab from the leg injury. Dalton let her go first, remembering a setting in an elevator at Microsoft where she physically dispatched a Chinese soldier with little to no effort on her part.

Dalton entered the car with her and hit the button for the lobby.

Most men would be intimidated. Maybe even a little scared.

All Zeb could think at the moment?

*My word, what a beautiful woman.*

She caught the goofy, twelve-year-old boy look on his face as they descended.

"What?" she turned. "There a problem, LT?"

"Nope. Not at all."

"Good, wouldn't want you jinxing this thing again."

"You still okay with this?" Dalton offered. "I mean, I could take care of it by myself some other time."

"Zeb," she stopped him, looking deeply into his soft amber eyes. "More than sure. The Locks were a special place for your mom. Seems especially appropriate to lay her to rest among the waves and boats."

A deeper, unspoken question still.

"You give any thought to the other request?"

"Well," he inhaled. "Gonna have to just take it one step at a time."

She nodded, knowing the complications and pain that would surface were he to follow through on his mom's dying wish.

"One last item," Dalton posed, looking to avoid the topic for now. "After the Locks. There's a little fish and chips place out on the private docks. Sound good?"

"Absolutely. White chowder, though, right? That East Coast red stuff is heresy."

"No argument there."

The surprising softness of the expression made a perfect match to her wit as they stepped out together, into the breezy Seattle evening.

*Before you go...*

## IF YOU LOVED THIS BOOK
Reader reviews are by far the #1 way people learn about new writers and stories. I would appreciate it so much if you would take a few minutes to leave your honest thoughts at the retailer of your choice.

## GET SOME EXCLUSIVE (AND FREE) ZEB DALTON MATERIAL
Building a relationship with my readers is one of the best things about writing. I occasionally send newsletters with details on new releases, special offers and other bits of news relating to the Zeb Dalton Military | Political Thrillers. And if you sign up to the mailing list I'll send you an audiobook copy of the prequel to the Dalton series (msrp $9.99) absolutely free. Set against the backdrop of Zeb's earliest days in the military, a young Dalton encounters an eye-opening off-base weekend in the border town of Ciudad Juarez, Mexico.

Get a free copy of *Juarez Liberty* at waynecstewart.com

## FIRST IN SERIES
If you haven't yet read the first full novel in the Dalton series, head over to Amazon and search for *When Totems Fall.*

# About the Author

*Wayne C Stewart* writes military and political adventure with a technothriller twist. His Zeb Dalton Series features an Iraq/Afghan Wars Veteran, working hard to make sense of his world with a keen mind and fragile, yet lingering sense of duty. The first book in the series finds Dalton in a Chinese-occupied Seattle. Book 2 calls him back into service as America's first female president tasks the team of Dalton and retired super-sniper Jessica Sanchez with fighting back an ancient Mayan scourge, set in motion by a jaded tech billionaire. The Zeb Dalton Novella (short read) Juarez Liberty rounds out the present work on the Dalton stories, set against the backdrop of Zeb's earliest days in the military and an eye-opening off-base weekend in the border town of Ciudad Juarez. Wayne is a displaced Seattleite, currently living with his family in Iowa.

# Acknowledgments

I write stories because I think stories matter. While "Totems" began as half personal dare and half rainy day downtime activity, I quickly realized the characters and scenes coming together on the page meant something to me. I hope they will for you, as well.

Thanks again to my wife, Breta, for her patience with the process and willingness to read first, second, and third drafts.

This time around I had the privilege of a larger beta reading group, many of whom are coming along for the ride as the Zeb Dalton series unfolds. Special thanks to Jeri Shelton, Melodi Jack, and Lois Archer for both encouragement and noting a few things that slipped by in the version they were handed.

Thanks to Mark Dawson, JF Penn, and Nick Stephenson for their challenge and instruction from a distance. Their podcasts and courses have been a tremendous help and education for this new indie writer.

Thanks to a growing list of readers. I so appreciate your willingness to take a chance on an unknown storyline and author.

All thanks to Jesus, from whom the one story that informs all others, flows.

Made in the USA
Coppell, TX
30 September 2020

39048790R10152